STRANGE ORIGINS

Jim Stein

This book is a work of fiction. Names, characters, places, and events are purely fictitious and stem from the author's imagination. Any resemblance or similarity to actual people, places, and events is purely coincidental.

Digital ISBN: 978-1-7335629-6-6
Print ISBN: 978-1-954788-03-9

First printing, 2021

Jagged Sky Books
P.O. Box #254
Bradford, Pa 16701

Cover art & design by Kris Norris
Edited by Caroline Miller

Legends Walk Series

*Strange Origins (a prequel)**
Strange Tidings
Strange Omens
Strange Medicine
Strange Shenanigans (a novella)

Also by Jim Stein:

Magic Trade School

The Heartstone Chamber
The Silver Portal
The Forgotten Isle

The Space-Slime Continuum

Planet Fred

* As a prequel, Strange Origins takes place before Strange Tidings (book 1.) This story can be enjoyed as a stand-alone or at any point before, during, or after reading books one through three.

Acknowledgements

Thank you to all the people who helped.

From cover design to editing and beta readers to developmental assistants (that would be my Great Dane Marley), all have been critically important to brining this story to life.

And thank you, the reader, for spending time with Phil, Ankti, Kay, and the rest.

A special thanks to those who are able to jot off a quick review online. As you venture along with the characters, think about what you like and don't so you can let others know. A simple headline summarizing your most lasting impression and a sentence or two only takes a minute to post and helps me immensely. So, again, thank you!

Visit **https://JimSteinBooks.com/subscribe** to get a free ebook, join my reader community, and sign up for my infrequent newsletter.

Prologue

T HE GODS gathered in a council of war at a great stone table where neither Light nor Dark held sway.

The horned serpent Uktena and Kokopelli, trickster god of life and music, brought forth evidence that the Dark Court again meddled in human affairs. Alliances shattered, reformed, and broke anew as fierce debate raged.

And so the great creator Damballa forged a powerful artifact, a staff to be wielded by a new council charged to keep the balance of all things.

Excerpt from *Chronicles of the Neutral Council*

Jim Stein

1. Skyfall

A THIN line of fire arced high overhead, followed by another deafening boom as the rocket exploded. Phil Johnson grabbed his ears, but couldn't suppress a grin. His smile sank into a frown when he realized the sacred ceremony drew to a close.

"It's almost over; we have to get in there." Phil's half-hearted lunge was blocked by a slender arm and coils of dark hair framing a suddenly stern face.

"Ain't happening, so just cool your jets." Ankti Naatoqa, his liaison with the local tribes, blocked Phil with practiced ease despite being nearly a head shorter than his lanky six-foot frame.

With feet planted wide and arms crossed, the striking blue jacket draped over her sturdy frame billowed out from the dark top and matching pants like a cape in the rising wind. Raven hair pulled tight and coiled into a traditional bun above each ear gave the added impression of old-style earmuffs. Though she was only a couple years older than him, her stance told Phil that getting inside was non-negotiable. He already knew she was no pushover by the way Ankti dealt with tribal leaders. Most twenty-somethings lacked her smooth confidence and self-assurance.

As a full-blooded Hopi, the young woman proved instrumental in getting him interviews with dozens of couples living on

1

reservations around Phoenix. His bureau papers and permission from the tribal council gave him authority to speak with those families still able to have children, but Ankti made it happen.

The experts back east would analyze the data Phil collected, but to his thinking little more than clean living might account for the local population's relative immunity to the C-12 virus. Still, he was only halfway through the month-long assignment and would keep digging.

A great place to start was the intriguing event underway behind the wooden gate Ankti guarded. Several tribes gathered inside the crude walls, conducting an ancient ritual to protect their people from the rampant manmade virus. They'd converged on this little corner of Arizona, defying the crumbling infrastructure and dodging the worst pockets of civil unrest caused by industry's collapsed.

Ankti had scheduled interviews with representatives from the Cherokee, Navaho, and Pueblo nations, but nothing was going to replace watching first hand. His palms itched to shove the girl aside for just a peek—something his superiors would want him to do—but the thought was just an idle daydream.

Whistling rockets and reports overhead punctuated the chanting and rhythmic drums from within. Sparks swam into the desert sky on the hot breath of some massive fire that must have raged in the center of the enclosure.

The gathered nations would be undertaking fertility rights, wearing ceremonial regalia and enacting rituals passed down through generations. They'd never let a white guy from Philadelphia through the door, and his face grew hot at the thought of violating the sacred event. But still…

Phil tucked in the tail of his dress shirt and slicked a sandy-brown lock of curls back, as if making himself more presentable would help. They'd come straight from an evening meeting that he was starting to think had been intended to keep him away from the ceremony.

"Maybe you can go in and just sort of...I don't know... take notes. This is the real thing, right, dances and music meant to protect the tribes from the virus? My report won't be complete without a good account. Are they doing the Sundance in there, Firedance, other rites? And since when do fireworks play into these things? I *need* to know." He gave her a crooked smile, letting it reach his blue eyes in the way that worked so well on the girls back in his college days.

Of course, Widener College had closed before he'd completed his four-year program in Communication Studies. Like everywhere else, there just hadn't been enough professors and supplies thanks to declining populations and pervasive riots. They'd been naive to think the country—the world really—could continue as usual as the population aged out and fear settled across the masses.

As the school's doors closed, the board of directors had handed out diplomas like consolation prizes. "The world's probably ending, but here, have a sheepskin." Still, it had gotten him into the statistics branch at the Disease Control Center, a blended organization of national assets often referred to simply as the Bureau. The DCC had people way smarter than him scrambling to pinpoint the source of declining birth rates and figure out a cure.

But his college, could-have-been-in-a-frat-if-I'd-wanted-to smile had the opposite effect on the serene woman with broad high cheekbones and perfect coppery skin. Ankti's lovely face darkened.

"We do not speak of such things. If you know enough to ask, then you should know the dances are not to be spoken of outside the tribe and—" an explosion overhead followed by crackling streamers that fell like stars cut her off.

"I swear I wasn't making fun," Phil said as soon as the noise faded. "You're right, I should have known better. Please forgive me. I just feel so powerless. Despite decades of data collection, all we know at the Bureau is a third world contraceptive virus went wonky thirty years ago and spread across the globe. Only three percent of the world population can still have children.

"But it's different among Native Americans here in the southwest. Birth rates of the Hopi and Pueblo people have only dropped fifty percent. Why so different from other parts of the world with similar climate and conditions? It's more than just a statistical anomaly, and my bosses are counting on me to find an explanation. Don't you see, Ankti? This might be the Rosetta Stone to decipher how to combat C-12 before things get even worse."

Her liquid brown eyes softened as his voice broke. The world might be on the cusp of the end of days, and it worried him. He'd been born a C-12 carrier, just like his contemporaries, and wouldn't be having children of his own unless some miracle cure could be found. But the doctors and scientists couldn't put the genie they'd unwittingly released back in its bottle. The virus core they'd spliced their little sterilizing agents onto mutated too fast, was too resistant, and spread like wildfire. For all intents and purposes, the virus itself had burned out, leaving an altered human genome largely lacking in reproductive capability.

"The tribes gather in times of great need as they always have." She reached out and took his hand. "I won't report on the gathering to outsiders, no matter how urgent the need. To do so would be disrespectful to our customs and ancestors." At his sigh of acceptance she hurried on. "You are correct though. Traditional ceremonies seldom use gunpowder or other pyrotechnics. We've borrowed from Chinese and Anglo traditions in an attempt to call more attention to our prayers. That started in North America when the tribes were pushed to celebrate Independence Day. We never truly assimilated the practice, but honored our warriors and other achievements during July. So why not steal some of the white man's thunder to aid in our ceremonies?"

She returned his smile as another series of booms sounded overhead and lit the sky with cascades of falling sparks. This really was the grand finale. Participants streamed out of the far gate. Several were observers in street clothes, others in grand regalia. Styles varied from heavy beadwork to grand flourishes of dyed leather. Other outfits tended to tight lines, colorful cloth, and simple headwear. Many dancers wore a minimalistic breechcloth or jerkin, preferring to decorate bare chests, arms, and legs with painted symbols and stylized art. Men and women shuffled from the enclosure to the beat of departing drums and low chanting.

"We can go in now," Ankti finally said. "I'll tell you what I can, but I doubt much of it will be news."

"You sure? Not everyone's gone."

A lone drum, maybe two, beat on inside to the low singing of male voices.

"That's just the fire vigil. It's been too dry to leave a fire unattended."

Lights from departing cars illuminated the dusty ground, throwing neatly cultivated cactus patches to either side of the gate into stark relief. This was the second drought year in a row. Maybe part of the ceremony he'd almost witnessed focused on bringing much needed rain.

He was about to ask Ankti about rain dances, but the shadows were acting odd and pulled at his attention. Instead of lengthening and dropping away as the last car departed, the ground brightened as eerie gold light bathed the area. A miniature sun came into existence overhead, burning like a military flare to light the enclosure up like midday. But unlike a flare that would arc away or drift down on a parachute, the blazing ball streaked toward them, silent, blinding, and leaving a sparkling trail.

"Rogue firework, something in that last barrage went haywire!" Phil got the words out just as the missile shot into the far end of the enclosure.

He shielded his eyes and ducked low, anticipating the concussive explosion of sky-borne rockets. But the thing hit with a zip, sizzle, and muted thump like a felled tree making the ground jump.

Vertigo washed over him, an acute feeling of being watched. Phil peered into the shadows along the fence line, but there was nothing there. Ankti startled him from the disorienting moment by darting through the gate. He followed close on her heels.

The bonfire guttered low in the center of a wooden enclosure forty feet across. Pungent wood smoke carried the scent of burnt herbs and incense. Smoke and dusk left a haze over the scene. Two older men and one younger sat on bleachers, drums on their laps keeping cadence with taut, precise blows. They wore street clothes, and had donned jackets against the cool night air. Whatever had struck didn't faze these hardy souls.

"Nothing out of the ordinary." Phil scanned the area.

Except for a few folding chairs, perhaps for use by the older participants, there wasn't much else to see. Whatever pyrotechnic had shot back along its trajectory must have fizzled out just as it landed, thankfully without exploding and scorching anyone or setting the tall wooden fence on fire.

Ankti bowed her head and raised a hand in greeting as they approached the drummers. Phil mimicked the gesture and was pleased to receive a wave in return.

Movement in the smoke opposite the fire resolved into a lone dancer. The figure crossed in front of the flames, a silhouette draped in skins and doubled over under a large pack. He shuffled in that oddly mesmerizing way of the indigenous people, moccasin feet stomping out tight little circles.

The smoke shifted, and Phil blinked. The man had surely been old and bent, with an impressive hook of a nose and feathered headdress. But now, although he still shambled in that shuffling gait, the performer looked much younger—certainly no older than thirty—with thick dark hair falling past his shoulders. The nose was still proud between wideset eyes, but not the caricature beak from just moments before—a trick of the smoke or, more likely, the dancer had pulled off a ceremonial mask. He'd likewise dropped the pack he'd been carrying. Tighter and tighter, the lone man circled, his feet weaving an intricate pattern, but missing a step here and there.

"He's hurt!" Ankti's exclamation pulled Phil's attention away from the pattern he couldn't quite follow, and she hauled him forward just as the dancer stumbled.

Phil reached out and caught the man as he fell to his knees. He reeked of sage and maybe burnt rosemary, as if smoked. Which might not be that far off the mark. The white leather tunic and pants were supple as buttered leather along the front of the outfit. But when Phil shifted his grip, the back of the man's clothing crumbled like old newspaper, and his hand came away black.

"He's burned." Phil eased him onto his side, which drew a grunt from both men. The guy was a slab of beef. "His tunic is charred through. We need an ambulance."

"No doctors," the injured man wheezed in a dry croak.

"Damned rocket. Fireworks burn hot. Sounds like his lungs might be scorched too." Phil fumbled for his phone.

"Make the call," Ankti said as she pulled several items from the pouch that passed for her purse.

Phil stood and punched in 911. Ankti balanced a small roll of gauze, bandages, and antibiotic cream on a silver packet and gingerly pulled away a patch of burnt leather along the man's shoulder. A tin sat in her lap, and she dabbed thick yellow liquid on the blistered skin she'd exposed.

"Quite the girl scout," Phil said after the first ring then cursed as static filled his ear and the line went dead. "Cell service is crap out here."

To be fair it was crap everywhere. He dialed again with the same result before reaching for his work phone. The DCC had a special contract that bumped up the priority of their service to nearly pre-virus reliability levels. But this time when he keyed in the number, the line exploded with screeching tones like an old-style fax machine. The battery heated up fast in his palm, and he hastily keyed the power button before the damned thing melted down. Ankti raised an eyebrow as he shook his head and blew on his tingling fingers.

"Did it bite you? This is nothing to fool around with. Second-degree burns along his side. Might be third degree ones hidden under there. I'll pull my car around. We'll need to get him to Painted Rock General." She unfolded the silver packet an impossible number of times, revealing a tissue-thin emergency blanket that she draped over her patient.

"No hospital." The man's voice was strong with an air of command.

Phil opened his mouth, but snapped it shut. *No use arguing.* Phil squinted through the smoke and waved. The drummers played on, ignoring the exchange.

"Little help here! We have a man down." No one so much as looked up. "Hey!"

Ankti shrugged, and Phil stood, intending to drag a couple of the men over. The fire wouldn't go out of control in the few minutes it would take to help figure out a plan.

"*You* care for me. Know medicine." Beady black eyes caught Ankti in a hawkish gaze.

"I know a little first aid." The woman tucked the blanket in tighter and shook her head as if to clear it before turning. "Phil, I can handle this. Let's just take…" she trailed off and looked back. "What's your name?"

"K—k—k." The man stuttered as if fighting to get his name out, the brash command gone from his voice.

"Poor man's freezing cold. We'll take Kay to my place." Ankti nodded, coming to a decision. "I've got the week off and can nurse him back to health."

Something about her idea sounded wrong. Phil squinted at the drummers. He took two steps toward them and paused. *What did he need to tell them?* Something about the hurt man. He looked back into shining black eyes that gazed on with a kind of pressure. Hopefully the guy wasn't fevered on top of the burns. That might not be easy to deal with at home, but…Ankti seemed competent. She'd be able to take care of Kay. A building anxiety he hadn't noticed flowed away with the decision. *Yes, Ankti can handle this.*

They loaded Kay behind the passenger seat. He'd dropped into a near stupor once they'd decided on a course of action. Away from the smoke, Phil found himself thinking more clearly. This wasn't going to be an easy recovery, and he didn't like the thought of Ankti alone with a stranger on her couch.

"The Bureau put me up in a three-bedroom townhouse. It's a corporate property that's too big, but it'd be perfect for getting Kay situated with his own room."

"But I need to watch over him." Ankti gently closed the rear door and went on to explain she'd once aspired to be a nurse. With several first aid courses under her belt, she'd even become the unofficial medic at tribal events—thus her pouch of goodies.

"I just don't think it's a good idea to be alone with a stranger, even if he's recovering. We don't know anything about this guy."

It wasn't a macho notion, just common sense. Phil eyed the muscular arms and broad chest that rose in shallow breaths in her back seat. Someone certainly needed to take care of Kay, and since hospitals were out Ankti seemed a good alternative.

"I've only got a studio apartment." Ankti sounded embarrassed and uncertain.

"Then it's settled. You can both stay with me. I'll be in that lime-green junker over there." He pointed to the expense report item that would offset the bill for his fancy digs. "Follow me to Stony Brook Gardens. It's a townhouse complex off I-15. I'm in 118, the last unit on the far end. Place is like a ghost town because the corporate folks aren't holding retreats anymore. Plenty of parking."

"I'll need to pick up clothes at some point, but"—she looked from Phil to Kay, perhaps thinking she was about to move in with two strangers instead of one—"it's a deal. Wait, he had a backpack earlier. Let's grab that."

They headed through the near gate and poked around behind the dwindling fire. A foot deep crater big enough to lay down in had been blasted in the hard-packed dirt, and bits of what looked like charcoal lay scattered about. The pack Kay had dropped must have been three feet long, but there was no sign of it now.

"Maybe the drummers took it when they left." Ankti shrugged, then pointed to a glowing branch that must have kicked out of the fire. "Oh, there's something."

Odd that he hadn't noticed the fire watch leaving.

Ankti walked over to the branch and picked it up! Drummers forgotten, Phil lunged to stop her, but pulled up short, blinking in confusion. Rather than holding a red-hot brand, Ankti's delicate hand wrapped around a two-foot length of gleaming wood with holes down the middle. One end tapered to a flat mouthpiece, while the other flared.

"A flute?" He shook his head to clear the cobwebs. It certainly had *looked* like a burning branch.

The wood was rich caramel with a leather wrap securing an ornamental block six inches from the tapered end. The little carving of a beast squatted with mouth open to expose delicate wooden fangs. The dying fire shimmered and danced in reflections across the polished surface. Simple animal carvings came to life near the neck and bell, seeming to sway and glow in response to the flames.

"Handmade and old." Ankti tucked the flute into her jacket. "Let's get Kay back to your place."

2. A New Normal

S KIN PRICKLED along the back of Phil's neck during the drive to his apartment. Tonight's gathering had been way out on the edge of town, and it was midnight by the time they'd loaded Kay up and got going. The deathly quiet streets put his nerves on edge. It just wasn't a good night to be out.

Ankti followed down the dusty back roads to the interstate, which slashed southwest through the urban areas like a scar across the desert. He liked that she followed at a safe distance instead of riding his bumper. But she drove with the dash lights turned up too high, which would cut down on her visibility and reaction time. On the plus side, it let him see all was well. She'd even given him a thumbs up and cute little wave before hitting the highway.

Twenty years ago, there would have been more traffic late at night, but people were abandoning these out of the way places to converge on industrial centers desperate for workers. The nation's core industries would thrive for a while yet, but many plants producing luxury and frivolous items had already shut down. Even the auto industry was on its last legs, no great loss given the stockpile of new cars sitting at loading docks and depots across the country. But all in all, the nation struggled.

Bands of outlaws had cropped up like it was already the end of civilization. Riots broke out at the slightest provocation, and people were scared. They had a right to be. National and local governments weren't going to hold together much longer. More and more often, the National Guard and military were dispatched to quell civil unrest despite both organizations being downsized to token forces.

High-beams lanced into the night as Phil scanned the gullies and scrub to either side of the road, certain something waited to dart from the dark. It was the time of night for fox, coyote, and possibly pronghorn, though he'd never actually seen any of the critters that looked more like dogs with antlers than true antelope.

"Damn it!" Phil watched his exit roll by behind a snarl of flat-leaved cacti.

The next ramp would put him on a frontage road that tracked back along the freeway. The detour would add ten minutes, no big deal, but the delay made him jittery. He hadn't felt like this since that South American assignment. His superiors ought to have known better than to send a pair of analysts to investigate population dips near drug cartels where guerilla warfare replaced law enforcement. Two days was all it took to realize the decline had little to do with the C-12 virus and dropping birth rates. Keeping their heads low and finding a plane out that wouldn't be shot down had taxed Phil's nerves and left him addicted to rum smoothies. Down there, the jungle had eyes.

Maybe tonight was a flashback, a bit of his PTSD stirring up the imagination. He slowed well before the next exit and hit the turn signal half a mile early. Ankti's midnight-blue SUV rolled down the ramp behind and made the smooth U-turn onto the frontage road just as two sets of headlights—the first he'd seen on the drive home—came barreling off the freeway. One car, a dark blocky model, fell in behind Ankti, while the other raced south with the screaming whine of a turbo diesel.

Ten minutes turned to fifteen, and their little procession pulled into the parking lot. By the shape of the headlights, the car behind Ankti must be a Hummer—a guess that was confirmed as the driver peeled off under the lights to park farther down the row of houses.

As they wrestled Kay inside, a slender woman and large man stepped out of the para-military luxury vehicle. She was trim and neat, wearing a bright pantsuit and jacket, her dark hair pulled back tight to expose a long face and sharp nose. Details were hard to make out from three houses away, but her eyes burned golden-orange. That had to be a trick of the lighting because the big man's wild hair and bushy red beard flickered under the streetlamp as if on fire. The pair watched them, a strange creaking and occasional clank of metal drifting across the brittle brown grass that passed for a lawn. Phil raised his hand in a tentative wave. There were few enough people in the complex, and being friendly didn't cost anything.

The woman inclined her chin as if in response, then flipped her head toward their unit. The Hummer's back doors opened. Two more people dressed in dark outfits jumped out and raced to the door. The woman followed with feline grace, the man in tow stomping and creaking like some medieval wooden war cart—or leather. That was it; he wore heavy motorcycle leathers with zippers that jangled as he strode to the door and they all disappeared inside. Phil shook his head as he absently draped Kay's left arm over his shoulder and hoisted their charge upright. Ankti took his other side.

Kay's dragging feet left twin furrows through the plush sage carpet as they maneuvered their patient past the kitchen doorway, leather couch, and dark wood coffee table. The front bedroom opened off the living room, and they lowered him onto the covers.

Ankti spread her first aid supplies across the dresser and sent Phil to fetch a pan of water and the bulk of his undershirts to clean the wounds. When all was ready, she got to work gently wiping away charred ash and soot so she could inspect the damage. She applied salve to most of the burns. Some got bandaged, while others were left open to the air.

It soon became obvious he wasn't needed, so Phil left to set up the other bedroom. By the time he finished making the bed, laying out towels, and scrounging up extra miniature soap and shampoo, Ankti was in the kitchen rummaging through the fridge.

"He'll be out for a while." She waved the milk jug at the closed bedroom door. "Burns are serious, but probably not life threatening. I'm more worried about the strange gouges and bruising along the nape of his neck—well, that and the fact he doesn't know where he is—or who he is for that matter. There's a nasty knot on the back of his head. A concussion might have his memory jumbled. Mumbled a little, but still couldn't come up with his name, still only got the first letter out."

"He need stitches?" Phil asked.

"Wounds aren't too deep, just strange, like big claw marks or something. I guess his mask could have been cracked and gouged him when he pulled it off. The butterfly bandages should close the cuts up, and there's triple antibiotic in that salve."

"Lucky you were carrying all that stuff." He grabbed two glasses and motioned for her to pour.

"Not luck really." Ankti hesitated, a blush darkening her lovely skin, but she got control in a moment and looked up. "Sometimes first aid is needed at the rituals. Between that and not having enough doctors, I just tend to come prepared." He must have looked too interested because she clenched her jaw tight, scooped up her glass, and headed for the living room. "That's all I've got to say on the subject. But I do need to run back to my place and get more supplies, not to mention some clean clothes. I could plant corn in this outfit."

Now that she mentioned it, his shirt felt gritty against his skin, like he'd been rolling in sand before getting dressed. All those stomping feet had raised tons of dust.

It still seemed odd that they hadn't found Kay's mask and backpack. Maybe one of the other tribal dancers was a friend and had circled back to grab Kay's stuff while they wrestled him to the car. But if so, why not stop to check on him? If he'd left with the others in the first place, he never would have gotten clobbered by the fireworks and Ankti wouldn't have to play nurse.

"So why'd Kay stay late? He didn't seem to be on the fire team."

"No, he wouldn't be in traditional dress for that." She sighed and downed her milk, perhaps considering whether the discussion strayed into privileged information. "I have no idea why he stayed behind. Maybe that knot on his head was from earlier and confused him, so he didn't realize the event was over.

"Doesn't matter, we're stuck with Kay for now. Keep an eye on him while I run home. Should take less than an hour. The first twenty-four are critical. If he doesn't wake up"—she paused at the door—"we'll *have* to figure out better arrangements."

Phil knew she meant take him to the hospital, but she didn't voice the thought. Phil found himself unwilling to say it out loud too. Kay didn't want a hospital, so that was that. Or was it? He'd been working on too little sleep lately and shook his head to break the cobwebs loose.

"Yeah," Phil cleared his throat with a nervous little cough, but couldn't bring himself to add anything useful. "We'll figure it out."

3. Day Off

K AY SLEPT on while Ankti went to retrieve her things—his rhythmic snoring made it easy to tell. Rather than the brash sawing of logs that Phil's uncle used to wake the whole house with, this was more of a mild fluttering deep in his chest like the rumbling purr of an annoyingly content cat.

Phil scrounged through his suitcases for a loose-fitting shirt and jeans. At some point the guy needed to get dressed. Ankti had him propped up on his side with a rolled towel so that the burns didn't rub. Blisters ran along bright red skin on his ribcage across to the right shoulder blade. The thick yellow salve made him look like he'd rolled in honey and was going to be a bear to get out of the powder-blue sheets. Though Ankti left those burns open to the air, there were two large patches on his upper back covered with gauze pads, and a small flock of butterfly bandages ran down either side of his neck closing up the gashes she's mentioned.

The skin that wasn't damaged—and there was a lot of that showing because he'd been stripped down to his oddly archaic underwear—gleamed in the dim light as if he might be running a fever. Olive skin took on a yellow cast under the dresser lamplight. Aside from his lustrous black mane there wasn't a hair to be seen on chest, legs, or anywhere else.

The bold nose fit his long face well, a curved promontory rising between high apple cheeks similar to Ankti's. His jutting chin fell just shy of being sharp, with a barely noticeable cleft that even Phil had to admit was quite dashing. He reassessed Kay's age, upping it by several years based on the slabs of muscle layered over shoulders and arms. Although unlined, the man's face held an ageless quality like those of Asian descent, but he certainly looked to be Native American. Ultimately Phil failed to settle on a number. Their patient could be anywhere from his upper twenties to early forties.

No matter what his age, all Phil's tee-shirts were going to be too tight for his burns to heal properly. Phil's lanky six-foot-two frame about matched up to Kay's, so the pants would be fine. But they'd have to pick up a couple of extra-large button down shirts.

"Knock, knock," Ankti called softly as she came in through the front door.

"No problems?" Phil stepped out of the bedroom and pulled the door partway closed.

"All's well." She hoisted a bright blue duffle bag with a big red cross on it and stood a rolling suitcase up by the sofa. "More cars than usual out there for some reason, but maybe those are just tribal reps coming in early for Thursday's event. How's our patient?"

"Sleeping soundly."

Cars weren't a problem, and whatever had him so uptight on the ride back certainly didn't seem to affect Ankti. Her demeanor always put him and others at ease. When not blocking his entry to forbidden events, the woman positively radiated happiness. Even her frowns seemed to glow with suppressed joy.

Hopefully she wasn't a morning person. Grumpy until nine and caffeine was Phil's normal mode. Living in close quarters with someone who was a morning ray of sunshine could be a problem. As it was, Ankti oohed and ahhed over the leather couch and granite kitchen counters. She checked out the entire common area and even poked her head into the coat closet.

"Bedroom at the end of the hall just past the bath is all yours. I'm up here near the living room."

"Let me check on him before I get settled." Ankti grabbed the blue bag and headed for Kay's room. "It's been a wild night, and I'm too wired to sleep anyway."

"I've got beer, wine, and seltzer. And I think there's some cheese and crackers. I can pull together a snack if you want."

"A beer sounds good, as long as it's something decent. Just give me a minute."

She moved quietly around the patient, checking the bandages and reapplying her salve. They'd have to open the windows soon because the place smelled like an herb garden.

By the time he had a snack plate together, she'd finished with Kay, stowed her suitcase, and returned from the bedroom wearing light flannel pants and a loose top covered with wild horses.

"Nice outfit." Phil couldn't help noticing how it hugged her ample hips.

"Get used to it. I like horses and being comfy."

"I wasn't poking fun." He held out a beer bottle as a peace offering. "Wait till you see my footy pajamas."

"That may fall into the category of TMI." She winked, took the bottle, and plopped down on the couch. "On a more serious note, what do you make of our guest?"

"Honestly?" Phil took the recliner opposite the coffee table and leaned forward to stack crackers, ham, and cheese onto a napkin. "Looks like a clean-cut guy. No knife fighting scars or anything. I'm guessing someone's noticed he's missing. And we do need to find him clothes at some point."

"Yes, I realize that." Her cheeks flushed prettily, and Phil had to wonder what was going through her head. "I'll put the word and a pic out to the tribal council. Tall fellow, but he sure looks full blooded. Can't place the tribe. His outfit could have been from any number of regions. Probably came in with an out-of-town group."

Phil nodded, and they drank in silence for a few minutes, each lost in their own thoughts. Tomorrow's three interviews would have to be moved to later in the week if they were going to keep an eye on Kay.

Ironically, he'd planned to spend the afternoon in the hospital records department, and two of the elders who'd agreed to meet Phil didn't speak much English. He needed Ankti to interpret and work her magic to put everyone at ease. Regardless of tribe, the locals considered her an honest broker.

Reservation boundaries had been redrawn as whites, Latinos, and other groups migrated to the coast in search of work in the collapsing post-virus economy. Sad that it took another catastrophe for tribes to gain back a bit of the land they'd lost. The free-for-all that had slowly unfolded over the past couple of decades left a patchwork of nation territories close in to the city proper. Hopi lands lay largely to the north, a smaller island surrounded on three sides by the Navajo nation and by Zuni lands to the south.

Native Americans were rightly proud of their heritage, and nations could have wildly different opinions, but individuals worked together well. So he had no intention of continuing interviews without this young woman by his side.

"What are we doing here?" Her question interrupted his thoughts. "I mean…you know, why?"

"Harboring a stranger?" That wasn't quite what she was asking, but any other way of stating things slipped from his mind.

"Well yes, but we shouldn't…It doesn't make sense…" she struggled for words.

Phil empathized. Something niggled at him, a thought that refused to surface. They were doing something wrong here. Maybe rescheduling those interviews was a bad idea. That would delay things. The Bureau liked interim reports, but wouldn't be expecting an update for a few days yet.

"I'm not a doctor!" Ankti forced the words through gritted teeth. Once they were out those that followed flowed easier. "I'm not a nurse either. What the hell possessed me to care for a stranger? I could just as easily kill the guy."

"Well…" Phil tried to kick his brain into gear. The beer helped loosen his thoughts, but they looped about in fuzzy, lazy circles. "Kay said no doctors. We didn't have a choice. Right?"

Ankti opened her mouth to reply just as dulcet tones drifted from the front bedroom, a handful of scattered, echoing notes that made him think of running water and sunsets.

"I left the flute on his nightstand." Ankti jumped up, and Phil followed her to the bedroom.

She pushed open the door. Kay hadn't budged. The wooden flute nestled between alarm clock and lamp gleamed in the dim light. The carvings along the bell shifted in shadow as the door widened to admit more light, and the surface brightened.

"Could that have been the wind?" Phil asked.

"Guess so." She squinted at the flute, then shook her head. "Evening temperature swings around here are notorious for producing interesting effects. We've got plenty of 'singing hills' nearby. It sure sounded like music there for a second, but he's still chugging along."

"Sounds like a happy pussy cat to me." Phil shook his empty bottle and offered to take the one Ankti still clutched. "Another?"

She handed over the bottle and closed the door before heading back to the couch. "I think I might need one more. Something to go with"—her hand hovered over the plate, and her eyebrows rose—"cookies! Now we're talking."

* * *

21

They stayed up a while longer, finishing that second beer and chatting. Although Phil had worked with the woman for two weeks there was a lot he didn't know, like how she'd spent four years in San Diego trying to put her paralegal degree from Arizona State to good use before returning to work for the Coalition of Native Nations. Ankti's parents—actual birth parents—had scrimped and saved to loan her money for the expenses not covered by scholarships. She'd loved the cool breezes and lifestyle on the coast, but even though she'd been able to pay back her folks, the high cost of living sucked away every extra penny. So she'd returned to give back what she could to her community.

A trace of bitterness colored her words. "I'll never have kids of my own so I might as well do what I can to help those who do."

Ankti had tested C-12 positive back in her teens. It was the one test everyone dreaded, a simple blood draw and exam to identify sterility and crush dreams. Trending statistics lumped ninety-seven percent of the world in with Ankti and Phil.

The three-percenters capable of bearing children were envied and sometimes in danger. A few desperate people would do anything to have a family. Underground human trafficking targeted the girls early on, making the database of resistant teens dangerous information that now was protected as a national security asset. Individuals of course knew their own results, but it was a rare thing for anyone to openly disclose they were resistant until that first child showed up. And, as in Ankti's case, the resistance to C-12 wasn't necessarily passed along.

After looking in once more on Kay, they both headed to bed, but checked hourly to make certain he still rested peacefully. The night passed without incident, interspersed with occasional echoing tones drifting on the wind.

The next morning, Phil thought back on the evening while brushing his teeth. He spit and grinned at the image of Ankti in her horse pajamas. They were going to get along just fine, and once Kay got better his interviews and investigations could continue. It had been foolish last night to worry about the delay and gnash his teeth over taking Kay to the hospital. The man certainly didn't need any doctors, just lots of rest.

The day passed as quickly and pleasantly as the prior evening. They talked and laughed over a breakfast of oatmeal and left-over cookies. Kay slept on, and Ankti headed out shopping, insisting they needed staples to get through the next few days.

After spending two hours on the dreaded quarterly projections, Phil called the hospital. Thanks to an unexpectedly strong cell signal, he was able to download to the bulk of the data he'd meant to review in person. Since the hospital staff had already scrubbed out personal information, the files were no longer sensitive and didn't require special handling. Kay still hadn't moved by the time Ankti returned, stocked the kitchen, and pulled Phil away from his computer and into the sickroom.

"His burns look much better, but you have to help me move him," she said.

"Ya gotta be kidding." Phil stifled a laugh and lowered his voice. "The guy's a side of beef. We aren't moving him anywhere. Just let him sleep."

"We need to turn him a little to prevent bed sores." Her jaw went tight when he grinned. "It sounds trivial, but if blood flow is cut off to a spot the skin dies, goes necrotic, and liquefies. If you want a cheap gruesome window into the body, let a patient lay in one spot for too long. Unfortunately, I've seen—and smelled—it up close. Go pull up pics online and you'll lose that smirk and probably your lunch."

"So do we just push him over?"

No was the answer to that question. She'd strategically placed a sheet underneath Kay and showed Phil how to assist her. In short order they had the man on his other side and angled toward the nightstand, avoiding pressure on the worst of his injuries.

Their evening was subdued. They ate tacos on Indian fry bread that Ankti made, surfed through the limited offerings on the big-screen television mounted opposite the couch, and settled on a local program about the big aquarium just over in Scottsdale, Arizona. It was odd to think the tourist attraction stayed in business, but the program made it sound like more of a labor of love. The locals couldn't bear the thought of thousands of sea creatures dying, and volunteers dominated the current workforce.

They turned Kay again before bed, and his eyes fluttered open—dark as midnight with irises barely distinguishable from the pupils of a cat about to pounce. The man's breathing caught, and for a moment Phil thought he might actually be awake. But Kay's eyes drifted closed, and that purring snore ushered his caregivers out of the room.

4. Don't Desert Me

T HEY NEEDED to do something with Kay today. Phil woke determined to talk about the elephant in the room, that topic they both kept skirting away from. He shaved, did his teeth, and dressed while repeating an inner mantra: "He goes to the hospital today. He goes to the hospital today. He—"

Hollow tones drifted in on the morning winds, this time bringing more than just a scattering of random notes. They held a definite pattern and grew stronger, seeming to come from all around. No, that wasn't right. Phil opened the window, but the melody—yes, it truly was a song—didn't get louder. At his bedroom door it did; music flowed down the hall.

Ankti poked her head out at the same time, just past eight according to the clock on his nightstand. They rushed down the hall, swimming upstream against what was now beautiful music. Ankti hadn't dressed yet, and Phil followed the galloping horses on her back to their patient's room.

Kay lay awkwardly against the headboard, his flute clasped in both hands and playing with eyes closed. Dark hair brushed the bandages on his shoulder as his head swayed to the haunting rhythm. The sheen of sweat was gone, though the room still reeked of herbs.

Ankti must have done something with his hair last night for it to look so clean.

"Kay?" Ankti called as she stepped into the room.

He didn't respond, simply kept playing, fingers flying now as the tune picked up momentum and energy. It crescendoed with a high trilling that crested into a pure single note and trailed off like the cry of a hawk.

"Kay, can you hear me?" Ankti moved to stand by his side, but his eyes remained closed, his breathing smooth and deep as though he inhaled his surroundings.

She reached out a tentative hand, and Phil's cleared his throat in warning. It might not be wise to—

Kay's eyes flew open, wild and bright, pupils huge. He sat up and winced as his bad shoulder brushed the headboard.

"It's all right. We're friends. I'm Ankti and this is Phil." She touched her chest and nodded toward the door.

"Hurt?" His black gaze settled on Phil as the word rasped from his dry throat.

"You were at the cleansing ceremony and got hit by a firework that misfired." She offered him a sip from the cup of water on the dresser. "Do you remember that?"

His head cocked at an angle, a bird considering the morsel of information. "Not that. Fell."

His words were stilted and heavy with an accent that managed to emphasize the vowels, but another sip of water helped his voice sound less harsh.

"You hit your head." Ankti spoke slowly and gently touched her fingers to the knot behind the man's right ear. He mirrored the movement and winced. "We've been calling you Kay because it's all you could get out after the accident."

"Except for the no doctor and no hospital commands," Phil said.

"No Kay. Name K—k…" He glared at Phil, turned his head away as if pouting, then tried again. "K—ko—k. Fine!"

"Head traumas mess with you." Ankti's voice and demeanor soothed more than just their patient, taking the sting out of the unspoken accusation in Kay's eyes—as if it was Phil's fault the guy couldn't remember his own name. "It's only been a couple of days. Give it a little time for things to come back."

"Is there a friend we can call, maybe someone who came to town with you?" Phil took a cautious step into the room, not wanting to spook the man further.

Ankti pulled an event flyer from the side pocket of her medic bag and handed it to Kay. "Do any of these look familiar?" A list of participating tribes and nations filled the bottom third. He squinted at the page and shook his head.

"That's okay. We'll figure it out eventually." She tried to take the flyer back, but he held onto it. "How about some food? We'll have to take it easy or your stomach might rebel. Eggs and toast?"

Breakfast was a silent affair involving several aborted conversations. Their guest was unsteady on his feet, but managed to get into jeans, a light-blue shirt, and slip-on shoes Ankti had purchased. They took turns trying to engage him in conversation, but Kay stayed withdrawn. When he did venture to respond, his accent and incomplete sentences made his answers hard to follow. The accident had addled more than just his memory.

"Not here," was all Kay said in reply to questions about where he lived. He didn't recognize city names or show much interest in the tribal regions. Phil even asked him to play more music, figuring that would be good therapy, but Kay shook his head and shoved the instrument through a belt loop so that it dangled from his waist like a nightstick.

"He seems stronger, but not very cooperative," Phil said under his breath as he and Ankti cleaned up after lunch.

"I admit he's hard to follow, but I doubt it's on purpose." She finished drying a white plate with decorative piping around its perimeter and handed it to him to put away.

"Can you place the accent? Maybe that's a place to start."

"It's certainly heavy." She tugged at the bun of hair coiled tight over her left ear. "Like our elders who are nearly octogenarians. But Kay's too young to have been brought up not speaking English; at least, it's uncommon for the people around here. I couldn't even guess where he might be from."

"How are we going to continue with interviews tomorrow with him like this?" Phil slammed the cabinet door with more force than he'd intended and grimaced an apology.

"I doubt he's dangerous or likely to wander off."

"Leave him here?" His voice cracked on the idea. "All day?"

"It's either that, push the meetings off until after Thursday's ceremony, or bring him along." She held up a hand cutting off Phil's protest. "You're the one on a schedule. How do you want to spend your last two weeks before heading back?"

"Maybe I can get an extension. It feels like there's something important hidden in the hospital data. A bit more analysis and…" Phil looking past Ankti. Kay danced around the living room like a madman, going still every few seconds to glare down at the coffee table. "What the *hell* is he doing?"

As they stepped into the room, Kay flung both arms up, leapt to the left, and glared down at the table. A moment later he dropped to all fours, big nose pressed to the wood and one beady eye focused on the ceremony flyer sitting near his glass of water. He studied the edge of the paper as if trying to see under it.

"Is there something—" Ankti jumped when Kay slapped his palm hard onto the wood.

"There!" He pointed at the flyer.

"You recognize a tribe?" Phil ventured.

With a curt shake of his head, Kay jabbed a finger at the top of the page where directions had been printed for those coming in via the airport or local roads. "Come from there."

The tiny map alongside the directions wasn't to scale. It showed only major highways, a roughly drawn scattering of mountains, and an arrow for where to park near the ceremonial enclosure. Kay's finger hovered above a thin blue line to the east where two roads merged near a small lake on the otherwise black–and–white map.

"Not much out there north of Salt River nowadays," Ankti said. "I think there used to be a few campgrounds and maybe a state park, but all that's defunct. Let's pull up a real map online. Maybe I'm forgetting something."

Kay's eyes gleamed with interest as Phil brought out his laptop and searched for a decent map. During the two decades of chaos in the wake of C-12, database updates had fallen by the wayside. He settled on a ten-year-old representation that let him toggle between a simple road map, topological features, and old satellite imagery.

"There." Kay stood over his shoulder and pointed to a blank area north of what was labeled as Lake Saguaro.

Salt River entered the mile-long body of water from the southeast as a wide blue inlet and left to the southwest as a pencil-thin tributary. Phil cursored over the mint-green area—an odd color for Arizona desert—about three miles north. Kay drove a palm into his shoulder and nodded at the screen as though urging Phil to climb in.

"Geez, calm down." Phil scowled as Kay gave him another ungentle nudge. "Not a damned thing there. Let's check satellite."

The bird's-eye looked down on Mars, except the dry hills weren't red, and a horseshoe of dark water glittered near the bottom of his screen. Zooming in showed a couple of dusty roads dropping down from Route 87, but they petered out into little more than dirt paths, or maybe just dry gullies.

"Up!" Kay tried to help him move the mouse north, then west.

"Slapping my arm isn't making this any easier."

As they moved east the terrain shifted from vast fields of erosion fanning north from the lake to varied and rocky landscapes. With some zooming in and out, single word commands, and much jarring and pushing, which made Phil feel like he was back in school doing homework for a certain bully, the cursor settled on an interesting feature. The rock promontory sat a mile above the river and a good way to the east of where they started.

"Go there!" Kay jabbed his finger at the center of the screen.

A flat spot sat to the east of a long ravine running south to the river. Judging by the scale, the area couldn't be more than a quarter-mile wide, a kidney-shaped plateau. A shadow stretched north from the landmass. Of course there was no way to judge the position of the sun, but by the shadow's length the flat area of ground likely rose several hundred feet, a squatter, wider Devil's Tower.

"Go where?" Phil threw up his hands, and Kay growled—actually growled! "It's nothing but rocks and ridges."

"Remember, that image is ten years old." Ankti used the reasonable voice that always helped get information from stubborn locals. "Could be anything out there by now. That's going to be on or near the Salt River Reservation, Pima and Maricopa land. Look, there *are* roads. We could drive out there. It's only thirty miles or so."

"As the crow flies." He zoomed out and traced the only path a car might use. "And calling these roads is generous. They look more like dirt paths. We'd have to circle this huge wasteland up along eighty-seven to the north-east and then drop down past the lake to get back to Phoenix. Fifty miles easy each way."

"Now. Go now." Kay pointed to the screen and collected his things—well, thing. He scooped the flute off the couch, gave it a loving caress, and settled it into his belt loop.

"Got something better to do?" Ankti gave a disarming smile that made it impossible to get mad.

Cheater.

They took her car due to the fact that Kay didn't have one and Phil's piece-of-crap barely had two-wheel drive, let alone four. Despite his reservations, the drive was pleasant, discounting the many times Kay urged speed by slamming the back of Phil's seat. It was like having a spoiled brat in the seat behind you on a crowded flight. But he settled down once Ankti turned on the radio.

They found a nice classic rock station and everyone grooved to the tunes. Kay picked up the songs' melodies quickly and seemed ready to sing along on the more iconic tunes, but contented himself with humming or whistling.

Suburban neighborhoods and lightly populated business parks quickly gave way to desert hills, then—surprisingly—to miles of farmland before opening on sweeping vistas. Shrubs and cacti dotted hills cresting into the distance under a blue sky that went on forever. The hazy horizon stretched wide, giving way graciously to rocky crags of multi-colored strata and water-etched landscapes carved by a thousand years of summer monsoons.

The desert offered muted beauty and quiet power. Back in Pennsylvania forests ruled, even before the disaster. Now, many neighborhoods and towns stood empty, the inhabitants consolidating as populations tailed off. Ghost towns might have been the purview of the old west, but abandoned mining outposts had nothing on what was going on across the nation, the world. And back east, as soon as people moved out, the forest moved in. As much as he liked trees, there was something refreshing in seeing the land exposed and raw, as if looking behind the curtain of the world's stage.

"Hang on!" Ankti called out as the SUV dipped off the main road, pulling Phil out of his reverie with a stomach-lurching drop.

The dirt road was well maintained—at first. But after they passed an abandoned wildlife recreation area, the surface turned to a teeth-rattling washboard and narrowed to barely wider than the car.

"I'm not so sure this is actually a road," Phil managed between chattering teeth as they bounced along. "Maybe a walking path."

"Out here, everything's fair game." Ankti grinned, but kept her eyes glued to the road.

She's enjoying this!

The GPS in the dash chimed and in a pleasant male voice told them to turn left into a rock wall.

Phil squinted at the satellite view he'd saved to the laptop. "Road splits off up ahead. Bear left. We'll head east for a little over a mile. The second right should be the one we want. A lot of ups and downs coming, but stick to the ridgeline for maybe two miles."

Washboard turned to cratered moon as the GPS prattled irrelevant recommendations. But programming in the latitude and longitude of the promontory that got Kay so excited did put a little checkered flag on the display. And they headed in the right direction.

The road swept down from the ridge on a treacherous grade that had them both white knuckled. Phil risked a glance into the back. Kay, oblivious to the height and drops to either side, had his cheek pressed against the window watching the sky. Phil had already yelled at him twice to keep the window up because he kept sticking his head out, which quickly filled the car with dust. The road leveled off, and Phil let out a relieved sigh. The expected tee in the road came into view, and they headed east.

"Faster." Kay slammed the back of the seat.

"Go ahead and do that just one more time, buddy, and we're going to have a problem."

"Another right up here?" Ankti verbally stepped between them with her overly cheerful let-it-go voice.

"Yeah." Phil spared one last glare for Kay, which rolled off the guy like water from a duck. "Should be the last one. GPS concurs we're directly north. The ravine will be twisty but plenty wide. Keep your eyes open; this doesn't look to have been used as a road in years. Unless we missed an approach from the south, I can't see how there's going to be a town between us and the river. We haven't even seen tire tracks since the rec area back there."

"Even if this turns out to be a bust, you have to admit it's a gorgeous drive." She was smiling again.

Definitely having too much fun.

Though sandy and winding, the final leg was not that bad. All told they'd traveled only five or six miles since leaving the blacktop by the time the rock wall rose to their left. At first, Phil thought the fifty-foot cliff face was their destination, but the ravine ran right along it. They continued on and the wall petered out, replaced by another steppe twice as high fifty yards off. Ankti stopped the car when a third edifice rose beyond that, towering hundreds of feet above them.

The GPS and satellite image confirmed this was the land feature they sought. With the sun casting shadows off the far side of the satellite overlay, he'd missed the shorter cliffs rising near the road like steps—a giant's stairway to rival any fairytale beanstalk.

"Lovely spot, but now what?" Phil asked.

As answer, Kay opened his door and jumped out. He strode across the rock-strewn expanse between road and cliff like something out of legend, back straight, dark hair flowing in the wind. He walked with purpose as if knowing exactly where he was headed. They scrambled out to follow.

A stone's throw short of the cliff Kay stopped, head cocked to the side as if listening. He turned in place three times, examined the sky, then scooped up a pinch of dirt and scattered it in the breeze. With a nod he angled to the left toward a dark patch at the base of the wall, a squared off cave entrance—a doorway! Kay crossed the threshold and disappeared into darkness.

"Come on, we're gonna lose him." Phil urged Ankti forward.

The last thing they needed was for Kay to get lost in a cave system or old mine. They'd have to get the authorities involved then for sure. But the woman slowed, stopped well shy of the opening, and let out an impressive snort.

"Just great." She crossed her arms and looked as annoyed as he'd ever seen her.

"We need to get in there before he gets too far ahead." Phil waved at the opening.

Ankti shook her head, sighed, and grabbed his arm. She pulled him over in front of her and pointed at the entrance. Kay stood just around the corner at a blank stone wall about five paces in.

"It's just a natural depression," she said, then called out to Kay. "You coming back?" He just stood there facing away. "We can still see you, you know."

After a long awkward moment, Kay backed out of the opening. "Something is wrong."

"Just the wrong place." Phil went for an optimism he didn't truly feel, and he certainly wasn't looking forward to the ride back to the highway given Ankti's daredevil driving. "In a day or two, something will look familiar."

"This right place." In one smooth motion, Kay pulled the flute from his belt and sank into a cross-legged sit facing the opening. "Perhaps wrong time. We wait."

He started in on another haunting melody that began with drawn out note pairs, each ending abruptly so that it pulled you in wanting to hear what came next. Long pregnant pauses had Phil hearing phantom drums as he involuntarily counted the beat off in his head. The notes built into short stanzas with the same truncated end note until the tune burst forth in a complex tapestry. This was not going to be a short performance. Phil raised a questioning eyebrow at Ankti, but she simply smiled.

"Good thing I packed lunch." She headed to the car and pulled open the hatchback.

He'd seen her throw a few items into the back, but had somehow missed the insulated sack containing bread, cheese, meats, and assorted snacks. She even had bottled water and a small blanket that helped keep the food out of the sandy dirt.

"You must have been a scout." Phil helped lay out the spread near some rocks made for sitting.

"Our community doesn't have the kind of scouts you mean, but I did get out and about with my parents a lot. So 'be prepared' is a familiar motto."

Kay played on as they ate and chatted, occasionally pausing between tunes to examine the cliff face and step back into the depression.

"This isn't normal," Phil said after a particularly bizarre break where Kay came over, grabbed a sandwich, and proceeded to walk around the base of the rock wall alternating between taking a bite and slapping the stones with open palm as if he expected them to do something.

"I'm not going to argue, but it's harmless. Better to let him get whatever he's doing out of his system than to drag him away. He'll wear down soon, then we can head back."

"Soon" proved to be a relative term. The sun was dipping low toward the horizon behind them by the time Kay put his flute away. Phil started out of a half-doze when he realized the music had stopped and he smelled smoke.

"Where did he get matches?" Phil nearly face-planted in his rush to get out of the car.

After eating and exploring a bit of the ravine, he and Ankti had moved to the SUV for softer seating. Kay peered into the tiny fire he'd started from scavenged deadwood and inhaled deeply. His eyes moved left to right as though reading newsprint in the shallow bed of coals the bit of wood and grasses left. The last of the actual flames blew out as a gust of cool pre-evening wind sent a chill through them all.

"We really don't want to be out here at night," Ankti said, echoing his own thoughts.

"I am done." Kay hung his head in the curls of rising smoke, sounding tired.

Whatever wood he'd found smelled of ozone and herbs. Although, that latter could have been the medicinal salve. How the man could stand dealing with fire given his burns was beyond Phil.

They scuffed out the last of the coals, loaded up the car, and headed back before sunset. The return trip to the interstate seemed much shorter, as was the way of such things. Of course Ankti's heavy foot might also have had something to do with that.

Kay sat in the back looking dejected, which brought the entire tone of the car down. Phil found himself missing the exuberant anticipation of the outbound trip, if not the constant seat pounding. They drove through downtown Scottsdale looking for a place to have dinner. As with so many cities, the bustling night-life had drained away with the reduced population, but a glowing neon sign steered them to an old-time diner for burgers and fries.

Ankti goaded Kay into eating by saying he needed the food to heal, and the calories brought him out of his shell enough to hold a brief conversation.

"What were you trying to do out there?" she asked around a mouthful fries.

"Go home," Kay said, as if they were both daft, but he looked uncertain. "Should have been there."

"Easy to get confused. Villages like to hide in that kind of terrain, or are you from a small town?" Ankti asked.

"No, no." This time he smiled, a mischievous grin that made those beady black eyes sparkle, but Phil couldn't tell if they shone with amusement or something more sinister. "No town. I live alone…I think."

So maybe they were looking for some hermit's cabin on a cliff somewhere—just not the cliff they'd visited today.

On the way out of town, Ankti looped north past a vast circular building with bold ribbons of blue painted like waves across the tan stone exterior. Vast, largely empty, parking ringed the structure.

"That's the aquarium we saw on TV." Ankti slowed and waved in excitement. "We *have* to go there before you leave. I've been meaning to go since I moved home, but things have been so busy that I never made time. As a kid, I absolutely loved the sea tunnels and tidal pool exhibits."

"Sure." Phil nodded as she made a U-turn and headed back to his town house. "We'll make a day of it after I get caught up on interviews. Speaking of which…"

"Kay, how'd you like to get out and meet some people tomorrow?" she asked over her shoulder. "We need to speak to some tribal elders and get down to the hosp—"

"Actually, I'm good on that last bit." Phil cut her off just in time. "It'll just be the interviews."

"Elders." Kay stretched the word out as if savoring the sound, then then snorted a laugh. "Yes, it is good."

Phil would be glad when the effects of the head trauma cleared up. Occasionally Kay spoke like a normal person, but much of the time his sentences were clipped or missing connective words, which combined with his accent to make understanding him a challenge.

The radio replaced conversation for the short drive home, but the mood was much subdued so they all simply listened. Dusk turned to twilight as they skirted the edge of Phoenix proper, and strange lights illuminated the darkening sky. Yellow and white flickered against an evening cloud layer that burned golden a few miles off.

"That's fire!" Phil said.

5. Riots

ANKTI TURNED onto Route 202 while Phil punched buttons on the radio in search of information. Satellite broadcasting persisted mostly intact, but local radio had dwindled to just a few stations. Most of those focused on news and information rather than entertainment. Music and talk shows were dying breeds. Losing the former was a true loss to society, the latter not so much.

As they approached their turn-off near the university, the glow on the horizon resolved into two, then three, distinct problems. Flames shot up off to the right, dark smoke pouring into the night sky from inside the old zoo. Unlike the aquarium, the animals had been farmed out to other locales and in some cases returned to the wild so the facility could be closed.

The smallest glow rose just ahead from the vicinity of the airport, but was overshadowed by what had to be a truly major fire further on near center city Phoenix.

"...can tell you, folks, is the police scanners are blowing up—" the male voice crackled from the stereo with just a hint of panic then cut off as auto-scan moved on. Phil cursed and poked the tuner back to settle on 88.9 FM. "...no way to tell. The abandoned section is burning in a bright line that has fire fighters asking the mayor to evacuate city hall. No official report from the zoo yet, but Sky Harbor airport reports a fuel truck caught fire near the arrival gates.

"I've just been handed a note." He paused. "Police are calling it arson downtown. They've stopped a small group dressed in leather and wearing red bandanas from lighting fires near Phoenix Mountain Preserve and Echo Canyon. Bands of looters are targeting grocery and department stores downtown, so authorities warn citizens to stay home. Again, we don't know exactly what's going on or who these people are, but sit tight and we'll keep you posted as more information comes available."

"Where the hell are you going?" Phil asked when Ankti blew past their exit.

"The ceremonial grounds are at Phoenix Mountain, and people coming in that couldn't find hotels are out at the camping area in Echo Canyon. I need to find out what's going on."

"Wouldn't it be better to wait until morning, after things have settled down? It sounds like the police are getting the situation under control."

"Hearing not good," Kay offered from the back.

"I agree." Ankti shot Phil a sideways look. "You must have heard something different than I just did. Looters downtown, fires at the airport. I missed the part about how everything being fine, and our people are out there camping for Pete's sake! Here." She handed her phone to him. "Call Brandon Owlfeather from my contacts. He's the council's event coordinator and head of Apache Reservation security. See what he knows, and tell him we're heading his way."

"Make call," Kay said with a helpful kick to the back of Phil's seat.

Phil counted to ten, found the contact, and dialed. It went straight to voicemail so he left a message, figuring Brandon knew Ankti's number. Echo Canyon was a mad house. Phoenix authorities had a half dozen squad cars, two fire trucks, and blue-light volunteer vehicles ringing the parking area. The flashing lights made Phil's eyes water, and a throbbing headache threatened as they pulled up to the portable barricade. Ankti spoke to the uniformed officer who then waved them in.

Beyond the lot, tents made the field look like a patchwork quilt under the blazing emergency lights. A pair of dumpsters off to their left smoldered and smoked under the watchful eye of several yellow-clad firefighters.

People in street clothes milled about, many looking behind them as if worried they were watched. Ankti spotted an older woman wearing jeans and a peasant top. Her hair laid across her shoulders in a wild array of black and gray, but her face was relatively unlined.

"Aunt Melody, is everyone okay?" Ankti asked as they approached.

"All's fine, my little Annie." The woman squinted at Phil and Kay, so Ankti made quick introductions. The woman gave them each a nod of greeting before continuing. "Hooligans started setting fires just after sunset. At first we thought they were just camp fires. But the trash went up like it had gasoline in it, and four young men started yelling for us to all go back to where we came from. The police chased them off."

"Good thing the cops showed up," Phil said.

"Good thing indeed." Melody gave him a humorless grin. "Otherwise, our young hot heads might have done something drastic. Luckily, Brandon calmed everyone down."

"Is he around?" Ankti asked. "We called and left voicemail. I don't want this messing with Thursday's schedule."

"He had the same concern, dear. Once things here were under control, Brandon headed up to check on the ceremony site. He had a roving patrol out in the area, but couldn't raise the man on duty. Not like there's much to protect but a few fences and benches, but if these troublemakers are setting fires…"

The unspoken words spurred them back to the car. Kay lingered to say goodbye to Ankti's aunt and bent to kiss her hand before releasing it. *Who does things like that?*

They found Brandon Owlfeather prowling around the back side of the palisade. Phil expected him to be in uniform, but the middle-aged man wore loose khaki pants and an Ozzy Osborne tee-shirt that showed he was certainly in good shape despite having twenty years on Phil. The glint of dark metal from a pistol clipped to his belt was the only evidence of office. His square face surrounded a generous mouth that split into a wry smile upon sighting Ankti running toward him.

"Should have known you would come up." Brandon gave her a quick hug then extended a hand. "You must be Phil, the DCC rep that's been talking to folks."

"Yes, sir. I'm just here for the month, but it's been a pleasure. Well, up 'til now." Phil eyed the scorch marks along the base of the fence.

"Tonight's getting stranger by the minute." Brandon nodded and released his hand. "Someone tried to set the enclosure on fire, even dowsed the benches in gasoline by the smell of things inside."

"Looks like you stopped them." Ankti ran her fingers over the wood near the gate where a light charring faded out knee-high.

"All I did was clean up the mess. Gas cans and a couple propane torches are in the back of my pickup. Wind must have blown out the flames." He turned to Kay as if noticing him for the first time and extended a hand. "Sorry I didn't catch your name, friend."

"This is Kay, a participant from out of town. He's staying with Phil for a few days."

Kay nodded and clasped the officer's forearm in an old-styled shake. Brandon raised a bushy black eyebrow, either at the antiquated greeting or the fact a tribesman bunked with Phil.

"I probably passed the vandals on the way in, two men and a woman wearing red bandanas and dressed in black walking down the road." Brandon shook his head. "But that was off our lands and there's no law against walking around. I drove back down after finding the discarded arson gear, but they were long gone. Probably had a car stashed off-road.

"My biggest concern now is finding Robbie. He's on night shift. There's no sign of the kid, but his car's still parked over by the head of the hiking trail. College kids can be unreliable, but he isn't answering the radio or phone."

"That's not good," Ankti said. "I assume taking a night hike isn't in character?"

"Nope." Brandon frowned under the dim security lights. "I tried calling down the trail, but that felt kind of stupid. I'll get some volunteers come daybreak to go down the ravine and see what they find."

"No one seemed to be hurt at the camping grounds," Ankti said. "Do you think it's safe to press on with rituals?"

The big man scratched his head and studied the fence for a moment. "If everyone's careful, I think it'll be all right. Let me check in with the police tomorrow though. I heard there were problems downtown and at the airport. Still have a handful flying in, so best to see if any flights are delayed. Should be able to make the call to proceed by midday. No real damage done here, but let me show you something."

He led them inside the fence and back behind the fire ring where they'd found Kay. Someone had been digging through the dirt near the crater left by their errant firework. Broken bits of wood and stone that hadn't been there the other night were scattered in a circle around the perimeter, and a twisted stick figure had been nailed to the fence inside the older scorch marks from the other night.

Phil realized they should have at least reported the accidental detonation to council security. Ankti hadn't mentioned making a report and now bit her lip in worry.

"Some of the pyrotechnics backfired Saturday night," Phil said and hurried on as a deep frown creased Brandon's brow. "After the ceremony of course, while the fire watch was still here. We assumed one of them let you know. We were outside, but rushed in to find that crater and the burn marks here."

The wood had suffered more under the impact of the small explosion than the deliberate attempts to torch the outside achieved. Kay stepped away from them and approached the sticks affixed to the center of the damage. Strips of bark and grass had been twisted together to form torso, legs, and arms. A knot of wood carved with roughly gouged eyes and a long sharp nose topped the little doll. It held a short stick in one hand and a little pole in the other. Two tiny black feathers stuck up from the back of the head. A thin, wooden-handled knife thrust through the chest secured it to the fence, really more of an icepick.

"I did get a rambling report from the lead drummer. He seemed to think someone stuck a roman candle or something right in the fire. We checked it out on Sunday, but this debris wasn't here and neither was that." He pointed to the knife.

"I would like this," Kay said as he reached for the doll.

"I'm not sure—" Ankti began.

"Hold up there." Brandon pulled out his phone and a roll of baggies. "You can have the doll in a minute, but I have to take photos and bag the knife for prints. It might help the authorities piece all this together. Riots are pretty commonplace anymore, but this isn't a local uprising. As far as I can tell these folks are from out of town. So why target us?"

They stood back and let the security officer do his work. After several minutes, Brandon handed the doll to Kay, saying there was no way to pull prints or any other useful information from sticks and grass, so he was welcome to keep it. With the late hour and immediate crisis handled, the three headed back to Phil's place.

On the way, the harried radio announcer continued to sputter out official updates. The airport had been forced to close a runway, but would be able to continue operations using the other two. The fire department managed to get the downtown blaze under control before it reached the courthouse.

Two looters were in custody, but most had fled into the night. As information solidified, it sounded as if the roving horde only consisted of maybe half a dozen individuals, likely some street gang making a play for goods to sell on the ever-expanding black market.

"No reports on the zoo," Phil noted as they turned down the road to his apartment. "That's only a couple miles from our digs down here. Judging by the number of emergency vehicles we passed things must be under control, but I'll be interested to hear what the heck went on up there."

Back at the complex, his new neighbors were home in force. Judging by the cars parked on their end of the building, they were throwing a party. Muffled voices punctuated by occasional shouts spilled from their unit, and he was glad they weren't in the one next door.

"Let's hope that quiets down soon." Phil held the door for Ankti and scowled when Kay rushed through behind her. "At least they aren't blaring music."

The voices didn't carry inside, small blessings. Having spent all day together, Phil was ready for a little alone time with his laptop and messages. A beer wouldn't be bad either. He looked through his small stash in the fridge. The others might like one too, but he wasn't certain if the antibiotics Ankti gave Kay would react badly to alcohol. He did seem to recall dairy products as being contraindicated.

"Hey, Ankti, do you wanna beer, and can Kay have…" he trailed off because she stood over the coffee table, hands on hips, and lips compressed in a tight line.

Kay sat in Phil's favorite chair with the crude doll laid out on the coffee table. Arrayed around the figure was a handful of the wood and stone chips they'd seen at the Phoenix Mountain enclosure. He arranged the chips to form little patterns, starbursts and symbols. His flute lay lengthwise across the bottom, serving as ground for the evolving scene, a person watching fireworks. But then what were the symbols that almost looked like writing?

"When did you scoop up all that stuff?" Phil joined the others.

"When no one watched," Kay said simply, placed a final gnarled wood chip, and sat back to study his work—though he did not look pleased. "This is not good."

"Can't expect to make fine art out of bits and pieces." Phil tried to lighten the mood; Ankti looked worried. "Big day, right? I've got a couple killer IPAs and a few porters left if anyone wants a beer."

Rather than answer, Kay rolled the flute up so that it touched the doll's feet and lifted the small figure up among the starburst designs. He rocked in his seat, breathed deep, then let out a barking laugh. "IPA? Do that on purpose, did you?" His next laugh came out richer, less strained as he swept the contents of the table into a pile. "This will not matter. Yes, I believe I must try one of your India Pale Ales."

6. Grandmother

"THERE IS power here, is there not, Grandmother?" Ankti nodded at the items arrayed on the old woman's kitchen table.

"Perhaps." Wikiwi leaned forward, her bony shoulders hunching to inspect the crude doll, wood chips, and stones Ankti had taken from Kay's room in the wee hours of the morning as the man snored softly.

Wikiwi was an elder of the Hopi people, a keeper of traditional ways, and experienced in elemental magic. Ankti had driven to the reservation where she'd grown up, to Hopi lands, hoping to decipher the riddle unfolding at Phil's apartment.

The doll gazed placidly up from the wood surface polished smooth by years of loving use, its misshapen body glistening in the late morning sun as if dusted in dark sugar crystals with lighter crystals along its feet—energy, not confections.

As an elder, Wikiwi eschewed many modern conveniences. Her kitchen was a small, simple affair of counter, stove, and sink surrounding the central table with its four spindle legs and wide-plank chairs. The rustic dwelling bordered on crude, a squat square hut constructed with beams and a slightly modernized form of traditional adobe that offered added insulation and strength. Still, it spoke of the dingy white sand architecture the Pueblo people had dwelled in along the cliffs of the southwest for generations. But this structure sat on reservation flat lands at the end of a little-used road on the outskirts of the village.

Though well respected, elders were not visited as often as they once were. Younger tribe members now sought answers electronically through help lines and chat rooms on the internet. Some still embraced the old traditions, but mostly just on special occasions or holidays. Ankti felt for the old woman who'd been her teacher and second mother. Nearly ninety, Wikiwi lived alone, her once-dark hair cascading down in a long white ponytail. She wore a traditional beaded top and skirt that were likely handmade by either herself or perhaps even her own mother.

Wikiwi had been Ankti's childhood mentor, a role that had become even more important since returning from southern California and coming into her full powers. Ankti's mother knew of and had been taught the basics of elemental forces, but the power skipped a generation, leaving Ankti to discover much on her own.

"There are definitely traces," the old woman said. "You have done well to bring this to me. See the dark sparks along the bits of fiber and rock, how they resonate on the doll. These are dark energies unlike the power of our elements—a seeking of sorts without using spirit or air to follow its quarry. This uses blood. These bits and pieces have been touched by someone injured, someone represented by this doll. They seek this person, and I do not believe for any noble purpose."

"I worried it might be something like that. We found a man injured and confused. I'm doing what I can to bring him back to health, but his mind is still scattered and bent. He doesn't even know his name. Who pursues him? Are they powerful, perhaps of some outcast tribe?"

"These are not of the people." Grandmother passed a hand over the doll and stones. "The energies come from elsewhere, from beyond my experience. They are strong, yet not as strong as the other power that has touched this. See how the feet glow, how the power infused within the twigs and grasses bring them back to life with tiny buds and a blush of green? Some of the stones too have been touched, cancelling out the darkness in them. I do not know what this is, but it is pure. And we see only an echo or accidental brush of that power."

"But should—" Ankti thought back to the scene Kay had arranged on Phil's coffee table, how he rolled his flute across the surface to raise up the doll.

The flute had touched the bottom of the feet exactly where there was now a twinkling of power so much stronger and brighter than the darkness encompassing the rest of the pieces on the table. She thought of the music of the flute, how it calmed and soothed as if whispering for her to help Kay, forgo the hospital, and stay with Phil. The flute shone in muted brilliance both with and in the absence of light, as though something hid within.

"I think I know the artifact that has that power," Ankti said. "This man we found has a flute. Could that hold such energies?"

"Well worn, well used, and well loved objects can absorb the energies of their owner. Perhaps this man has found such a relic and even as we speak it attempts to keep him safe without his knowledge. The energies that have touched this doll would neutralize the seeking spell so that it cannot lead anyone to the person it represents. It seems reasonable to assume that person is the injured man you found. You must be on guard for signs of danger, Granddaughter."

"But if he has this flute, this artifact, couldn't he...I don't know, use it further? He plays well."

"Impossible to say. You should bring him to me when you can. Music will resonate with the instrument, helping release its power to

49

follow the will of the player. If this man's desire is to protect himself, you, and your other friend, that may be all it takes to avoid his pursuers. I can tell you no more at this point." The old woman stood, the chair and her knees creaking. "But perhaps you will stay and take midday meal with an old woman?"

"Of course, Grandmother."

A shallow and heavy cast iron pot already simmered on the stove in the tradition of the people to always have hospitality ready for visitors. Wonderful aromas filled the tiny kitchen, taking Ankti back to her childhood when Mother prepared such dishes, to a simpler time. She inhaled onions, sage, roasting carrots, and lean venison.

As Ankti waited, Wikiwi rolled out dough that had been proofing under a towel by the window and popped it into the oven. Within minutes a wonderfully yeasty scent join the others and made her mouth water. She'd have to stop for groceries on the way home and maybe treat the men to home-style cooking, that was if the rioters hadn't forced her favorite market to close. She could always stop in north Phoenix where there hadn't been problems.

Word from Brandon on her way to the reservation told her the police had all but closed their investigations, which seemed an odd choice considering the damage done just the night before. They of course continued to watch important infrastructure points and institutions, but since the bulk of the attacks focused on the Native American populations in town, the prevailing sentiment was that tribal security could take care of its own.

Blame for the damage done down-town and at the airport fell squarely on the shoulders of the two men they'd taken into custody. The pair had been handily shuffled off for a speedy trial at the capitol for arson, theft, and inciting riot. Some in the department actually claimed these were the only ones involved and the rest of the rioters were simply down and out citizens desperate for help and goaded by the strangers—who thankfully did not appear to be of Native

American descent. The absurd theory contradicted the original radio reports of black-clad people with faces hidden behind red bandanas.

There was still no word on what had transpired at the zoo. But with the airport open, tomorrow's ceremonies were a go. Brandon had already called on neighboring tribes for additional security. Hopi, Apache, and the Salt River tribes would all send people to help keep the peace and ensure no one interfered with the upcoming event.

Tomorrow would be the critical culmination of the ceremonies held earlier in the year. The pattern built by successive rituals wove an intricate and powerful request to the spiritual world so central to the people. Each fit that pattern in a precise way and served a specific purpose.

Saturday's rituals had called for a new beginning among the people, for the young women of the tribes to flourish and bear children. Ankti had itched to participate. She did have power, just not the best control yet. But Grandmother had pointed out it was more important to safeguard the gathering from the young white man the government had sent, from Phil. She'd been charged with keeping their traditions and ceremonies safe from prying eyes, to ensure some—but not too much—information was exposed to the rest of the world.

So Ankti had bowed to the wisdom of her elders. She'd spent two weeks shepherding Phil Johnson around to speak with those who did not believe the tribes' resistance to C-12 was due to anything more mystical than happenstance and clean living. And here she was again, letting others prepare for and conduct the most important ceremony of all.

Tomorrow's event would celebrate balance and respect to cement gains made by prior rituals. Prayers for prosperity and health would always be answered, even when sent up by individuals. This would be a much larger gathering than the others. All the tribes honored traditions to maintain balance. Those who communed with the land and nature were much more numerous than those who called to the great spirits of fertility and protection. The powerful ceremony *had* to go off without interference.

7. Who Took my Car

ANKTI DROVE south with Grandmother Wikiwi's words dancing in her head, the things the old woman hadn't said evoking just as many images as the little she had. Ankti's focus always grew clear in the presence of her mentor. What she'd readily attributed to a trick of the light, the sparking and sparkling of the doll and stone, resolved into true traces of power. That much her grandmother had confirmed. But Wikiwi implied so much more. Who were these mysterious people that sought Kay? The old woman couldn't—or wouldn't—say.

Ancient and wise, Wikiwi likely knew more than she had chosen to share. More prodding over lunch only added to Ankti's frustration rather than her knowledge. After eating she'd said her goodbyes with a promise to bring Kay to see the old woman as soon as it could be arranged.

Ankti needed answers from their absent-minded stud-muffin, but Kay might not even remember how he acquired the artifact, the flute. Still, it was worth a try. If his instrument was indeed an artifact of power, he needed to be mindful of how he used it. So far the flute seemed to be protective, but there was no telling what such a device might do without warning. Yes, a good talk with Kay was in order once she got to the apartment.

The afternoon meetings she and Phil had scheduled would take them back up to the Phoenix Mountain station to talk with another clan elder, Tommy Roundbush. From there, they'd head into town to meet with council legal advisors who wanted to ensure the paperwork Phil had signed was fully binding. The tribal council meant to review and approve any information the DCC planned to make public.

It promised to be a busy afternoon, but Ankti made time for a grocery stop just above town at a quaint little market run by a Latin-American family. The wife in particular was a dear and talked her into buying spices and peppers that might prove dangerous. She herself had developed a taste for the spicier fare that made its way up from South America, but she would have to be careful with the fresh ingredients if she didn't want Phil's eyes streaming.

The thought made her smile. He was such a milquetoast man, kind and respectful—and not too hard on the eyes. Those baby blues lit up with his easy smile and charming hint of dimples. She'd certainly caught him eyeing her up and down when he thought she wasn't looking. But he'd proven too courteous to act on any male impulses—or too shy.

All just as well. He wore his heart on his sleeve, as they used to say. Phil was cellophane, transparent and predictable. Little he did or said came as a surprise. She found it refreshing to work with someone stolid and dependable.

But a bit of mystery made a man somehow more real, made a girl work to get to know the things that made him tick. She'd had a couple short flings in the past, but couldn't imagine living with someone she had all figured out. Where was the excitement in that?

Ankti blushed as the apartment complex came into view and a realization struck: she currently lived with *two* men. Of course the arrangements were temporary, but if only her mother knew. Mom would spot the problem with Phil immediately and write him off as a romantic interest for her daughter, but the dark, smoldering, and mildly confused patient she'd been attending to might be a different story. Fierce heat rose to her ears.

"None of that now." She let the heat flow out with her words. "You're just getting him back on his feet, out of bed—not into it."

The poor choice of words had her face going crimson again as she parked in front of the apartment and consulted the dash clock while gathering the groceries. It was nearly two, but Phil's car was gone. They must have needed something from town. Hopefully he'd get back in time to make their three o'clock meeting. The front door flew open, and Phil raced out to the car.

"Where the hell have you been?" Phil shot the question at her before she finished pulling the bags from the back seat.

"Visiting my grandmother at the reservation and errands." She raised the bags to illustrate. "Don't worry, we have plenty of time to make the afternoon appointments."

"That's not the point." Phil stomped in frustration, yet still offered to carry a bag. "You should have at least left a note. I had no idea—"

She rolled her eyes, cut him off with a curt head shake, and stormed inside to the kitchen. While unloading her haul she jabbed a finger at the yellow sticky above the water dispenser on the stainless-steel fridge. "You mean a note like that?"

"Well…yes, fine. But he's taken my car!" Phil threw up his hands.

"Kay?" Ankti paused and glanced around the quiet apartment. "Kay took your car?"

"Damned right he did."

"I don't suppose he left a note?"

Phil opened his mouth but froze, apparently refusing to walk into the same trap twice in as many minutes. Together they scoured the living room, kitchen, and Kay's bedroom, finding nothing to indicate where the man had gone. Ankti thought it unlikely he'd just run off without extra clothing and—more importantly—his flute. The instrument sat gleaming on the nightstand exactly where she had placed it that very first evening. She gave the nightstand a wide berth and eyed the old instrument.

"Think he shoved a Post-it inside that thing?" Phil asked.

"Not bloody likely."

"That car's a rental! If he wrecks it, the company is responsible."

"Tell you what, forget about the car for now. Let's go to our appointments. I'm pretty sure he wouldn't leave this behind if he wasn't coming back." She jutted her chin at the flute.

"Guess you're right." Phil let out a big sigh. "But the guy's just not right in the head."

"We've been over that. Just—" she rubbed her eyes, too weary to rehash old ground. "Just go get ready. I'll drive."

As Phil went to pull himself together, Ankti studied the flute. Such an innocuous-looking thing, not quite two feet long, simple wooden design with a squat carved block shaped like an animal head near the mouthpiece. Stick-figure animal carvings decorated the wood to either side of the single row of holes, sparse but with a few more at bell and neck.

She couldn't say what type of wood was used in its construction. The unstained surface looked a couple of shades darker than traditional cottonwood. She crossed her eyes, letting the flute drift out of focus. Grandmother had taught her the trick of seeing without looking to use the gift of true *sight* that ran in her family. Looking beyond the mundane physical world at will took years of practice and even then was an imprecise and capricious ability—as if the world preferred not to be spied on in such a manner.

The flute swam and doubled in her vision, gleaming in the wavering sunlight streaming through the curtains. But ultimately it remained a simple carved hunk of wood. No sparkling energy as she'd seen on the doll, no muted aura of power, no sensation of any sort came off the instrument. If this was indeed an artifact of power, it hid its true nature or required special action to activate that power.

She laid a hand across the holes and cocked her head at a quiet hum and ghostly whisper. The phantom sounds disappeared the moment she focused on them—just a fancy of her imagination.

* * *

The ride out to the mountain took all of twenty minutes. Despite police department attempts to put the town at ease, people stayed home in the wake of the riots. Traffic was blessedly light. But the October sun slanting through the windshield made the ride uncomfortable despite the unseasonably cool weather and roaring air conditioner. She'd have to get the system recharged before spring, or face melting when temperatures really took off again.

They arrived at the ceremonial grounds just before three and shuffled across the dirt parking lot to meet a short man in his early seventies. Robust and outspoken as he'd been in her youth, Tommy Roundbush had grown to match his name. The old Zuni was as wide as he was tall, an oddity among the desert tribes, especially with his crop of wild hair that—while technically not curly—headed off in so many directions it too resembled the gnarled branches of desert brush.

"I'm honored to meet you," Tommy said after Ankti finished introductions. "Come into my office."

The office in question was the front section of an outbuilding where the events coordinator stored miscellaneous equipment, chairs, and tables. As a community asset, the ceremonial grounds could be booked for anything from picnics to sacred rites. Judging by the bed in the corner, stove, and fridge, Tommy pretty much lived with his gear. In his youth the man had left the tribes to see the world as a Navy quartermaster. He'd excelled at his profession and returned to fulfill a similar role for the tribal council.

The old man pulled two folding chairs from wall pegs for his guests, and plopped down in a faded leather office chair, which creaked under his bulk.

"What do you need to know, young man?" Tommy turned a cheery smile on Phil, clearly at ease talking to people outside the tribes.

Phil had his notebook open. Ankti liked the fact he didn't use a computer or his phone during interviews. To do so would be a sign of discourtesy, especially when speaking with elders. Hand scribing notes was a longstanding custom—not as old as their oral traditions, but he conveyed respect by not burying his nose in an electronic device.

"As you probably know, I'm talking to people in the communities up here on behalf of the Disease Control Center." Phil launched right into his spiel. "The Bureau has been tracking the effects of the C-12 virus for thirty years. As a field agent I travel to areas that have fared better or worse than the general population when it comes to retaining the ability to bear children.

"Phoenix and its surrounding areas have only experienced a fifty percent drop in birth rates over the decades. That's statistically significant, and digging into hospital records confirms the region's Native American population is skewing the data. The sterility rate across the tribes averages out to just twenty-five percent.

"This isn't the type of interview where I'm expecting you to know any secrets for resisting the effects of C-12, but every scrap of information helps paint a picture. Data about lifestyle, diet, and activity level will get compiled with climate and other ecological factors to hopefully forge another nugget of understanding that may one day lead to a cure."

"Well put, young man. Very diplomatic." Tommy leaned back, brown eyes twinkling beneath bushy brows. "But I can tell you exactly why the tribes here fare better than the rest of the country."

"Oh, really?" Phil's forced smile and the act of laying his pen down said more than words that he expected whatever came out of Tommy's mouth next was going to be a tall tale instead of useful facts. "Why's that?"

Ankti held her breath, uncertain of where the old Zuni was going with this. As a rule, elders generally held their tongue around outsiders and were well known for safeguarding tribal information. Tommy was a wildcard, and she'd been surprised he showed up on the council's approved list of interviewees. He often skirted formal channels and tended to be a loner.

As a fringe element of tribal society, she supposed the council thought Tommy wasn't likely to have guarded knowledge to share. Or perhaps they selected the salty quartermaster because his demeanor tended to negate whatever wisdom the man espoused. Ankti actively sought opportunities to cultivate respect for elders among a younger generation lost in its digital world, but perhaps ensuring respect was firmly in place within the ruling body would also be in order.

"The gods are on our side!" Tommy quirked the right side of his mouth in a lopsided grin, eyes narrowing above pudgy cheeks.

"Gods, as in religious beliefs?" Phil ventured, clearly trying to frame the statement in a way he could understand.

Tommy leaned forward, his chair groaning as he dragged it closer. "We call on the great spirits. We call on the land. We call with our voices, our song, and our dance. With Kachina we honor and represent the spirits, dolls to learn and masks to commune. The gods of fertility answer and shower our people with prosperity and protection. Alosaka, Ololo, Kokopelli, and others answer our prayers at the great renewal ceremonies. All of this sings together in harmony to wrap the people in protective forces, to keep us apart from the ravages of your manmade virus."

"Okay," Ankti interjected, needing to steer the discussion to safe waters. "I think Mr. Roundbush is agreeing with your comment. The strength of our spirituality and our respect for the land keep all things in balance. It brings the tribes and people together so that the comradery and closeness of our communities helps keep the C-12 effects partially at bay. It doesn't hurt that reservation lands tend to be far-flung, away from the white man's cities. We just aren't getting exposed and bombarded by all the germs and viruses that plague others."

Phil's brows drew together, but then he nodded, scooped up his pen, and scribbled out notes, mumbling to himself as if in agreement.

"There are instances of aboriginal tribes that haven't borne the full brunt of the C-12 virus. Island nations, desert communities, and the like maintain elevated birth rates, statistically significant but not quite as good as we're seeing here."

"Protects us from more than just your germs." Tommy shook his head like an irritated bear. "Stops the demons that sneak down from the hills too!"

That's news!

8. A Bold Perspective

P HIL'S LAUGH choked off into sputtering and nervous throat clearing when he realized Tommy Roundbush wasn't smiling. If anything, the old man looked offended, as if Phil mocked his beliefs. For that matter, Ankti's scowl and knitted brow set him back. Why was she suddenly so serious? The educated, well-spoken young woman couldn't possibly be concerned about evil spirits. She must be frowning at poor Tommy, a respected elder who clearly was a few cards short of a full deck.

"You mean those devils that keep vandalizing stuff, right? Not demon...demons." Phil put air quotes around the first "demon," shoved his hands in his pockets and watched the pen roll to the bottom of the notebook in his lap.

He looked from old man to woman, but Ankti refused to meet his gaze. She eyed the elder warily as if willing him to change the subject.

"I certainly do mean 'demon' demons." Tommy gave a vigorous nod that slapped his tangle of hair forward. "I'll tell you what else. These are some sort of fire demons. Not good, not good at all. Black armored hide that creaks as they shamble along. Skull faces too, with flames streaming off the tops of their heads in place of hair.

"Can't tell me it's not true; I've seen them coming around trying to torch the place. Fire demons like to burn things, but the ceremonies stop them. Stop them dead because the great spirits look out for us. Yep, old Tommy knows when he's on the right side of things."

The tiny room grew uncomfortably quiet, not that the old man seemed to notice. Tommy leaned over to rummage through the small apartment-sized refrigerator. His chair creaked ominously, bringing to mind demon mercenaries lumbering through town setting fires, gliding across the ceremonial grounds like ponderous wooden ships, their black bodies straining against the mystical energies protecting the place.

Phil shook away the odd vision and rolled his eyes heavenward in silent prayer for the poor sailors that would have endured similar tall tales while trapped at sea. The old story-teller certainly knew how to get under your skin.

Aside from a tattered events calendar and chairs, eclectic art hung from ceiling and walls: hand-crafted blankets, simple ornaments, and dreamcatchers. A few old movie posters featured what had to be offensive stereotypes for Native Americans. Then there were more contemporary pieces with swirling colors and psychedelic images more suited to old Grateful Dead concerts. Maybe the old man had a thing for recreational drugs. That would explain a lot.

"Want a can?" Tommy held out a diet cola. When Phil shook his head and Ankti scowled, he shrugged, popped the top, and took a giant swig. "All I'm saying is it's a good time to gather the tribes. Even if the outcome results in these weird blended ceremonies, more people and belief means more power. That keeps the spirits looking out for us. Although…can't say as they did a great job the other night."

"You mean when the Red Scarfs tried to torch the fence?" Ankti's question had Phil raising an eyebrow at the odd term. "Well,

'Red Scarfs' is what the news dubbed the gang members who swept through town, blocked the airport, and set fires at the camping grounds. Red must be their gang color or something, but calling them red-bandanas apparently isn't catchy enough. So now they're Red Scarfs. Tommy, were you up here the other night when they came with the torches?"

"Ah hell, I'm always here." Another slurping swig yielded a quiet burp. "But I was asleep. Heard the ruckus and cursing, looked out, and the damned demons were already inside the compound. Busted through that joke of a lock, no problem. By the time I grabbed a light and my gun, they were high-tailing it down the road and big Brandon came roaring up in his four-by-four. Probably just as well. Owlfeather's and my guns won't do much against their kind."

"So we *are* talking about this rogue gang of thugs," Phil interrupted. "No flaming hair, just a bandana pulled up over their heads. Besides, supernatural demons wouldn't carry cans of gasoline to get the job done. Would they?"

Tommy scratched his stomach and leaned back, again torturing the poor piece of office furniture as he went on the offensive. "Shouldn't get this close in the first place. Protecting spirits are supposed to keep them out. Never should have gotten into the ceremony area. Certainly shouldn't have been able to try to start a fire. Good thing there's a little power left to keep them from actually lighting things up, but it's enough to make a man question the big truths in life."

"Phil, do you have any more...normal questions for Mr. Roundbush to help finish your survey?" Ankti looked tired and exasperated.

There wasn't much to add, and Phil doubted asking more about tribal lifestyles would yield productive information. Tommy might be an elder, but the old man was off the rails. Phil was used to attitudes ranging from belligerent to downright hostile. People didn't always like talking about their personal lives, especially when it touched the raw nerve of being unable to have children. But this had been the oddest interview yet. He scribbled the date and time in the margins, closed the book, and shook his head.

"Nope, I think that covers enough for now. Is it okay if I stop back with more questions if something comes up?"

"That'd be fine." Tommy took one last pull of his drink, crushed the can, and tossed it into a recycle bin in the corner. "You know where to find me—as long as the devils don't burn the place down."

They left Tommy pulling together equipment for Thursday's big ceremony. With all this talk of spiritualism, Phil desperately wanted to see what went on behind closed gates. He looked to Ankti as they headed for the car, uncertain how to read her. At first he'd thought she felt sorry for the rambling elder. But by the time they left, he wasn't so sure.

On the way downtown for the tribal council meeting, he mentioned the upcoming ceremony, hinting at the idea of getting in to observe just part of the proceedings. He tried to approach the idea from several different angles, but Ankti blocked them all. The atmosphere in the car turned cool and brittle, and they drove in silence for a good three minutes. Judging by the growing traffic, people were coming back out of the woodwork.

Ankti broke the tension with a bitter laugh "Tommy's a bit off his rocker. Think about it. Black creatures with flaming heads that moan and creak? I mean, he's clearly talking about these red bandana people, but the fact that they're arsonists has him all confused. He's mixing reality up with legends. A lot of the elders have a funny way of looking at the world."

"So he's speaking in metaphors?" Phil ventured.

"Yeah, something like that. And Tommy…Well, he's not the most reliable person. I hate to talk ill of any elder, but he has baggage."

"Seems the council knew that before sending us out there." Phil said, and she had the decency to look abashed. "One might even assume they threw me a red herring, something to occupy the gringo and keep him out of the way."

"Not like that—"

"It's okay." Phil gave a wry smile. "I know I'm the enemy, the guy from the government that's here to help. We all know that's always a load of crap. I'm used to being unwelcome. But still, Tommy Roundbush is a colorful character. Gotta give him that."

"For sure!" Ankti's laughed and looked at the dash. "We've got forty-five minutes until the meeting, and I'm famished. Care to get a bite?"

"Honestly, I'd rather find my car."

"A sandwich back at the house then." Ankti took the next ramp as if the decision was made. "Kay's probably back by now. You can get your keys and maybe consider keeping a closer eye on them in the future."

* * *

Back at the complex, Phil's beater-of-a-rental sat diagonally across two spaces in front of his apartment with the right-front wheel up on the sidewalk. Its dingy green paint was even duller than usual.

"Wasn't out taking driving lessons. Looks more like he's been off-roading again. Looks like your car after that oh-so-productive picnic in the hills." Phil traced a clean streak through the dust and grime that coated the car from bumper to bumper. "Man! I *just* got this washed."

"Do you think he headed back to that plateau?" Ankti asked.

"Don't know, but I'm going to find out." Phil stormed in through the front door. "Kay, what the hell were you thinking?"

Their houseguest sat bare-chested on the floor beyond the couch in front of a roaring fire. The teepee of logs on the television burned merrily, one of those channels promising the feel of being one with nature without bothering to leave your house. Between the crackling flames, chirping insects, and distant call of a coyote on the soundtrack, Phil imagined the sharp scent of burning wood mixed with the ever-present smell of herbs from Ankti's salve.

Phil waited for a response, but Kay simply sat with eyes half closed and swayed to some unheard rhythm. The moment stretched on, stoking a sullen anger in Phil's gut.

"Thank you for the use of your vehicle," he said just as Phil was about to lose it.

Kay opened dark, shining eyes and half turned. A small hiccup came from Ankti as her breath caught. He could well see why. The man's bare chest glistened with an artistic sheen of sweat in the flickering simulated fire. Dark olive skin stretched over perfectly toned shoulders and pecs.

"Keys are on the counter. I would have filled the tank, but well…" Kay shrugged and gave a wry smile. "No pockets."

"At least ask next time." It was surprisingly hard to stay mad at the man, and the car was just a crappy rental. "Especially if you're going off-road. I can't afford to pay for damages on that heap. Did you at least find what you were looking for this time?"

"It was just within reach, so close." Kay reached out as if to pluck the answer from the air, shook his head, and let his hand drop. "But no. I could feel it, almost touch it. Something is in the way."

Another catch of breath and little sob escaped Ankti. *Strange reaction.* But then Kay stood so that the couch no longer blocked Phil's line of sight. The man wasn't just shirtless; he was buck naked.

"Hmmn." Ankti cleared her throat and tried again. "Perhaps um… some clothes." Her voice cracked.

Was the guy an exhibitionist? No, that didn't seem right, but Kay just stood there for all the world to see while puzzling out her words.

"Yeah, at least shorts, dude." Phil tried to catch Ankti's eye, but she seemed unable to look away. "Um, Ankti." He cleared his throat and spoke louder. "Ankti, lunch?"

A touch on her elbow broke the spell, and color rose to her cheeks.

"Yes, lunch, and maybe a cold drink." Ankti bustled into the kitchen, refusing to make eye contact.

Making sandwiches would give Kay time to pull clothes on. Phil spared a backward glance and mouthed the word "pants" to a now grinning Kay.

"He can't be a psychopath; he just can't be," Phil muttered under his breath, but the guy certainly didn't comprehend social taboos.

Kay opted out of lunch, leaving the two of them to eat at the kitchen table. Phil mixed up instant lemonade to go with their sandwiches. The icy drink eased his sore throat. Dust and smoke always got to him, and his nose had been right, there was residual smoke in the house. Given how color still flushed Ankti's cheeks, Kay might not be a suitable lunch topic, but Phil couldn't help himself.

"Can you believe he stole my car? For what? To go sit in the desert? From the smell in here, I bet he build another fire out there and stared at that cliff face all morning like some kind of loony. His clothes are probably stinking up the bathroom."

Ankti's ears turned a pretty cinnamon-crimson and her eyes went wide at some thought she didn't share. "I think it's a ritual similar to something you'd see in a sweat lodge. Meditation can open the mind to insight and knowledge. He's just looking for answers."

"I guess." Phil still worried that Kay might be off his rocker. "But that doesn't explain stepping into that depression in the cliff as if he thought it led somewhere."

"Definitely odd behavior. We need to have a serious talk when we get back tonight and find out what exactly he thinks is out there in the desert."

"I doubt it's just wisdom." Phil nodded agreement.

It was high time they figured out who they'd ushered into their apartment. Phil's own ears burned this time. Why on earth had he thought of it as "their" place?

As they were putting dishes away, Kay emerged from the bedroom—thankfully fully clothed—and took the extra sandwich they'd made with a nod of thanks. His eyes lingered on Ankti, looking her up and down as if memorizing every curve and smoldering every bit as hotly as the pseudo-fire he'd been watching earlier. Goosebumps rose on Ankti's upper arms under the blatant scrutiny. She shivered, spun on her heel, and headed for the door.

"I'm taking the car keys." Phil glared at Kay then slid a pointed look to Ankti's retreating back. "You need to cool your motor, if you know what I mean. Just hang here for the afternoon."

"Not a problem," Kay agreed, but his wicked smirk belied any sincerity.

Phil sighed. If the guy continued to be a douche, they'd have to reassess this living arrangement.

* * *

"Ah, geez! I smell like smoke." Phil sniffed at his shirt as they waited outside the tribal offices.

The walls were finished in sandstone with matching travertine tile floors. Polished stone trimmed stairwells and doorways, giving the community building the feel of an art center. Pedestals and glass cases lined the alcove opposite the reception desk. Phil stretched stiff legs and ambled through the displays of pottery, intricate clothing, and tools—examples of traditional artifacts and art from the southwestern tribes.

The door to the outer office behind the receptionist slammed open, making the young man minding the long polished desk jump. The kid was flighty, apparently from one of the tribes and with the look of the young and impressionable—no doubt an intern consigned to taking calls and keeping schedules.

Four men and a woman exited the office followed by a haggard looking tribal liaison. The men filled the tiny reception area, big, square, and cut from the same cloth, with wide jaws and narrow eyes that scanned the path to the elevator as if expecting an ambush. Their leather pants flared at the cuffs, more like midnight black chaps, matching oddly heavy jackets given the time of year. A red bandana rode above each scowling face.

"Red Scarfs," Ankti hissed as the lead pair bulled past the flustered intern, clearing the way for the two familiar figures following in their wake.

The woman also dressed in black, a sleek elegant outfit of artistically dangling zippers, form-fitting pants, and tailored jacket. Her dark hair was pulled back tight as it had been the night they'd first brought Kay home. A narrow face, sculpted cheeks, and sharp nose gave her elegant beauty in contrast to the rustic Viking by her side. Easily as large as the two leading and wearing similar black clothes, the woman's partner needed no bandana. His flaming red hair billowed as the group strode to the elevators. One last Red Scarf walked backwards at the rear of the group, waving off the blustering liaison.

"Hey there, neighbor." The red-haired man quirked a grin and gave a mock salute.

Uncertain how to respond, Phil simply raised a hand in acknowledgement. What on Earth were the new tenants doing at the tribal offices—and with Red Scarfs in tow?

The procession stopped alongside the display cases, and the man in front impatiently jabbed a knuckle down on the call button, ignoring the fact that the light came on readily and the car was several floors away. The red-haired man turned away, but the woman inclined her head and pulled him back around by the elbow.

"Let's be courteous to our new friends, Erik. I am Kasandra." The woman turned wide-set brown eyes on Phil—or were they hazel? The color shifted under the artificial lighting as she extended a hand and inhaled through her nose, a long sensuous pull as if breathing in an intoxicating scent. "And you are?"

"Phil Johnson." Out of reflex he took the delicate, long-fingered hand she extended. "I live down in the end unit, and this is my friend Ankti."

"Ah, yes." She nodded, still clutching his hand, and drew another long breath through her nose.

"I was just telling Erik how nice it is to live near such an adorable couple. And that aroma—you've been playing with fire, haven't you?" Her gaze slid sideways to Erik, and she finally released Phil's hand.

"Perhaps we can get together for a cookout soon." Erik's rumbling laugh rolled over the double ding as the elevator arrived and the doors slid open.

And just like that, Phil knew he'd been dismissed. His palm prickled as though he'd gripped a hot pipe instead of the woman's hand. The elevator lights flickered as the group entered, the car creaking and straining under the weight of so many large men. For an instant, the acrid smell of burnt rubber mixed with the sage and wood smoke still wafting off Phil's shirt.

Bandanas rippled with the changing air pressure between lobby and elevator, giving the impression that true flames licked up from the bandana-bound heads—a fleeting image of whimsy with Erik's bushy beard and wild hair a roaring conflagration compared to the others. Phil gaped until the doors slid shut on the bizarre hallucination.

"What the hell are *they* doing here?" Ankti glared at the display as it marked the group's descent, then rounded on the liaison as if to demand answers.

But the haggard-faced man was busy taking his frustration out on the poor intern, jabbing a finger at the paper calendar on the young man's desk then back at the office door. Phil felt for the wilting intern, who was clearly being blamed for the visitors getting the better of the tribal liaison.

After one last glare, the painfully thin man scurried over with hands clasped before him in apology. "So sorry to keep you waiting. We had a bit of unexpected business to attend to. I am Havkin, this month's appointed liaison. The council will be ready for you in just a few more minutes."

"What's with creepy Natasha and the Red Scarfs?" Phil jerked his chin toward the elevators.

"That would be our unplanned meeting." Havkin frowned. "No concern of yours, just other council business."

"Business with the people who torched the airport and camping grounds?" Venom leaked into Ankti's words. "Please tell me they were here to make amends and promise not to interfere with any ceremonies."

"I'm sorry. Anything discussed is privileged information." The skinny man looked more nervous than apologetic. "You'll have to take that up with Councilman Orrick. All I can say is that we are looking forward to Mr. Johnson's status update and the opportunity to review the information he's gathered before it leaves per our prior agreement."

"Of course," Phil said. "Today is just a verbal update, but I'll have a hard copy to review by the week's end."

The meeting went as expected. Havkin and Jasper, the cultural outreach officer, sat to either side of Orrick, politely listening and occasionally chiming in with questions. They seemed particularly interested in the talk with Tommy Roundbush.

"That's old Tommy, nutty as a squirrel." Jasper waved away the idea of demon spirits with a large, gnarled hand, then backpedaled under a reproving glare from Orrick. "No disrespect intended. The man's inventories and logistics work are spot on. If it weren't for Tom, half our events wouldn't happen. But we all know he tends to over-imbibe and spin tales."

Nervous looks passed between Havkin and Jasper. Rather than wade into what was clearly a sensitive topic, Phil nodded and plowed on with his summary of findings from the hospital records, which constituted the bulk of hard evidence confirming that local birth rates among Native Americans remained well above the rest of the country.

"I'll want to see how that's written up," Orrick said as Phil concluded his briefing. "Some tribes are more sensitive than others about disclosing information, and of course we don't want to release any specifics that identify individuals."

"Certainly. You'll find I've aggregated samples to prevent drilling down to small groups or families. Nothing should be traceable back to specific names. I'll send my draft over this weekend, and we can correct anything that concerns the council."

"Excellent!" Orrick nodded and rose. "Then I believe we are done here."

The three men headed for the door while Phil gathered up his charts and notes.

"Why on Earth did you have those gang members in here?" Ankti's question stopped Orrick in his tracks.

The old man's startled expression shifted to a bemused smile. "Believe it or not, they want to conduct interviews much like you two are doing."

"Interviews by arson?" Ankti's eyebrows rose high.

"Well, they did apologize for a handful of rogue members that got carried away. Even offered to pay for any equipment damaged near camp and the ceremony grounds. I'll have to talk to Tommy about what inventory needs replacement." He directed that last at Havkin, who nodded and took a note on the pad that appeared in his hand like magic. "They're looking for a distant relative who has an inheritance of some size coming." Orrick shook his head as if to clear it. "It's all very confusing and hush-hush. I wouldn't worry. They'll be done and on their way in a few days anyway."

"You just handed them permission to poke around after what they've done?"

"Give me some credit, young lady. I told them to work with the police like anyone else seeking a missing person and to stop sniffing around reservation land."

"I seriously doubt they'll pay to replace equipment if you sent them packing," Ankti said.

After a brief futile discussion, Phil left the office with a surreal sense of unease. The council worked with criminals, and the gang leaders had moved into his apartment complex. He thought of the way the woman inhaled his scent as if cataloguing and memorizing, of the flickering image of flames rising from the departing Red Scarfs.

"Something just doesn't add up," Phil said as the elevator approached their floor. "How did Erik convince Orrick that only a few Red Scarfs were out of control?"

There had to be more to the story than some bull about searching for lost inheritors. No way could a reason that lame ring true to the council, yet they hadn't seemed to question the lie. At least they hadn't given the gang permission to canvas the tribes. Ankti gave a sullen shrug in response, the elevator doors opened, and Phil followed her in.

"What the hell?" Phil squinted at several dark smudges along the ceiling that hadn't been there on the trip up.

It looked as if vandals had tagged the elevator ceiling with black spray paint. A dark swath drawn between the doors split into four lighter branches that each ended in a blackened patch—one at each corner of the car. He swiped a finger through the spot above his head. It felt dry, but his finger came away black with fine power.

Ankti raised an eyebrow in surprise. "Soot?"

9. BBQ

"**I** CANNOT live in the same development as those people!" Phil slammed his briefcase into the corner by the coffee table. He really needed to smooth that final draft, but instead headed to the fridge for a beer to wash the bad taste out of his mouth. "You saw how they vandalized that elevator. Jeez, they practically melted through the ceiling in a bunch of spots. I don't want to wake up one night to an apartment full of smoke. Beer?"

Flute music drifted from the closed bedroom door as Phil held up a can for Ankti. The lilting notes should have been calming, but he was simply too wound up. Ankti nodded and took the offered can. Phil carried his own to the couch, plunked down, and popped the top while she took the seat opposite and threw back a long swig. She grimaced as if biting into an under-ripe lemon, but it wasn't the beer.

"I don't think these are just arsonists or simple gang members." Ankti framed her words carefully.

"Are you saying this is organized crime?" Phil scowled and took a bitter gulp full of cocoa nibs and coffee flavors. "Perfect."

Crime had increased a hundred fold as the country fell apart, catering to demands for luxury goods, offering "protection" for hire to vulnerable areas, and generally manifesting as a sort of brutal feudalism that swept through society. But the existence of true crime bosses and mobsters wasn't a problem according to the mind-numbing security training the Bureau forced employees to sit through. Mob or not, the main office should be willing to move him. There had to be other empty housing available.

"No, not the mob or anything like that. These guys are different, more dangerous, and I honestly don't know what to do."

"Well, the tribal council sent them to work with the sheriff—"

"The police can't do shit!" She lurched to her feet, sucked in a deep breath, and turned serious eyes on him. "Phil, Tommy Roundbush is *not* crazy."

"If you say so." The sudden topic shift and intensity left him ungrounded, breathless, as if he dangled from a cliff.

"Great spirits *do* protect the nations, and the Red Scarfs aren't—" she licked her lips, looked left then right, and lowered her voice. "Phil, they aren't human. Don't laugh, this isn't funny. It's dangerous, they're dangerous. The council shouldn't even talk to them, let alone buy into their stories. That Orrick didn't give permission for Erik and his crew to go among the people tells me at least some of the protections are working. But if the tribal council can't counter the Red Scarfs fully, the other elders won't have much better luck."

"Um…that's kind of crazy talk." Phil thought back to Tommy's descriptions. "I don't mean to disrespect your beliefs, but we haven't seen anything out of the ordinary. These are just hoodlums with a fetish for lighters and propane torches."

"Of course they look human. That's how glamour magic works. Without it, demons and deities alike could never walk among the people. We both saw the illusion slip, saw the flames as they entered the elevator. Your eyes gave you away."

"What I saw," Phil began, but swallowed the rest of the sentence. What had he seen? A trick of the air currents flapping bandanas and hair, making them look like the flames that had been planted in his subconscious by Tommy Roundbush's tall tales? The odor of scorched rubber and plastic had seemed real, and for just an instant he'd glimpsed the impossible. But that's how the human mind worked. Right? "I don't know what I saw."

"You saw what I saw." Ankti squeezed her beer tight. "I have certain abilities. I can't see through all illusions, but I'm pretty sure this crew wasn't too concerned about hiding their true nature. Maybe because the council didn't fully welcome them, or maybe they plan to come out into the open soon. Either way, it can't be good news."

The front bedroom door creaked open, and Phil realized the music had stopped. Kay stepped out, went to the fridge, and grabbed a drink. *So glad he's made himself at home.*

"She is correct. It will be difficult to deal with these creatures."

"Kay, you don't even know what we're talking about or your—" Phil took a deep breath. Kay was actually speaking in full sentences. But was it dangerous to remind a person with amnesia about their problem?

"There might be a lot I don't know." Kay gave the truncated concern a lopsided grin and leaned against the back of Ankti's chair, putting Phil in the minority "But I'm fairly confident I know a *lot* more than I currently recall when it comes to things like this, and I can guarantee that is more than you know."

"Isn't that wonderful," Phil scoffed, but couldn't muster much rancor. "And I'm pretty sure I know less than I think. But I'm also confident that demons aren't walking around and randomly attacking the greater Phoenix area."

"Oh, I agree with you there," Kay said. "I doubt much of this is random at all. People like this make definite plans. I know the type— don't ask me how, just have a little faith. We all need to be careful." He trilled out a little riff on his flute then hooked it back on his belt.

The room fell into brooding silence. Phil picked at his label while Ankti sipped quietly and patted Kay's hand, which had fallen on her shoulder in a gesture of support.

"Once the ceremony is over, you both need to come with me to see Grandmother Wikiwi. She can explain this better, and I think she'll be willing."

"Willing to talk to an outsider?" Phil immediately regretted his harsh tone and smirk of skepticism.

"Yes, I think it's time." Ankti gave a sharp nod and turned to Kay. "She wants to meet you anyway, if you're okay with that."

"Always happy to speak with elders." Kay's face screwed up in confusion. "Though I can't recall doing so before. Bah, I'm sure it's a wonderful experience. Now that *that's* settled." He sniffed loudly and turned his prominent, beak-of-a-nose toward the front door. "Does anyone else smell smoke?"

They all jumped as the front door shuddered under a series of heavy blows, as if someone knocked with a sledge-hammer. Although the sun had already set, orange and yellow flickered beyond the window curtains—flames. The pounding sounded again.

"We know you're home, so come on out," a deep voice bellowed.

Ankti rushed to the door and peered through the spy-hole. "It's one of the Red Scarfs from this afternoon."

"Not big on social graces are they?" Phil scanned the room for something that might work as a club, gave up, and looked through the curtains. "Well…that's not what I was expecting."

The man pounding on the door was just out of sight, but three others stood by the sidewalk tending the flames that still cast light through the window.

"What are they burning now?" Ankti leaned over to look out with him.

"Do I smell hamburgers?" Kay asked.

Flames ringed the front of the apartment, but rather than leaping from burning debris or hate symbols in the dry grass, they sprung from metal barrel halves mounted on rolling carts—barbeques. A lean Red Scarf danced between the grated cookers, wielding a long metal spatula like a conductor tending to a symphony of searing meat sizzling over the flames.

While the pit master attended to the food, others in black leather and bright headwear took up station along the sidewalk like defensive linemen—and women—in some bizarre ball game.

The door shuddered under another blow, and Ankti yanked it open. Caught off-guard with fist descending to strike again, the startled man filling the doorway floundered. He managed to check his swing without hitting the small woman who'd suddenly appeared before him or pitching through the doorway at the lack of resistance.

"Have a little respect!" Ankti went on the offensive. "You'll pay for any damage. What on Earth can be so important to have you acting like a damned fool?"

A square face sat atop the man's blocky body, curls of raven black poking out from beneath his crimson bandana. He looked left and right and cradled the meaty fist he'd used to pummel the door as if it was a grenade with the pin pulled and he couldn't decide where to throw it. Wheels turned behind hazel-brown eyes as he processed his predicament and Ankti's outrage.

Given the noise, Phil had expected to find a pair of the thugs wielding something like a police battering ram. Dents deformed the steel security door where the man had knocked. Phil wasn't exactly a weakling, but he'd be hard pressed to do that to an aluminum door.

The man finally had the decency to look abashed and lower his fist as he scuffed at the sidewalk with a boot. "Um…Kasandra sent us to—" he relaxed the fist and turned both giant paws palm up, a grizzly asked to explain mathematics. "That is, Kasandra said you're supposed to…"

"Start with something simple like you're name. I'm Ankti." She nodded to her right. "This is Phil. And you are?"

The man steeled himself and gave a curt nod as he regained his bearings. "Trevor. You can call me Trevor."

"Nice to meet you, Trevor," Ankti said. "So why do you have our car and apartment surrounded with grills?"

"Three." Trevor scratched his head and craned his thick neck in an attempt to look past Ankti and Phil into the apartment.

"Okay," she said. "Why do you have three barbeques?"

"No." The shaggy head wagged in denial. "There's supposed to be three of you."

Phil looked back, noting the beers on the coffee table. The third can was gone, as was their guest, and the bedroom door stood closed. Kay must not have wanted any part of the gang outside— not a bad notion, except his beef-cake guest was probably best suited to make a stand if it came to a fight.

"Just Ankti and me." It wasn't worth dragging the unpredictable man into this if he didn't want to be involved, so Phil stepped into the doorway, blocking further inspection. "Trevor, you were telling us what you want."

"It's a…a…"

"It's a barbeque in your honor." A tall giant dressed in black strode up behind the knocker, voice as smooth and oily as his complexion and hair.

Where Trevor was nearly as wide as he was tall, this well-proportioned giant stood six-eight and simply looked overtop Phil's head to scan the interior with feral gray eyes.

"Name's Uhnar. We're making enough food for everyone. So where's the other guy?" He drew in a long sniff and glared as if daring them to deny there was another person. "I can almost smell him."

Phil didn't like any of the Red Scarfs he'd met, but sinister intent rolled off this man, making Trevor seem positively friendly by comparison.

"What is with you people?" Ankti asked as a scatter of flute notes drifted from the back of the apartment. "You aren't bloodhounds. There's no one else here, case closed."

"Wait." The huge man sniffed again. His brow furrowed and he shook his head in resignation. "It's gone now. What the hell? Kasandra promised."

"Well, it's been wonderful meeting you both." Ankti pushed the door partway closed, using it as a shield. "Enjoy the burgers and please keep the noise down."

"Wait!" Trevor held out a hand, but stopped shy of actually blocking the door's swing. "You're supposed to come out and join us."

Ankti's eyebrows shot up, and Phil was certain she'd slam the door. But her expression changed, and a sly smile spread across those full lips. "Sure, I guess we could eat."

Phil nearly choked on a tense laugh as he shouldered into the doorway, his back to the strangers.

"Are you insane?" he mouthed the silent words and was annoyed to see a sparkle of amusement in her eyes.

"We need info," she mouthed back, pointing from herself to him and tapping her temple.

He wanted to argue, to tell her stepping out with the enemy might not be the best idea. There was no good reason for these folks to want to spend time with them. If anything, these brutes were the ones hunting for information. And hadn't Ankti just been trying to convince him that the Red Scarfs were more than they appeared, that maybe they weren't even human? Or had he read that wrong?

Phil suddenly wished they'd been able to finish that discussion. The fact that the two at the door wanted to be certain no one was left in the apartment made him think they meant to ransack the place the next time everyone went out.

But he'd known the young woman long enough to recognize the steel in her expression. This wasn't something Ankti could be talked out of, and he supposed joining the group outside would take their focus off Kay.

* * *

Phil sat on the steps eyeing the two-inch-thick burger and pile of beans suspiciously. To his right, Ankti bent over her own plate, closed her eyes, and inhaled. But instead of simply smelling her food, she passed her left hand over the plate, fingers moving in a subtle pattern as though she read braille in the air above the meal.

"Don't worry." She gave him an encouraging nod and picked up a tiny white spork. "It's safe."

Sure, demons are known for their home cooking.

Phil snorted at the thought of monsters tending the grills. The bizarre circumstances, Tommy's stories, Ankti's claims—all of it combined into something insidious that chipped away at the foundations of reality. Possible versus impossible, truth versus fantasy. The lines blurred as seeds germinated in the fertile soil of his imagination.

And whatever witchy spell Ankti used to declare their food fit to eat fell right in line with his little mental breakdown. With the deteriorating state of the world, a vacation from reality might even be nice. Phil smiled at the notion, shrugged, and picked up his burger only to find he had another problem.

"Damned thing has to weigh two pounds. I can't even fit my mouth around it."

"You know what they say about eating an elephant." Ankti tore a corner off her own burger and chewed thoughtfully. "Funny how they're sort of ignoring us."

She was right. Besides Trevor and the towering Uhnar who had met them at the door, there were four other men and two women who sat around in small groups enjoying the food and an odd green drink that came in tall glass bottles. Empties were piled by the grills, but no one had offered either of them one. Aside from the occasional glance, they were indeed being ignored.

The Red Scarfs spared more looks for the front door of Phil's apartment. More often than not those looks were followed by furtive glances to where Erik and Kasandra lived two doors down—as if the gang members were worried their leaders would catch them partying.

Trevor noticed them studying the others, broke away from the woman he'd been talking with, and joined them on the stairs. "Good food, huh?" He eyed their nearly-intact burgers and ran a surprisingly pale tongue over his lips.

"Too much." Ankti rubbed her stomach and waved at her plate. "Help yourself."

A childish grin lit the man's face as he scooped up her sandwich in one meaty hand and took a massive bite.

"Your people out here seem uninterested in Ankti and me. Weird considering how adamant you were about us coming out." By the time Phil got his thought out, Trevor had—impossibly—finished the burger.

"We're not real social." He wiped ketchup from the corner of his mouth with the back of one hand as he looked around the small patch of lawn. "But Erik and Kasandra said it was important, so here we are."

"They're the leaders of the Red Scarfs, right?" Phil asked.

"Red Scarfs?" Trevor cocked his head.

"No offense intended," Phil backpedaled. "That's just what the news has been calling your group on account of the bandanas."

"Huh, makes sense. I like it."

"What's the deal? Why the interest in us, and why the worried looks back to your apartment down there? Something doesn't add up." Ankti had that oh-you're-going-to-tell-me look.

Phil had been on the receiving end of that expression enough times to feel sorry for Trevor. Ankti was an awfully nice woman, but when she put her mind to something the gloves came off.

"I don't think I should talk about it." Trevor set his jaw and turned away.

"Are you from Jersey?" Phil asked, trying to keep the man from shutting down. "I can't quite place your accent, but it sure sounds like something from the north shore area."

"Not exactly, but close." Trevor turned back, his eyebrows lifting in surprise. "I just love it up there. Things run at a different pace. You ever been to the Greensward? They have the best grub. And man, the people you see."

"Nah, too ritzy for me," Phil waived away the other man's adoration. "Never had that kind of money."

"True enough." Trevor nodded and pantomimed picking up a cup of tea with his picky extended. "A lot of hoity-toity, self-important folks. Of course, it was a lot worse back in the day. Things have been thinning out everywhere."

"So is everyone from New Jersey?" Ankti asked.

"We're from all over. I just like visiting that area. You could sort of say that I grew up near there." Trevor smiled at some inside joke. "A couple of these others are from my…neighborhood. Big shots like Erik and Kasandra, well, they've got their own special places where guys like me can't go."

"Sucks to be shut out." Ankti nodded in commiseration.

"Nothing like that," Trevor said. "They have their own place because…well…they're just above us. You know?" When Ankti didn't respond, he continued. "And it's not like we're worried about them. It's just that they expect certain tasks to get done while they're out." He scanned the courtyard. "We've done the best we could."

"We've all been there," Phil said. "Ballbuster bosses. I can't tell you the number of times the Bureau wants an area needing a month of study to be wrapped up in under a week."

"See, you know what it's like." Trevor gave him a friendly pat on the shoulder that had the unintended effect of slamming Phil into Ankti so that their heads cracked together and he saw stars. "This time of year, I'd rather be back east. Not everyone likes seeing fall come in, but I do. The leaves, the scents, the land preparing for winter's sleep. But there's a job to do. The bosses have a right to be demanding."

"When this is over maybe you can go back to your day job or whatever it is you do in the northeast." Ankti gave his knee a reassuring pat. "I know Phil will certainly be happy to get back."

"Yeah, maybe," Trevor hedged. "There's always another…job, but still, maybe. And if you guys get back"—it was Trevor's turn to shoot a furtive glance at the Red Scarfs' apartment—"I guess just enjoy things one day at a time." He eyed Phil's burger. "Do you mind?"

* * *

"That was monumentally uninformative," Phil said as he shut the front door.

After twenty minutes of discussion with Trevor and several failed attempts at calling it an evening, the group outside finally gave in and let them head inside. Unbelievably, the skinny cook was out there throwing fresh slabs of meat onto the grills where the raging flames refused to burn down. If they weren't careful, the fire department was going to show up in response to the haze of charred meat smoke curling up into the clear night sky.

"We know they want something in your apartment, and that their leaders are going to be pissed they didn't get it." Ankti plopped down on the couch as Phil bolted the door. "I don't know how they expected to sneak back in with us right there. Heck, no one even tried."

"They expected all three of us to be home. Maybe not knowing where Kay was made them cautious." Phil sat across from her as his other houseguest shuffled from the bedroom. "Speak of the devil! Nice hiding job. We could have used a little backup out there."

"Things would have gone very differently had I shown my face," Kay said. "I did manage to overhear some of their plans while you spoke to Mr. Door-knocker. You have more to worry about than their interest in me. They want to stop the ceremony. From the sound of things, their enigmatic leaders are downtown working plans with the police even as we speak."

"Why would the cops work with these thugs?" Phil wasn't buying it. "They won't lift a finger to help vandals. For that matter, how could you hear anything, seeing as you were locked in your room the whole time?"

"Maybe I was inside." Kay gave one of his sly little smiles to Ankti, as if sharing an inside joke, and slid onto the couch beside her. "But then again, maybe I wasn't. A man needs his secrets." Ankti actually smiled back and a musical titter escaped her. *Ah jeez*. "Suffice to say, I did get close enough to hear the cretins. Apparently the city police are willing to deputize a chosen few so that the Red Scarfs can keep their rogue members in check. But they will use that authority to close roads and turn participants away from the Phoenix Mountain Preserve tomorrow."

"We've got to get to Brandon," Ankti said. "I'm sure he can talk sense into Police Chief O'Donnell."

"The police won't listen to reason." Kay held up a hand to forestall argument. "Logic and personal relationships won't change things. These Red Scarfs have heavy influence, if you know what I mean." Kay pointed to the bundle of sticks that had been twisted into human shape. The rudimentary doll lay on a side table, staring blankly up at the ceiling.

For some reason Ankti's eyes went wide as she looked from doll to Kay and nodded. "If they have that kind of power, we're screwed. Over a hundred people are supposed to participate tomorrow. We need the roads open to get to the ceremonial grounds...unless." Ankti jumped up and rushed to her bedroom, leaving Phil to stare at Kay in confusion.

Those two were communicating on a different wavelength. Subtleties he couldn't grasp ran beneath this discussion. That the tribal council had sat down to listen to Erik and Kasandra was one thing, but for city officials to hand over authority made zero sense. Yet both of them acted as if it was perfectly reasonable to assume the Red Scarfs had leverage over the police. Before he had time to puzzle out an answer, Ankti returned and slapped a laminated map on the coffee table.

"Deputized officials won't have authority on reservation land." She traced a finger from Mount Phoenix north through back country, then looped east into Hopi lands, and finally came south along the border between the Apache and Salt River reservations. "One good fallout of the population crisis is that rather than maintain failing infrastructure, the state's been ceding land back to the nation. It's a convoluted route, and we'll need all-wheel drive vehicles. But people can funnel all the way to the ceremony without straying onto public roads. Deputized or not, Red Scarfs won't have any jurisdiction, and tribal security will have free rein."

"Gonna take time to coordinate," Phil said as he headed for the door. "You two stay here. Pull an overnight bag together, call Brandon, and give him a heads up. We ought to at least confirm what Kay heard about deputizing before going too crazy with backup plans. I'm going to extract the car from the barbecue zone. When I pull around back, hop out the window."

"Be careful." Ankti slid her phone from her pocket.

10. Face Off

T HE RED Scarfs partied outside like their lives depended on it. The pile of empty bottles had grown to monumental proportions, as had the array of meat smoking over the flames.

Eyes bored into Phil as he strolled down the sidewalk to speak with the cook, his steps measured and deliberate in an attempt to slow his racing heart. Ugly glares replaced the feigned indifference and boredom from earlier, making him feel like a prized pig sauntering toward the pit master—a stupid notion that had sweat popping out along his forehead.

There was no way any of these people could still be hungry, yet the grinning cook now stacked steaks and less-identifiable hunks of meat onto his grills. Trevor had downed at least three massive burgers during their conversation, and Phil caught the man going back for more while they'd headed inside. This group ate like professional athletes.

Including the cook, he counted six Red Scarfs. Trevor wasn't anywhere to be seen—disappointing. Small as it was, they'd formed a connection with the big man, and Phil would rather speak to him about getting his car out from among the grills. At a minimum, having someone that wasn't staring daggers would be preferable to facing the towering cook alone. The chef's posture didn't exactly invite a friendly exchange. He stood with arms crossed, a wicked serrated spatula rising over each shoulder like a pair of jungle machetes.

"Hi." Phil coughed in an attempt to bring his voice down half an octave and pointed at the nearest hunk of sizzling meat. "Best burger I've ever had, real gourmet fare. You could make a fortune with a restaurant."

The tall man looked blank, as though Phil spoke a foreign language. But perhaps that wasn't a fair assessment. There was emotion in those coal-black eyes, a smoldering malice accentuated by flickers of flame reflecting off the raised spatulas.

"Well, your work is top-notch so keep it up." Phil reached into his front pocket, pulled out his car keys, and jangled the set for emphasis. "I have to head out for a while and need to move a couple of your grills so I can get into my car."

A sneer pulled the man's lip up on the right side, and a sonorous growl rose from his throat. As if in response, the flames licked higher, the odor of charred meat suddenly cloying, oppressive. Light blazed off the mirrored surface of his spatulas, bathing the tall man's long face in shades of orange and yellow that made his bandanna seem to jump and flap as if in a strong updraft.

This was the elevator scene all over again. The flight of fancy, the illusion bolstered by the all-too-real backdrop of roaring flames, had Phil squeezing his eyes shut against the sudden glare. He blinked away stinging tears, but instead of returning to normal the scene turned more bizarre.

His beater rental was barely visible through the fires, and matching orange flames rose from the cook's head sending sparks streaming into the night sky. The man's face grew pale and chalky while the zippers and snaps of his leather outfit melted away, leaving coarse pebbled skin. The apparition stood tall, a flaming skull above leathery body with black talons clasping a pair of gleaming spatulas-turned-machetes.

Phil stepped back, heel catching on the first of three steps at the parking lot end of the walkway to his door. All the Red Scarfs were on their feet, quietly closing in on him, heads aflame over grinning skulls. Some were wide, others tall and gangly. They shuffled forward with odd rolling steps on knees hinged to swing forwards and back.

"Forget about the car. We'll just order what we need online." Phil turned and ran for the door, knowing he wasn't fast enough, certain he'd go down under ripping claws, burned by searing skulls as chiseled teeth tore out great mouthfuls of living flesh.

It made no sense—had to be a hallucination. *What was in those burgers?*

The Red Scarfs slowed, letting him make the landing, but their eyes followed. Devils should have glowing embers for eyes, steeped in the fires of hell. Hate and anger filled every gaze, but the eyes were normal—the only feature on each that hadn't changed. They grinned as one when he shouldered the door open and stumbled inside.

Phil gulped down a lungful of air, grateful to be away from the miasma of charred flesh. His eyes stung, and the cloying odor filled both nostrils like the smell of burnt hair. Ankti looked at him with concern from the window where she'd watched the confrontation. Kay stood by his bedroom door, expression unreadable.

At the coffee table, Phil picked up his open beer with a trembling hand and took a swig. He wanted to tell them what he'd seen, to be rushed to the hospital to treat whatever condition caused the hallucination. None of this was possible, but neither words of explanation nor denial would come. He took another long drink and approached the window with deliberate steps, willing his pulse to slow. Outside would be a group of thugs gathered around the parking lot just as they'd been all evening, nothing more.

Ankti slowly pulled the curtain aside. Outside, the Red Scarfs had gathered into a knot around the cook, flaming heads bowed together in discussion, black talons flexing and grasping at the end of leathery arms. The vision hadn't dispersed. Ankti laid a reassuring hand on his shoulder. He leaned into the warm human contact, not trusting his voice.

"Demons are real, Phil." Her liquid brown eyes were filled with compassion.

It took another can of beer and soft words from the Hopi woman to talk his frayed psyche down from its ledge. One misstep and he'd surely tumble into insanity. She was kind and patient, but insistent.

Tommy Roundbush's outlandish claims were in fact an accurate description of what descended upon Phoenix. And if Kay had heard right, these demons planned to destroy the tribes' collaborative magic—real magic released through their ceremonies. But there was more.

His head hurt. The beer helped dull his senses, which was good and bad. Phil stood at the fridge, but realized he needed his wits about him and grabbed a water bottle instead of another brew. The liquid eased his parched throat. His encounter with the cook had sucked him dry.

"You're saying it's more than just stopping the ceremonies, that they're looking for something?" Phil asked.

"This is a seeking charm." Ankti picked up the crude stick doll they'd found that first night. "A kind of effigy made with dark magic. They've been looking for Kay."

His oddly arrogant, half-amnesic houseguest merely nodded at her declaration.

"But why?" Phil asked.

"That I don't know." Ankti raised an eyebrow at Kay, who simply shrugged. "Regardless, we need to get out of here, find Brandon, and warn the tribes. The fact that these creatures are trying to interfere is ample reason to ensure tomorrow's ceremony stays on track."

"Well, *my* car isn't going anywhere anytime soon," Phil said.

"Which is why it's good that mine's at the end of the street." Ankti reached behind the couch and lifted her blue bag. "Let's stick with your plan, except I drive. We gather our things, climb out the bedroom window, and get the heck out of here before these things decide to break down the door."

"I'm surprised they haven't done that already," Phil called over his shoulder as he went to grab his overnight bag. "Unless they just want us under house arrest."

"It's a matter of protective energy," Kay said. "You've been in this place long enough—we've been here long enough—that it's a home of sorts. Energy at the threshold keeps them at bay. Didn't you notice when they first tried to draw us out? They were careful not to cross your threshold even when Ankti yanked open the door and caught them off guard."

"We still have to go," Ankti said. "Cell signal is crap. I can't get Brandon's phone to ring or even go to voicemail. There's a bunch of interference no matter who I try. My last attempt got the all-lines-busy recording, which makes me wonder if the Red Scarfs are doing something magical to interfere."

"Or maybe they simply blew up a few cell towers."

Sarcasm colored Phil's words, rising from a stubborn corner of his mind where hope for a rational explanation still huddled despite the evidence dragging his intellect kicking and screaming to the impossible reality. Ankti shot him a you've-got-to-be-kidding look.

"Worse than that," Kay said. "If Erik and Kasandra return, I doubt the threshold has enough power to keep them out. There's something familiar about that pair. Tickles the back of my head, but I can't…quite…" he shrugged and relaxed, dark eyes twinkling with the carefree grin Phil was coming to hate. "Nope, it's gone."

Ankti narrowed her eyes as if trying to see into the man's mind. Phil looked from one to the other, then to the flickering light still playing against the curtains, and came to a decision.

"I *like* plan B. Grab your things! We leave in five and get out before the super bad guys come back."

Spurred by the threat of something worse than burning skull demons, they were ready in a flash. With a short drop into an alcove behind the apartment, Ankti's window proved easiest to climb out. The building sat on a canyon ridge so that the ground sloped away under the other windows. A handy maintenance path ran along the foundation, and the hill would hide them from anyone out front.

Phil slipped out first and offered a hand back to Ankti. But the lithe woman simply threw him her bag and jumped to the ground. Kay—the show-off—vaulted through the window to land silently next to them.

"This is an end unit." Phil kept his voice low. "Hug the building around to the right. The hill should keep us out of sight. This trail runs along the ravine out to Thistle Avenue. That's where you parked right?"

"It is, but—"

Ankti froze as Phil tried to hand over her bag, standing with mouth open and staring past him. Stars twinkled in her wide eyes— no, it was more like the reflection of a blazing campfire. In fact an orange glow lit the entire alcove.

Phil turned and found himself facing a nightmare. A massive demon with flaming head lumbered into the alcove and raised its arm high, talons extending and ready to slash. Dark hazel eyes gleamed from skeletal sockets beneath the flames. Was that—

"Trevor?"

The deadly claw poised above his head pivoted from side to side in a half-wave.

"Hey, Phil." The sonorous voice from dinner sounded dejected. "Why couldn't you just have sat tight?" Trevor let out a massive sigh that caused the flames along his brow to flicker low. "Come out front; have some more burgers. They're good right?"

"Sure, they're great, but we've got to…go." Phil couldn't believe he was arguing with a monster, but Ankti was right—they needed to warn the tribes.

"And I have to stop you." Trevor squared his shoulders so that he fully blocked the alcove.

Kay stepped forward with a hand raised. At first Phil thought he held a weapon, perhaps a knife or club. But it was just his flute. The guy was buff and probably stood the best chance of any of them against these creatures. But he was just as likely to get fried to a crisp, clawed, or snapped in half by the brute. Phil laid a restraining hand on Kay's shoulder and turned back to what had been the man they'd spoken with earlier.

"Trevor." Phil cleared his throat to buy himself time to think. "You don't even like your job. You said so yourself. I mean, you want us to stay, but we've *got* to go. Things get ugly, someone gets hurt? It's just not worth it.

"Say you never saw us, that we slipped out…magically." Phil pushed that last word past reeling senses that clung to the reality he'd known. On its way out the word grazed those mental tethers, casting him into uncharted territory, but he focused on what the *man* had told him earlier. "Head back east, Trevor. Leave this madness. Go home, see the North Shore, and enjoy the coming winter."

"Can't do it, Phil." That blocky flaming head rocked left and right as a frown pulled down the corners of the skeletal mouth—so not boney, just chalky white flesh. "You don't know them. It just wouldn't work."

There was true pain in the big creature's voice, the big man's voice—hell, Phil didn't know what he was dealing with. But he did know the feeling of being trapped and alone, of having no say over your future.

"I know it seems that way, but you really can choose. Don't let others drive your life."

Phil had been trapped in a well-paying dead-end job that crushed his soul. Driven by aptitude tests and well-meaning parents, he'd rushed to his fate, never pausing to think through what he truly wanted. Chained behind a desk by mind-numbing work locked him away from a world he yearned to experience, and at the time he'd been certain there was no escape. Yes, he'd been in Trevor's shoes until he'd found his passion and forced a change.

Gentle music lilted as Phil told the story of how he'd taken those first steps out of the trap. The flute wove a light soothing tune, and Kay melted into shadows under the window as Phil described his moment of revelation and how he'd known there was a better life out there waiting. Trevor's brow drew low, the flames along his head burning down until they resembled a glowing halo more than roaring torch.

"Do you really think so?" Trevor asked. "Because I'd like that, to just go back—away from all this."

Phil blinked in confusion. Under the dim moonlight a dark-haired man beseeched him with hazel-brown eyes, his beefy hands clasped before him like a hopeful child. The misery and sadness that drew down the corners of mouth and eyes slowly lifted, replaced by a dawning look of wonder as the flute notes trailed off. The night grew still as if not just Phil but the world held its breath.

Trevor stepped aside, and Phil took a tentative step toward the trail. A second step went unchallenged, so he pushed Ankti ahead. Kay slipped the flute into his belt, nodded, and took her by the hand. The two headed off along the building.

"Thank you and good luck." Phil stuck out his hand.

Sausage fingers wrapped fully around his knuckles, and for a moment he worried his hand would be crushed to a pulp. But Trevor shook gently, almost reverently.

Phil followed the others, looking back at the man they had just met and uncertain if his own words or some other power had swayed Trevor. The big man faded silently into the night as the three hurried toward the road.

Furtive glances back showed no signs of pursuit. Ten minutes later, Ankti slid into the driver's seat of her SUV with Kay beside her and Phil in the back. A long slow U-turn got them heading toward the highway, hopefully without attracting further attention.

11. A Longer Road

E XCEPT FOR light evening traffic, the roads to the camping grounds were clear with no evidence of any Red Scarf road blocks. That was to be expected. Players wouldn't start gathering for the ceremony until tomorrow afternoon.

Despite all they'd been through and the emotional wringer that had neatly hammered, rolled, and stretched Phil's belief system into something unrecognizable, the camp proved suspiciously quiet—a calm before the storm. Ankti swore her magic *sight* showed the air full of tense expectation. Phil felt it, a kind of building electricity like the moment before a thunderstorm. They scoured temporary pavilions and white travel trailers masquerading as offices, but couldn't locate the chief of security.

"Yeah, Brandon's not around," Jack Fletcher said when they caught up to Brandon's second in command coming off rounds on his four-wheeler. "I expected him back around dinner time. Must have gotten sidetracked."

"We've got problems." Ankti didn't mince words. "We think the Red Scarfs plan to stop people from getting to Mount Phoenix for tomorrow's gathering."

"Yep, we know about that," Jack agreed. "That's why he went downtown to talk sense into the sheriff. He called around four to say the police were a bust and that he had another avenue to pursue. I'm guessing his phone died because no one's been able to raise him since. Hope he hasn't gone off and done anything crazy."

Jack stood a hair under six foot with a proud visage and the high cheekbones of the Apache—reminiscent of Ankti's, but set along a longer face with a strong nose and boney brow beneath fine brown hair that lay straight as an arrow. His shoulders were broad and sturdy without being overly muscular like, say, Kay's. Phil was no expert, but Kay's appearance didn't fit neatly into any particular group. Perhaps his lineage included several tribes—and a bodybuilder or two.

"Brandon is as by the book as they come," Ankti said. "I'm worried too, but doubt he'd be off on a wild chase. In the meantime, we have an idea to avoid the Red Scarfs. Let's go inside and talk."

They headed to one of the modest office trailers. Jack pulled in two of his officers to hear Ankti's plan. The group worked up a more comprehensive route and contingency plans for stragglers. Not everyone was at the camping grounds. New players would be arriving on early flights, and several contingents would drive in from northern territories. With the phones largely inoperative, Jack's people set up runners to intercept the people still inbound, get them off the main roads, and hopefully avoid the roadblocks.

"Problem is, we don't know what roads they'll block," Phil said as they studied a huge map with topological overlays.

"You can bet the approach to Mount Phoenix will be one." Jack stabbed a finger at where the main access road to the preserve split from the highway. The narrow road to the ceremonial grounds wound through hills just inside reservation borders marked on the map. "If you're right, and they stay off our land—and they better—this will be the last chance to stop people. Same with the airport access road. Hustling people out of there without being spotted will be tricky."

"Hopefully Brandon shows up with more information." Ankti traced along the back roads they'd settled on for the approach to Mt Phoenix. In several spots the participants would be forced to cross out of reservation lands. In other places proper roads didn't exist between legs. "We need to get calls and runners out to the tribal council and elders to ensure these routes are open and put safeguards in place for anyone who needs help along the way. Probably about a two-hour haul from here, and it's convoluted. We don't want people getting turned around out there."

"Jump on the phones tonight and do what you can." Jack nodded to his two helpers. "If the cell towers keep acting up, get runners with copies of the route moving first thing in the morning. We need to have this whole thing in place by noon, sooner if possible. I'll spread the word across camp for everyone to hang tight until we start sending groups out. Intercepting those out-of-towners is going to be tricky. Shit, put on a pot of coffee too—the big one."

"We'll run up to the Hopi Reservation at first light," Ankti declared. "Grandmother Wikiwi is best suited to keep the roads through our lands clear. And you two"—she pointed to Phil and Kay—"need to meet her anyway."

It was well past midnight by the time they finished planning and Jack had the runners set to go. Brandon still hadn't showed up and didn't answer his phone on the few occasions they managed to get a call through. Ankti stifled a yawn that Phil managed to catch and complete for her.

"Listen, take my tent." Jack said as things wound down. "It's got a decent space heater and extra sleeping pads. I'm going to try a few more of these dead phone numbers and finish making copies of those mini-maps. It won't be the first time I've crashed at the office. Go get some shut-eye."

After offering a token argument, they left Jack and his helpers to finish up and picked through loose rows of tents to the far side of the compound. Stars shone bright in the clear sky, and the cool desert night wrapped the quiet camp in a crisp, brittle embrace. Most tents stood dark, but a subtle glow illuminated a few, casting the occasional shadow of someone within hunched over to read or work into the wee hours of the morning.

Though dead tired, Phil's mind buzzed with all he'd seen and heard. Sleep wouldn't come easy, especially in a makeshift tent, on a hard cot, and with scratchy army surplus blankets. But his vision of bivouac-style accommodations shattered as they pushed through the double-folded tent flap into a well-appointed space. A tapestry depicting desert and prairie landscapes hung along the back wall of the warm interior, and thick sleeping pads were piled with soft handcrafted blankets. The fringed pillow, woven of cloud-soft fibers reminiscent of alpaca, called to him as he and Kay set up on the right side of the tent, while Ankti took the left. Ankti pummeled her pillows, lower lip clenched between her teeth as they settled down for the night.

"Jack seems like a solid man," Phil said, taking a stab at what bothered her.

"He is, but this is a huge undertaking." She slapped her sleeping pad. "I'm worried about Brandon. It isn't like him to go off on a wild goose chase. Something's wrong."

"Not much we can do about it tonight." Phil looked at his watch and winced. "Make that this morning. Try to catch a few hours of sleep. We can test the route between here and your grandmother's as soon as the sun's up." Phil looked to his left where Kay sat cross-legged in front of the little heater that cast an amber glow across the fabric of the tent. "Kay, you've been awful quiet. What's your take on our plan?"

Wind rose outside, snapping and flapping the material in a soft, hypnotic rhythm. The other man's shadow jumped and billowed as if dancing on the tent wall. The weak light cast the flute at his belt into a long shadow, like a staff rising up behind him instead of the simple wood instrument. Phil rubbed his eyes; he really needed sleep.

"I think our little Ankti has put many wheels in motion." A slow smile spread across the man's face as he looked at her. "Things will be as they will be, but you have done well to protect your people and the coming ritual."

"Back at the apartment, you sure had a lot of opinions about these Red Scarfs," Phil pressed. "How about a few tips on defending ourselves if push comes to shove? You two have pulled me into this crazy world of spirits and magic. Isn't there a spell or something to keep them at bay, maybe send them back to where they came from?" Of course, in Trevor's case that was apparently New Jersey.

"If it were only that simple." Kay barked out a laugh. "There would be little need for balance in the world, and a great many problems would be simplified. But we have a few tools at our command. Ankti's plan should avoid most of the conflict." He dropped a hand to his flute and stroked the polished wood while considering his words. "As for magic, I cannot help you there. Perhaps your elder will have some ideas."

Ankti gave Kay a wry grin. "I hope she does."

They agreed to be on the road by seven to give themselves a few hours of sleep and still beat the morning rush hour, such as it was. Phil recalled nodding in agreement, thinking he'd be lucky to get any sleep at all with his mind racing. But between the wonderfully luxurious sleeping pad and the insistent pressure of heavy blankets, sleep found him with little effort. One moment Phil lay studying the fluttering material overhead, the next he was falling until he whumped onto a hot griddle that seared his back. But the surface shifted as he thrashed and closed his fist around a handful of scorching sand. Sunlight blazed in an azure sky, and white birds soared overhead calling out with mournful, hungry cries. *I'm at the beach.*

A shadow blocked the light, a woman's round pixie face with raven hair trimmed in a cute bob that dripped seawater. Her pretty blue eyes lit with playful mischief.

"Wake up, sleepy head, or you'll get fried." Simone leaned in close and planted a kiss on his forehead.

Her halter top slipped, exposing a vee of creamy white skin the sun had been unable to reach. He had little time to appreciate the sight because she shook her head like a wet dog, sending a cold spray that had Phil gasping as goosebumps rose across his front. As she'd predicted, his chest was already turning pink.

"What time is it?" He grabbed the towel and patted himself dry.

"Almost two," she said and laughed. "If you're done imitating a lobster, we could get food up on the boards."

"When have I ever turned down that offer?"

They'd come to the beach for a weekend getaway, a rare opportunity where the stars lined up a break between his trips for the Bureau and her clinicals back at Bryn Mawr hospital. They'd met in Philadelphia, but with so many businesses closing and entire areas evacuated, it was nice to spend time at Ocean City. The quaint seaside town along the Southern Jersey coast had been a playground for nearby city-dwellers for almost a century and remained a bastion even as the few thousand people remaining in Philly consolidated into an area of the burbs christened New Philadelphia.

It was no surprise his girlfriend was hungry. She barely ate between twelve-hour shifts on the nursing floor. Phil liked that she wasn't a food prima donna who insisted on veggie-based this and low-fat that. Simone loved life and attacked it and her food with enviable gusto. Phil smiled at the thought.

Although some of the boardwalk magic had dwindled as storefronts closed, the notorious pizza shops and custard stands thrived through the summer. Between those, fudge, and taffy, there was no shortage of arguably-unhealthy but wonderfully satisfying delights available along the weathered raised walkway separating beach from city. Slammed by waves, fried by sun, and eating until you burst was half the fun of a trip to the shore.

But first a little retaliation was in order. Phil finished toweling off, scooped up a handful of sand as he stood, and flung it across her thighs earning a squeal and shriek as she spun and darted for the boardwalk. He hurried to catch up, feet sinking deep into hot shifting sand that clung to his ankles like molasses.

Simone looked over her shoulder, laughing eyes encouraging him to hurry. He pushed on, but the sand redoubled its efforts to drag him down. Phil wouldn't let this one get away; a well-hidden ring back in their apartment attested to that. It might be an inventory sell-off from a closing jeweler, but the ring sported a quality third-carat diamond and fell firmly within the budget dictated by his entry-level position with the new Disease Control Center.

Simone clomped up the wood steps to the weathered boards that made up the three-mile-long walkway overlooking the beach. The sun had somehow dropped low on the horizon, making her shadow stretch across the sand, sand that was still too hot. Phil's own shadow stretched back toward the water, toward the blanket where they'd set up for their day of sun.

Something was wrong with his shadow; it had depth and substance, and grabbed his ankles to drag him backward. He clawed at the sand on all fours, but the hot material seemed alive with an irresistible undertow.

"No!" He screamed as he was pulled along the length of his own shadow away from the woman he loved.

The sand grew slippery beneath the shadow, and Phil shot past the blanket and towels, but slowed to a stop just shy of the foamy line marking high tide. A dog thundered toward him along the crashing shoreline, a big long-legged animal with gray and white fur. Ears flapped as it galloped with the sound of horse-hooves beating the sand, tongue lolling from the side of its mouth in a happy grin. But as it approached, it changed. The fur grew dark, turning into cracked leathery hide. The animal's head sharpened to a beak as it sucked its tongue in and the snout elongated with ears flaring wide into a horny mantle. Fire erupted from its coal-black skin as it passed him, leaving the scent of sulfur and burnt plastic, a pint-sized dragon racing across the sand—actually more like a miniature, flaming, triceratops.

Phil followed the creature away from the water to where it disappeared beneath the elevated boardwalk. He crossed from scorching sun to cold shadows, picking his way through wood pilings that supported the walk like telephone poles rising from the sand.

Phil continued on for an impossibly long time. The pilings turned knotty with coarse bark. Tree trunks rose all around him, and the shading boards overhead became a tangled canopy of leafy branches. He pushed on into the forest, shuffling through loamy soil rich with decaying organic matter and insects.

A clearing opened beyond a final massive tree. An unfamiliar species, the broad tangle of wispy branches held no leaves and terminated in complex knots of twigs that hung down like woody fruit shaped into the semblance of matchstick dolls.

A familiar woman sitting in the grass rose to her feet, walked to the tree, and picked one of the low-hanging dolls. Her skin shone bronze and perfect. Dark buns of hair were pinned behind elegant cheekbones, a lovely vision.

"Come with me." Ankti motioned him onward.

Phil followed along a dirt path through lush green grass that soon gave way to ugly brown stubble. They crested a hill, but instead of following the path down the far side they climbed higher, flying above a parched landscape. Ankti worried at the doll, pulling at knotted branches as if trying to undo its form.

"Where are we going?" Phil studied the ground far below.

Long dry rivers and veins of erosion cut through the rocky landscape, exposing the bones of the world in sedimentary bands of tans and reds. Nature had carved deep, intricate designs, a spreading history, a story. The patterns left him with a vague feeling of unease and wonder, but like hieroglyphs of some forgotten language there was no key to unlock their true meaning.

Wind whipped his hair into a wild frenzy that broke the mesmerizing view. He should be terrified. What held them up? Ankti smiled, tucked the doll under her arm and held her hands out, palm up. Impossibly, they rose higher.

He remembered now—magic was real. The woman helping him was some kind of…well, he didn't know what to call her. Maybe a witch or simply someone who harnessed spiritual energy? They hadn't had time for much discussion. The doll glowed from the crook of her arm. Hadn't that done something too, something bad?

They soon arrived atop a tall mesa ringed by rocky crags and rising beside a winding river that cut through the desert landscape. The air smelled of salty brine, but a sluggish stillness replaced the ocean's crashing waves.

Ankti knelt, dug a hole, and planted the twig doll, covering it over with dusty soil. A wave of her delicate hand brought a shower of water to darken the dry little mound. The scent of cool moisture mixed with backing stone. Seagulls called in the distance, followed by a defiant scream unlike anything at the shore. The third call twisted into a harsh, electronic wail.

Phil's eyes flew open. Muted light filled the tent. Ankti silenced the alarm and stretched with a theatric yawn.

"Well, that felt like ten minutes." She gave a resigned smile.

Phil wasn't certain it had even been that long, but amber sunshine filtered through the canvas. Rumpled blankets twisted in knots around him told the story of his uneasy slumber, but the sleeping mat to his left was empty.

"Where's Kay?"

The man was gone, but his bag sat near the door. Ankti looked around, sucked in a breath, and her cheeks turned bright pink.

"You have the most obnoxious alarm." Kay sat up on the far side of the woman, a beaded necklace slapping against his sculpted bare chest. He too scanned the tent, eyebrows lifting in surprise. But when his gaze fell on Ankti, his lips stretched up into a huge toothy smile.

"I…I." Ankti pulled her blanket up to her neck despite the fact that she was fully clothed.

"I tend to move around in my sleep," Kay said by way of explanation.

Though clearly amused at Ankti's persistent blush and downcast eyes, Kay had the decency to extract himself from the nook and knee-walked back to his own sleeping pad.

"I had the weirdest dream, and you were in it," Phil said, throwing out a lifeline to change the topic and only realizing his mistake when the woman's face blazed a deeper crimson. "No, nothing like *that*! You picked something off a tree and planted it."

"Fascinating," Kay said as he pulled on a shirt.

The material covered his perfect, hairless chest, but not his muscular thighs. Ankti had a right to blush, the guy had only been wearing a flimsy loincloth! Phil felt heat rising to his own face. He tried to keep in decent shape, but sitting next to Adonis here really undercut a guy's self-esteem.

"Fight any monsters? Save a princess?" Kay asked with a mischievous grin.

"You were…" Phil searched his fading memory, but couldn't finish the thought. It felt like Kay was there. But the tattered remnants of the dream drifted away like smoke. Phil shrugged in defeat, grabbing hold of the one thing he did recall. "Maybe you were the dog."

* * *

They pulled out at five past seven, cruising north along Highway 101. Phil finished dialing for the third time only to again receive an "all lines busy" recording.

"Still can't get through to your grandmother." Phil shoved the phone into the cup holder in disgust. "Would she even be up this early?"

"You don't know much about Grandmother Wikiwi," Kay said from the back seat, as if he did—*jerk*.

Ankti bit down on a laugh, but it escaped in a wet burst when she saw whatever expression crossed Phil's face. "Don't worry; she'll have been up for hours. Grandmother is a tribal elder, a keeper of knowledge and spiritual ways. She raised me from an early age, and

I can't ever recall waking before her. No sense trying to call at this point; we're only a few miles out."

"Seems like we should have stuck to the backroads that we spent all night mapping out for the ceremony," Phil said. "Highways might not be safe."

"The Red Scarfs were watching that old beater of yours." Ankti kept her eyes on the road, but her jaw tightened. "I don't think they'd recognize my car. Bet you have four flat tires by now. Plus, I didn't want to lose the time this morning. Grandmother will have to mobilize a bunch of people and should have protection to help keep us safe from these creatures. She needs as much time to prepare as we can give her."

"You mean something magical, don't you." It wasn't a question.

Phil grimaced at the thought, but couldn't say why it upset him. Thinking back, Ankti had made a number of references in the time he'd known her that likely held extraordinary meaning he hadn't picked up on at the time.

"She'll know how best to handle the Red Scarfs." Ankti nodded in agreement.

"In for a penny…" Phil let the old saying trail off under his breath.

Magic, demons, spiritual energy keeping the C-12 virus at bay— he shook his head at the absurdity. *If Mom and Dad could see me now.*

For that matter, what if Simone could see him? Phil looked at the beautiful woman driving, and felt a stab of anxiety. Perhaps it was better his fiancé remained in the dark. He'd of course told her about his work with Ankti, but she'd been wrapped up in a particularly busy training session in recent weeks, racing to complete her nurse practitioner certification. The entire kerfuffle over these ceremonies would be over by the next time they spoke, which gave him time to figure out what exactly to say. It wasn't like he could simply spout off about magic beings and the other bizarre things he'd gotten involved with.

Ankti turned off the main highway and headed through an old abandoned section of town that ringed Hopi lands. Boarded up storefronts lined the empty street, but something big glinted in the intersection ahead. Three cars parked sideways, blocking the road.

12. Grandmother Knows

T HREE FIGURES dressed in black tactical gear at odds with their red bandanas stood defiantly in front of the road block. The mismatched outfits screamed surplus store bargain hunters rather than SWAT team elite.

"They might not know your car, but the Red Scarfs apparently have the best approaches into Hopi territory covered," Phil said.

Ankti slowed the car as they studied the scene. The three blocky vehicles were parked bumper to bumper across the front edge of the intersection. There was no way around. Blue and red lights flashed from a temporary bar slapped on the roof of the gray Suburban in the center—civilian vehicles, nothing official, just big heavy hunks of steel that made any thought of trying to crash their way through untenable.

A deputy's star glinted in the morning sun like a silver heart on each breast. The women standing to either end of the barricade each held a riot gun, while the man in the middle stood empty handed with feet spread wide, arrogantly waiting. He held his hand up palm out, commanding them to halt.

"No turning around either." Kay pointed out the back window.

Two other cars crept along the line of storefronts, effectively hemming them in. Ankti sucked in a breath, compressed her lips, and let the air escape through her nose in a long exhalation.

"Hang on!" She mashed her foot down on the accelerator and the car leapt forward.

"Are you crazy?" Phil clutched the center console and the grab bar above his door as Ankti jerked the wheel hard and they veered left.

She wasn't going to try plowing through the three tanks, but the alternative didn't look much better. They bore down on a shack, an old corner newsstand, but there wasn't enough space between it and the abandoned glass storefront. They tore through the structure like papier-mâché, splintered wood and fiberglass exploding across the hood. The front left bumper caught the brickwork below the display window with a jarring crash that had Ankti fighting the wheel to keep control.

Glass and metal framing showered down. Something heavy caught the windshield dead center and a crack shot across it from edge to edge. But they were through, swerving onto the street beyond the roadblock.

Behind them three sets of angry eyes turned to follow their progress, and flames erupted as the Red Scarfs shifted into their demon forms. The nearest raised her shotgun, which now looked more like a long spear with a wide bronze head. A crimson fireball exploded from the tip and raced toward their fishtailing car. The energy slammed into an empty drugstore, splintering the window displays, and flames hungrily engulfed the storefront.

As they pulled away, the center vehicle backed out to let the red transit van that had tried to hem them in give chase. Ankti had a good head start, but their lead narrowed as buildings flashed by.

"Half a block back." Kay called off distances as they raced on.

The driver's flaming skull was clearly visible through the windshield, and Phil wondered how he managed to not burn a hole in the roof.

"Coming up on the reservation border," Ankti said through gritted teeth and pointed at the green placard off to the side of the road ahead.

A high entryway constructed of simple wooden beams straddled the road. A long plank inscribed in flowing script, presumably Hopi, hung from the crossbeam. Other than the signs and thinning buildings, there was little to the demarcation between public and reservation land. The blacktop stretched uninterrupted past the gateway into open land spotted with an occasional outbuilding.

"Those things don't look like they're going to stick to jurisdiction limits just because of their badges," Phil said as they shot under the sign.

Subtle energy washed over the car, leaving a sense of relief in its wake, like the feeling of arriving home after an exhausting trip. But they were far from safe. The transit van still roared toward the gate. Phil felt like Ichabod Crane racing away from a vengeful spirit.

The screech and squeal of tires had them looking back as the van slammed on its brakes and stopped just shy of the border.

"Well, how about that." Phil shook his head at the absurdity.

"Grandmother's definitely awake," Ankti said through a fierce grin.

The pursuing demon jumped out of his car, opened the rear panels, and let...something out. At first the flicker of flames made Phil think the black form was another Red Scarf crawling on all fours. But it stayed down and was half the size. The driver unhooked something from around its neck and motioned the beast forward. The creature's head lifted high, and it surged forward, racing past the signs with no trouble. It was quick, but nowhere near as fast as the car, and soon dwindled to a small speck.

"What the hell's that?" Phil had no idea if a hound, demon, or something else entirely, like a pet dinosaur—*strange thought*—chased them.

"Tracker," Kay replied. "It won't give up, no matter how far ahead we get."

"Why could that cross and not the Red Scarf?" Phil wondered aloud.

"I don't know." Ankti took the left fork in the road and headed toward the town sitting at the base of a ridge perhaps five miles off.

Simple houses and a few larger buildings rose from the dusty soil along the outskirts. They pulled up in front of a modest single-story home of stucco and wood, or perhaps it was a more traditional material like adobe. Herb gardens wrapped the front and sides of the house, and an old, straight-backed woman stood in the shaded entry as if expecting them.

"Greetings, Grandmother Wikiwi," Ankti said as they spilled from the car. "This is Phil Johnson, the man studying the virus that I told you about, and Kay, who's been staying with us while he recovers."

"A long overdue meeting," Grandmother said. "But time is short, and I fear you bring ill news. Everyone inside."

Wonderful aromas filled the interior: herbs, spices, boiling potatoes, and things just as pleasant yet less easily identified. Phil sucked in a big breath, enjoying the scents and feeling a calm that made little sense given their situation.

"We need your help, Grandmother," Ankti said as the three took seats at the kitchen table. "There's a group of fire demons in human form trying to stop today's ceremony."

Grandmother Wikiwi bustled about the room while still somehow managing to give her granddaughter her full attention.

"I think they are probably the same ones who left this." Ankti nodded to Kay, who placed the twig doll they'd found that first night in the center of the table.

Grandmother Wikiwi looked from the doll to Kay, squinting at the man as if trying to read something scrawled across his forehead, her lips pressed tight. "You, young man, are an enigma, coming here bold as day and looking like a young stallion sniffing around my granddaughter." Ankti squawked in protest, but Wikiwi pressed on. "Yet, you don't *feel* young at all. Your aura is confused and tattered, but also partially obscured. So be it. You must remain a riddle for another time." She wagged a gnarled finger in warning, letting it settle to point at the flute hanging from his belt before turning to face Ankti. "Speak of what you need."

Something in her words made Kay smile in genuine amusement instead of the sly trickster smile that so often preceded trouble. Then his eyes clouded in confusion, as though he could not remember what was so funny.

Ankti summarized their woes, starting with how they'd run across Erik and Kasandra leaving the tribal offices. She told how the Red Scarfs had detained them and of their escape from Trevor, ending with last night's work with Jack when they'd found Brandon missing.

While the young woman spoke, Wikiwi collected spools of colorful twine and metal clips from the cabinet next to the refrigerator. She nodded, encouraging Ankti to continue as she strung the twine along each side of the alcove coming in from the back door. The woman tied a bright red thread to a clip that she wedged into the hinge of the storm door leading out back, propping it open. More string formed a decorative network of fibers across the lower panel on the open door, leaving the path outside clear.

The rest of the clips connected the twine lining the inside of the small mudroom to the door frame, and she wove a final network of strands across the entry into the kitchen. By the time Ankti finished, the old woman had fashioned a kind of cat's cradle on three sides of the entry area, leaving the rear doorway from backyard to mudroom clear of decorations. Wikiwi inspected her handiwork, stepped back, and smiled.

"Are you even listening?" Ankti asked, a note of petulance clear in her tone.

"Now, Ankti," the old woman chided. "Who taught *you* how to listen?"

"My apologies, Grandmother." Ankti dropped her gaze to the tabletop.

"Never fear; all is not lost." Wikiwi crooked a finger at Kay. "Come stand here, my young—yet not so young—visitor. You two hold still. There is something we must attend to first."

Kay gave a bemused smile and let the old woman guide him by the shoulders to stand in front of the rear entrance facing the backyard. Phil raised an eyebrow at Ankti, receiving a huff and shrug of resignation in return, which made him snicker. It was oddly reassuring to see his friend was just as confused as he was.

At the old woman's glare, they fell silent. Stillness settled over the kitchen as if the house itself held its breath. A scrape sounded outside like mice scurrying around the foundation. The sound traveled from left to right, but there was nothing to see through the open door except shirts flapping on the clothesline and spikes of aloe rising from the garden along the back fence. A tick sounded overhead, followed by another, as if birds strutted across the roof. Whatever it was scurried to the back edge of the house, and a muffled thud sounded off to the right of the back door.

Quiet chuffing followed another scrape. Phil tried to ask what was going on, but couldn't bring himself to break the silence imposed by the old woman. A colorful blue-striped blanket flapped into view as the wind shifted, obscuring the spikey green aloe plants. Wouldn't clothes drying outside get awful dusty and itchy—

A shadow fell across the doorway, blocking Phil's view and cutting off his wandering thoughts. No, not a shadow; the black body of a creature the size of a Great Dane with flames licking up from its long black snout. Wide, flat horns swept back to protect either side of its neck.

The creature crouched low like a big cat, scented the air, and lunged directly at Kay, foreclaws gouging deep furrows across the linoleum floor. Kay didn't have time to move; it all happened too fast. Powerful hind legs launched the dark creature at Kay's throat, razor claws extended from massive forepaws.

A great flash of energy erupted when the creature hit the red and blue twine strung across the kitchen entry, and it let out a mighty yowl. The searing flash threw the monster back, and caustic fumes replaced the kitchen's pleasant aromas.

Stark white burns crisscrossed the thing's chest. It swiped out with a claw trying to sever the strings, but jerked back when the innocuous looking twine released another blast of power.

Grandmother Wikiwi calmly reached up, grabbed the red string trailing in from the back door, and gave it a hard yank. The storm door banged shut. The startled creature spun around and mewled as it slammed against door then walls, releasing more blasts of power and acrid smoke. But searing energy blocked it on all sides. After a couple of minutes, the creature stopped flailing and curled into a half-ball to lick its wounds—an odd sight especially given the translucent fire flickering along its body like the clear yellow-blue flames from a Bunsen burner.

Grandmother gave a sharp nod of approval. "Now we can move on to your other business."

"What the hell is that thing?" Phil's voice didn't quite crack, but he cringed at the unintended volume, expecting to be reprimanded.

"Something that should not be here, and it's looking for that." The old woman turned and pointed at the twig doll on the kitchen table. "But the creature is safe enough for now. Let us address your other concerns. I will deal with this creature later."

Even Kay looked rattled as they all reluctantly sat down and tried to ignore the black demon creature in the room. Over the course of the next hour, Grandmother called several people to the house and sent them off again to organize waypoints along the route to the ceremony. When it was again just the four of them, Wikiwi went to the back room and returned with two cloth bundles the size of walnuts tied onto a cord. She gave one to Ankti and the other to Phil.

"These prayer bundles will provide protection against many of these creatures." She waved a hand at the thing in the mudroom, which now chewed on a moccasin it found, sneezing when curls of smoke drifted up from the sodden leather. "But there will be more powerful entities to deal with. Use what I have taught you, and do not be too proud to accept help from your friends." She looked from Phil to Kay, her gaze lingering on the other man and making Phil think that was the quarter from which the old woman truly expected help. "To you, my puzzling gem, I can offer nothing close to what protection you already have." She waved at the flute, as if *that* would keep the man safe. "I believe your search will soon be over. But you may find that which you need rather than that which you seek."

If there was one thing consistent about Kay besides his spotty memory, it was his flippant attitude. Phil held his breath waiting for the disrespectful response, but Kay simply nodded and bowed his head. "Thank you, Grandmother."

"That's it I guess." Ankti clapped her hands, looped the prayer bundle's cord over her head like a necklace, and stood. "We'll run down the reverse route to the camping grounds to ensure it's all clear with no washouts."

Phil gave what he hoped was a respectful nod and headed for the door with Kay close on his heels.

"One last moment of your time, Granddaughter," Wikiwi said. "We have one final preparation to discuss."

Phil checked his watch. Getting back by noon would be cutting it tight. He sighed and turned back into the small living room.

"You guys go start the car." Ankti waved the men out the door. "Try to get a call through to Jack and let him know that everything is good on this end. I'll be out in a few minutes."

*** * ***

With the exception of some kidney-bruising stretches of washboard road, the ride back proved uneventful. Jack had the camp fully mobilized with participants broken into small groups and assigned to vehicles that would head out three at a time. Even the two groups of participants due in by aircraft had been hustled from the airport without incident.

Covert runners mapped out the Red Scarf roadblocks and managed to guide a van coming down from Apache lands through safely, but two other carloads were detained and had dropped out of contact. Nothing could be done about that at this point. They had sufficient participants, and filtering people out to set up for the ceremony was the top priority. Hopefully the people that had been detained would not be harmed.

"I think we've done all we can," Jack said to the group gathered in his office. A handful of his trusted officers had joined Ankti, Phil, and Kay, and it was standing-room only in the small trailer. "Anyone else coming in from out of town is on their own. We have a couple of roving intercepts out there still, but the rest have gone silent—presumably taken by the Red Scarfs since our comms remain solid."

The security team used high-powered handheld radios that bounced signals off repeaters scattered on strategic high ground. Cell towers had been dropping off-line all morning and phone calls no longer an option.

"We'll look for anyone unaccounted for later, but for now the ceremony takes priority." Jack nodded to Pamela Redcliff, his second in command.

"I'll give the word for people to start moving out." The thirty-something woman gave a two-fingered salute and strode toward the door. She had the long lean build of a marathon runner.

"Before the cars roll, there's one more arrangement to make." Ankti looked to Jack. "We'll need extra sound gear. Are you still in contact with Tommy Roundbush?"

"Yeah, sure." Jack looked as surprised as Phil. "He's up at his gear shack waiting for us and feeling a bit lonely. Says the Red Scarfs are keeping their distance though and haven't come onto nation land. But they got up to the palisades once, so we'll have a line of security people armed to the teeth in place before things get rolling."

"Good, that's where I'll be too," Ankti said. "But first, let's get Tommy on the line while everyone else makes sure the cars are ready to roll."

13. Take a Stand

ANKTI FINGERED the prayer bundle hanging from her neck and willed herself to take a deep, calming breath as she peered into the gathering gloom. Jack's security team fanned out to either side, forming a picket line across the inbound roadway fifty yards from the palisade. Several more people hid among rocks and scrub to either side of the road ahead. Most were armed with shotguns or small caliber weapons equipped with homemade scattershot consisting of rock salt or silver.

Lead bullets wouldn't inflict much damage on the creatures they faced. But Grandmother assured her that salt was a bane to dark forces and disrupted their magic, while silver often proved the best defense against supernatural creatures. The tribes were not rich enough to have much of the latter on hand, but a few special rounds had silver powder mixed with the rock salt, several of the crew carried silver-bladed knives, and one enterprising soul wielded sharpened antique silverware. Heaven help *that* poor man when his wife discovered he'd plundered the family heirlooms.

Phil and Kay flanked Ankti, the former having opted to carry a wood cudgel and the latter—standing tall and proud on her right, a rising wind plastering his loose tee-shirt against that magnificent chest—stood weaponless except of course for the power of his mysterious flute. The instrument dangled from the belt of his deliciously tight jeans. She'd grown quite fond of having both men around, but Kay sparked something primal deep within. Despite his flippant attitude and spotty memory, the man was gorgeous, from that flowing hair and regal nose to those long delicate fingers that moved so well when he played.

What's wrong with me? Ankti shook her head to dislodge the rogue thoughts. This was no time to start swooning. *Focus, girl.*

A half mile distant at the base of the road winding up to Mount Phoenix, two dozen cars had gathered along the highway off-ramp. The Red Scarfs abandoned all pretext of their human forms. Dozens of matchstick heads flickered along the boundary to reservation lands, milling about and waiting. None of them had dared cross onto the reservation proper, but Ankti knew that wouldn't last.

The twig doll they'd found the night Kay got hurt pulsed in her hand, somehow connected to these beings and their leaders. The dark energy Grandmother had helped Ankti sense built in response to its creator. Something powerful approached.

Behind the defenders, drums beat atop rhythmic chanting rising from within the ceremonial enclosure. A hundred voices lifted skyward calling for the spiritual intervention needed to maintain fertile lands and people. They called in many languages, odd and discordant, yet bound by a single purpose that lent beautiful harmony to the whole.

The ceremony had started just before dusk. The main ritual that called on ancestors and spirits was better than halfway done, but they weren't out of the woods yet. Another half-hour was needed to complete the ritual and rites. The dancing, drums, and prayers of thanks would continue as long into the night as possible, but it was paramount to complete that core ceremony without interruption.

Grandmother knew the detailed inner workings of the series of rituals the tribes used over the years to improve the livelihood and health of their communities. She'd confided in Ankti, saying she feared it was ultimately a losing battle. Yet they fought on. This final cross-tribal ceremony would cement gains made to date and embody the spiritual support so desperately needed throughout the tribes.

"So far so good," Phil said from her left as he squinted into the distance. "Nice of them to stay lit up so we don't lose track of anyone. But a few spotlights wouldn't hurt either."

"Rituals have to be by natural light." Ankti had to admit the few dimly glowing streetlamps didn't improve visibility much. "Firelight and moonlight should be all that enters the circle. We'll have to make do."

"Sure. Gotta keep the ceremonies pure." Phil nodded, but kept frowning back at the enclosure whenever he thought she wasn't looking.

The minutes ticked by slowly. She knew he was disappointed to again be excluded from witnessing things first-hand. After all, the Bureau had sent Phil to determine what factors kept the C-12 virus at bay out here, and the tribal ceremonies were obviously a big part of the answer. His wistful gaze shifted from the wooden enclosure to the parking lot.

"Didn't we have more cars staged to head up here?" Phil bounced a finger along, counting the line of dusty vehicles.

Ankti had worked until the last possible second with Jack's security people, enlisting Kay and Phil to help reload and issue ammo while participants made their way toward the ceremonial grounds. By the time the three hopped into her much-abused SUV and brought up the distant rear, security was already in place, the palisades shut and barred, and the ceremony underway.

She scanned the twenty-odd cars scattered across the parking lot and the row of four-wheelers security had neatly lined up alongside Tommy's equipment building. *Most* of the vehicles were here.

"Tommy sent some drivers off to pick up supplies on the off chance we don't have any problems. Dancing and chanting is exhausting work, and as hosts we usually provide late night refreshments." Ankti studied the ground as she spoke.

Her answer sounded reasonable. Heck, at this point she could probably tell Phil about the new arrangements. Energy surged through the doll in her hand.

"Youch!" Ankti dropped the twig figure and shook out her stinging fingers, all thoughts of car counting forgotten as the sticks smoldered. "Here they come."

A sleek black sports car rolled down the off-ramp from the highway and parked behind the assembled Red Scarfs. The driver and a passenger got out, dark blobs in the dwindling light, except a mane of flowing red hair and matching beard sprouted from the head of the larger person.

The demons made way, burning figures parting like two fistfuls of birthday candles to clear a path for the newcomers. The car, the deference, the red hair—this had to be Erik and Kasandra. The pair paused at the simple archway marking the reserve's entrance.

Hope surged. The boundary held, the inherent power of ancestral lands denying entry to the demon's leaders. The rhythm of the drums changed, adding a double beat as the first lone rocket sizzled skyward from within the enclosure to explode high overhead in a shower of crackling red sparks. This was the final stage of the ritual; they just needed a few more minutes.

Kasandra crouched low, studying or perhaps drawing on the roadway, then stood, and the pair strode forward onto reservation land. The smoking doll at her feet burst into flames as they breached the threshold, burning white-hot until nothing but a scorched outline remained.

Ankti felt the intrusion to her core as if the land itself shivered at an oily stain spreading across its soil. Kasandra and Erik stepped to either side of the road and ushered the others through, holding the way open for the less powerful Red Scarfs. The group hesitated a moment, but once that first flaming figure stepped across the floodgate was open. They came on in a ragged mob. Once the last passed between them, Kasandra and Erik stooped low as if tying their shoes before straightening to leisurely follow the pack.

Some demons carried the energy throwing spears they'd seen at the roadblock, others had short batons or lengths of chain, and the rest held no visible weapon—except of course those wicked claws. Jack watched from off to their right where he could keep an eye on the picket line and his people hidden along that side of the approach.

"Should I give the signal?" Phil asked.

"Just a few more yards," Ankti said. "We need all of them in the crossfire."

The roadway was contoured to their advantage, with rock outcroppings rising high to either side. That's where Jack's people hid, ready to fire down from both sides while her own line blocked the road where it spilled into the parking lot. They had to pin down the Red Scarfs long enough for the ceremony to finish and couldn't afford springing the trap early. If the enemy scattered in an end run around the rocks, Jack's people would be exposed. To be effective they needed the demons to come head on at the protective prayer bundles. Grandmother cautioned that the artifacts were not a permanent solution. But they just needed to buy a little time.

"Almost there…" Ankti raised her hand, and Phil lifted his tactical flashlight, ready to flash an open-fire signal to Jack. "Wait for it…"

They just needed Erik and Kasandra to cross the mouth of their trap, just a few more yards and—

Screams erupted from either side of the road, high-pitched and frantic followed by ringing shotgun blasts. Several shrieks cut off too abruptly to be anything but terrible news, and those shots weren't aimed at the road.

A pair of fireworks launched from behind, and the sky blossomed into bright green and white starbursts, painting the landscape in sharp contrast. Dark shapes ran to either side of the road, darting between the rocks.

"Damn it!" Phil cursed. "They have more of those cat-things with them."

But these had no flames to give away their position, and no one had seen the handful of pets coming through the shadows. Now they raced behind the rocks hamstringing the trap. But Jack raced to help with the reserves he'd kept aside. The gunfire changed from sporadic chaos to deliberate salvos.

They must have wiped out the animals because guns soon trained on the road and opened fire. The demons howled and surged forward, several staggering under the barrage of gunfire. The front line stopped in their tracks twenty paces from Ankti's defensive line as they came up against the power of the prayer bundles.

Heavy pressure squeezed her chest in pounding waves as the enemy tried to break the invisible barrier. Phil staggered next to her and clung to his own bundle as the onslaught continued, but this was what they had come to do; the plan was back on track.

The air between the two groups thickened and vibrated in response to colliding energies. The distance between them shrank, but the spiritual magic held as the security folks to each side of their line opened fire. At point blank range, Red Scarfs went down.

Rather than bleeding, the creatures' pebbly hides turned white and ragged where salt-shot struck. Glancing hits to an arm or leg caused the skull fire to dim, while taking a shotgun blast full on extinguished a demon's flames completely. Ankti felt the rhythm of the process as salt interrupted the demons' innate magical power.

Once flameless, they were vulnerable, and the next shot would put them down.

Pressure behind the front line built as more demons slammed into those up against her barrier. One got smart, stepped off to the side, and leveled its staff. The fiery ball flew over the heads of the others, heading straight for Ankti, but the energy dissipated in the gap between the lines. He adjusted fast and fired the next ball off to her left where the bundles had less power. Rocks along the road exploded, spraying shards across the woman holding the end of their line and sending her staggering away. The others spread out to cover the gap.

A few more of those would put them out of commission or blast open the embankment and allow an end run. Jack came to their rescue once again, and the staff wielder went down under a volley of rock salt, his once-glowing staff now dark and powerless.

"We're doing it." Phil forced the words out between ragged gasps, hands on knees as though catching his breath after a run.

Ankti's natural abilities allowed her to pour forth power to bolster the effectiveness of her prayer bundle as the artifact called for energy. Phil had no such mechanism.

"You achieve nothing!" an angry voice boomed above the gunfire and pyrotechnics bursting overhead.

The demon horde parted as they had before, allowing Erik to step forward. Ankti gasped at the electric shock that shot through her as he touched the barrier. She wouldn't hold up against much of that.

Kasandra followed in Erik's wake. Once trim and elegant, her features had turned sharp and angular with eyes taking on a feral intensity. Although she hadn't turned black or flamed out, she looked every bit the demon and moved with the stalking grace of a predator.

"This foolishness has delayed us long enough." Erik slapped a palm against the barrier, rocking her and Phil back on their heels. "Stop your childish games." A second slap drove Phil to his knees, and Ankti staggered as deafening gunfire erupted. But the shots never landed because Erik erected a barrier of his own.

Kasandra lifted her face to scent the air, nostrils flaring. "The interloper is here too, my lord."

Ankti's thoughts flashed back to the burning twig effigy and Grandmother's warning that someone tracked Kay. Her eyes went round as she looked to the right, intent on telling him to leave the fight, to run. They couldn't let this pair get their hands on her friend. But a frantic scan told her Kay was already gone. Perhaps he sensed the danger, or his arcane flute gave the man warning. She breathed a sigh of relief, hoping he ran hard and fast and never looked back.

A third strike of Erik's hand shattered the barrier, flinging her and the others back. Screams and lights spun in a confused whirlwind. She landed hard alongside Phil, and the enemy poured through the breach they'd been defending.

A barrage of rockets roared from within the fence line, followed by deafening reports as more streaked skyward a few seconds apart. Drums and chanting rose to a fevered pitch. They were so close— so damned close.

The Viking-of-a-man strode forward and placed his palm flat against the thick timbers of the gate. The sturdy wood polished smooth by generations of use exploded inward, dark energy blasting the door to splinters.

What on Earth is this thing? Grandmother had warned of entities more dangerous than simple demons. Perhaps Erik was a greater lord among them, a fae of the mythical Dark Court, or simply a powerful mage of old. And what did any of those make Kasandra? His lapdog? No, her magic was wild and shifting with an undercurrent of corruption that even the hulking man lacked.

Whatever the woman was, she was barely in control herself, let alone controlled by another.

Ankti fingered the hard little cylinder in her pocket, but she needed to keep Grandmother's final gift in reserve. It might make a difference before this was over. Her own magic churned in her belly, useless at this point. Calming emotions or calling desert creatures would do little to stem the tide as the remaining Red Scarfs stormed after their leaders onto sacred ground.

14. Shell Game

P HIL STRUGGLED to his feet, feeling as though he'd been kicked in the chest by a mule. His hand flew to the pouch around his neck. Torn material dangled from the leather cord. The sacred material that gave the prayer bundle power had scattered when Erik broke their defense.

He dropped his hand and winced. Something in his right shoulder had torn. A sharp ache like hot needles pressed into the joint from the top of his bicep, but he seemed to have full range of motion.

Ankti had landed nearby. Phil offered a hand as she rose and flexed her left hand, which had been scraped raw. But she waved him away and staggered after the Red Scarfs. Groans and moans filtered through his ringing ears. The entire team was down, but most picked themselves up, so he hurried after the woman.

Miraculously, the celebrants carried on, their voices calling into the night with drums steady and strong, ignoring the demons pouring through the shattered gate. Ankti darted inside, close on their heels as a mighty roar of anguish rose from within.

Those people are doomed. Phil cursed and hurried to follow, clueless as to how he might help. He stopped dead in his tracks and blinked in confusion at the scene within. Erik stood off to the left, hands raised high and sparking with crimson energies as he unleashed another angry scream overtop the chanting voices. Kasandra stood next to him, toes of her forward foot just touching the ground and head cocked to the side as though frozen mid-stride and uncertain of how to proceed. The remaining Red Scarfs shied away from their angry leader, pulling into a milling mass.

A crackling fire blazed in the center of the hard-packed dirt, much as it had for last week's ritual. But instead of a hundred tribal dancers, the demons and their overlords faced down one old round man on an office chair, empty beer cans scattered in the dirt at his feet.

Tommy Roundbush sat frozen, his long-necked lighter hovering halfway to the fuse on the next brick of fireworks. Charred, spent cartons littered the ground behind the old quartermaster, but a handful of unused fireworks remained.

Aside from Tommy, the arena was empty, yet the chanting and drums continued, blaring from twin stacks of speakers along the fence line.

"What is this?" Erik roared.

"Deception," Kasandra hissed in response and with a wave of her hand threw out a blast of energy.

The speakers sparked and exploded, as impressive as any of Tommy's display. Cords caught fire and melted, dropping into the dirt. Tommy watched Erik with narrowed eyes, lowered the lighter, and took a slow deliberate drink from the can in his other hand. He spotted Phil and Ankti standing just inside the gate and smiled.

"Hey, Ankti. I guess the show's over." He raised his beer in mock salute.

The wavering firelight made reading expressions difficult, but rage darkened Erik's face as he turned to glare at them. He rushed forward, unbelievably fast, knocking Phil aside and grabbing Ankti by the throat. His meaty hand caught her under the jaw, fingers and thumb wrapping up around either side of her startled face and lifting her onto tiptoes.

"Where are they?" He bit off each word, pushing power into the question that filled the air with a static charge.

Angry eyes bored into the woman as she clawed at Erik's forearm and growled through gritted teeth. Phil's club was long gone. He scooped a heavy board out of the debris and slammed it hard across the back of Erik's head. The wood splintered, leaving him holding the stubby end as his arm and elbow exploded in white agony. He blinked back tears only to find Kasandra's gaunt, snarling face filled his blurred vision. Her nails lengthened into talons that she held up for his inspection in clear warning, and those glowing red-rimmed eyes dared him to make another stupid move.

Shotguns roared as Jack led a handful of people through the gate. With a wave of his free hand, Erik threw the group back through the opening without ever taking his eyes off Ankti. "Where have you hidden them? Tell me or die."

"Go to hell!" Ankti struggled for breath as he lifted her fully off the ground, but she managed to launch a wad of spit right in his face.

"So predictable for a would-be medicine woman."

A massive explosion sounded from high overhead, followed by a second and third in rapid succession. Tommy looked about wildly to ensure his fireworks hadn't accidentally ignited, but these explosions were more distant than his aerial display.

"Lord, over here." Kasandra was at the gate in a flash, looking across the hills rolling off to the east of Mount Phoenix.

The red-haired giant dropped Ankti like a sack of flour. She hit the ground and sucked in air. White finger imprints stood out in stark contrast on her lovely skin under the silvery moonlight. The outlines flushed red as she rubbed her jaw and groaned through a weak smile. Phil let out the breath he'd been holding. She'd have some nasty bruising, but seemed to quickly regain her bearings.

More detonations echoed overhead. Phil helped his friend to her feet, and they stumbled back to the entrance—oddly, funneling out through the shattered gate alongside curious Red Scarfs with flaming heads turned away to scan the horizon.

Erik and Kasandra stood as dark outlines against sporadic fiery geysers that rose from perhaps two miles away, the display far more impressive than what Tommy had managed or even what had been used during the last ceremony. These flew higher and spread wider than any fireworks he'd seen, like signal beacons cutting into the heavens.

"Damn it!" Ankti cursed under her breath. "They weren't supposed to use pyrotechnics."

It took Phil a moment to catch up: the missing cars, the speakers in the enclosure, Tommy tending the fire and fireworks. Now that those speakers had been silenced, Phil could just make out the echoing beat of drums in the distance between explosions. And if that humming undercurrent wasn't his abused ears bleeding, it just might be chanting voices.

"You moved the ceremony?" Phil whispered.

"And it's just about over." Ankti nodded and gave her fiercest grin yet, though she winced and rubbed her jaw.

"The humans are down there." Kasandra jabbed a sharp talon into the night. Power flowed from her other hand in a fine silvery whip she used to lash the demons into a run "Go!"

They loped off into the foothills. If the ceremony was as close to done as Ankti seemed to think, it should be over before the Red Scarfs arrived. But the flaming heads dwindled impossibly fast as the demons stretched and ran on all fours. Kasandra and Erik were gone too, though they hadn't run after the others.

Phil used his flashlight to take stock. Jack's people were in bad shape but regrouping, the more mobile helping those badly injured.

Some bled freely, while others nursed breaks or sprains. Most would be of no further use tonight.

"The plan was sound and bought us time." Jack limped over holding his dangling left arm. "But I'd like to throttle whatever idiot slipped fireworks back into the performance. Those people down there are in danger." He shot an accusing glare back at Tommy.

"Doesn't matter now," Ankti said. "I've got one last trick up my sleeve."

"We're about spent." Jack gave a half-shrug with his good arm and handed Phil a folding jack-knife. "Guns haven't helped since the red-bearded giant showed up. Take Susan and Ira, use the ATVs to catch up. Keys are in the ignition."

Phil must have been glaring at Ankti as they hurried to the vehicles because she finally answered his question. "Yes, we moved the ceremony as a precaution. Grandmother's idea and Jack concurred. While we finished preparations, drivers ferried people down into a hidden valley in the foothills. We thought they'd be able to complete the ceremony while all eyes were on us here. It pretty much worked. And before you complain, we had to keep it secret. Only Jack, me, and the drivers knew. We couldn't afford word spreading or someone being overheard talking about a change."

"I guess," Phil grumbled as he threw his leg over one of the red four-wheelers and Ankti took the next in line.

"The valley down there is powerful, a sacred place of balance and peace. We have to stop these things. No more time for discussion." She thumbed her starter.

Phil nodded and did the same. The other engines growled to life in quick succession, and four ATVs raced into the night, headlights washing across the rocky terrain. Phil worried they'd hit a hidden ravine and break their necks, but Ankti lead them along a relatively smooth path. Of course she knew the terrain; she'd snuck over a hundred people down to the alternate location.

They wound around flowing hills toward the continuing display, and an orange glow painted the landscape ahead. Too spread out to be the ceremonial fire and with individual points of light gliding along hills, it had to be the pack of Red Scarfs. They closed half the distance, topped a rise, and finally spotted their destination.

A bonfire blazed through billows of smoke rising from the shallow valley ahead. The cool night wind carried rhythmic drums and voices, but the aerial explosions came more rapidly, turning the valley into a warzone.

They accelerated, abandoning the last bit of caution, but still the Red Scarfs arrived first. Phil and the others hit the valley, cut their engines, and ran the last few yards through thick wood-smoke smelling of ozone and—oddly—fresh laundry.

Erik and Kasandra stood before their minions, confronting a hundred tribespeople in ceremonial regalia. Drums fell silent, dancing feet stilled, and the smoky air vibrated with tension as the two groups squared off under what had the feel of a final barrage of fireworks.

Did they finish?

Soft chanting still drifted from a few hardy souls in the back, but many of the players simply looked shell shocked—as did several of the demons, which made sense given the ridiculous amount of firepower in the sky overhead.

Roaring flames illuminated the thick haze, making the air itself glow. One last massive mortar seemed to shoot straight out of the flames. But the launch platform must simply be hidden behind the fire ring. As the shot blossomed overhead into whistling streamers that faded into the night, a figure emerged from the flames—another trick of the confusing scene, as the bent man must have stepped from behind the fire. Perhaps he'd been the one launching rockets.

Though hunched, the man danced into view with arms spread wide, wearing white buckskin fringed and beaded to imitate feathers dangling from each outstretched arm. An elaborate headdress swayed with his movements, three feathers standing high and proud from the crown of his head.

Details flowed and ebbed with the drifting smoke and surreal atmosphere. Though a hunchback, the dancer stood tall and moved with quiet grace, executing complex steps and flourishes—small movements of great import that drew the eye and mesmerized those watching. His impressive ceremonial mask blurred in and out of clarity under the flickering light.

Phil had read of Kachina masks worn in rituals among some tribes. This one depicted an ancient soul, old and lined with baggy cheeks and an imposing hook nose. An impressive caricature that even bent and flexed to mimic facial expressions as if the dancer was truly ancient. Deeply lined cheeks rose above the hint of a smile as he dropped his arms and lifted a flared pipe to his lips. Music flowed pure and sweet, and the drums joined the simple tune.

"You call, and I have come, my children." A familiar voice rang out as the notes trailed off, though the tone was gravelly with age.

"Kokopelli," several dancers whispered in awe.

The figure bowed deep, its impressive hump making the man look like a giant beetle as a sudden downwash of smoke obscured their view. He walked forth through the haze—it must have been the same man; there were no others near the fire. But the elaborate garb was gone, replaced by jeans and his faded red tee-shirt from earlier. No longer hunched nor wearing a mask, Kay strutted toward the huddled Indians like an actor accepting accolades, his infuriating grin plastered firmly in place as though unaware of the dangerous situation.

15. Tripping

"**G**ET OUT of there, you dang fool." Phil couldn't believe Kay put himself between demons and people.

He gripped the silver-edged knife Jack had given him, but throwing himself in front of the flaming demons wouldn't help the lunatic.

"The trickster and his games return." Kasandra purred the words into the quiet clearing.

Kay's brash confidence faltered. He blinked and took in his surroundings as if waking from a dream. One eyebrow and the corner of his mouth quirked up in confusion. Whatever he'd been up to fled as the amnesia muddled his thoughts.

"So, the maker remains unmade." Kasandra's smile widened into a predatory mask. "And weak."

"And vulnerable," Erik finished for her, a grim smile stretching his own features. "Bring me the old man. We can end this all in one stroke. Dark ones, listen and obey." His voice rang out, and every flaming head turned. "Relieve these people of their claim to this world."

Odd choice of words, but his intent was clear. The Red Scarfs howled like eager hounds and stalked toward the tribespeople, weapons and claws raised. Kasandra slunk forward, cautiously circling Kay as if wary of what he might do. Contrary to Erik's words, Kay certainly wasn't old, but Phil doubted his gym muscles could match the lithe predator Kasandra had become.

A shot rang out. With an angry flick of his hand, Erik swept Susan and Ira back with invisible energy. They landed in a crumpled heap and lay still.

"Shit!" Ankti swore and fumbled in her pocket for a small stick. No, it was a wooden cylinder about four inches long.

She looked from demons to woman as if trying to decide on the greater evil. Kasandra used the distraction to strike from behind. She grabbed Kay around the throat and hauled him back off his feet. Ankti rushed toward the pair, cylinder poised to throw, but stopped dead as a scream ripped from the crowd.

A young woman in front fell clutching bleeding gashes across one shoulder. The middle-aged man next to her fended off the demon's next strike with a sharp blow of his ceremonial staff to its stomach. But the wood was light, blunt, and not silver. Nothing the players carried would keep those demons at bay.

"Damn it to hell!" Ankti spun, hauled back, and threw the cylinder into the crowd of demons.

White light erupted where the small device landed, a brief strobe that hugged the hard-packed ground for a moment before fading. *Complete bust.* The monsters ignored the flash, each trying to claw its way to the front, eager to complete the grisly task their master ordered.

The damn knife was useless against so many, but an attack on their flank might split their attention. Phil tried to catch Ankti's eye, but she continued to stare intently at the ground as if unable to believe her flash-bomb failed.

With the demons' backs to them, there'd never be a better opportunity. Phil dashed forward and jabbed the three-inch blade into a leathery back where a kidney would be on a human—a cowardly move. *These are monsters*, Phil reminded himself as he darted in for another stab.

Each stab wound turned silvery-white, similar to the effect of salt, and dark blood sizzled and spat on the metal of his blade. The Red Scarf snarled and spun. Phil ducked back from a claw slash, darted around the next demon over, and slashed at its side in hopes of turning the two monsters against each other. It didn't work. Both demons turned on him.

The ground shuddered, a pulsing vibration Phil barely noticed as he retreated. Pinpricks of white light sparkled in the dirt around the angry pair. The field of shining stars went unnoticed as it spread beneath the horde of Red Scarfs. Delicate tendrils of light sprouted like seedlings from each pinprick and curled upward, questing. Spectral white leaves budded out as the thickening vines twined around clawed feet.

Phil danced back, but the glowing vines weren't interested in humans. The two demons closing on him stumbled and clawed at the tendrils that now encircled their thighs. Slashing claws and weapons had no effect.

Soon the entire snarling, wailing group fought the magic unleashed by Ankti's device. The vines retracted, clutching their prey and dragging the demons into the earth. A few called for help from Erik or Kasandra as they went under, but those two had their own problems.

A thick mass of twisting power snaked toward the Red Scarf leaders. Kasandra sliced out with an impossibly long arm, claw tips sparking with their own power to hold the vines at bay. But keeping hold of Kay hampered her effectiveness. Erik was not similarly encumbered. The giant of a man strode forth, wading into the winding energy. A massive obsidian battle axe appeared in his hands. He swept it through Ankti's spell in great scything arcs to severe the massed vines, leaving glowing piles that blurred and sank out of sight.

In short order the axe put an end to the magic, but not before the spell dragged away every lesser Red Scarf. The huddled drummers and dancers had no one threatening them—for the moment.

"Go, go, go!" Phil urged the dazed people to move, then actually chased them into a run like a flock of startled chickens, not knowing where they might head. Anywhere was better than here.

Waves of anger washed off Erik as he rounded on Ankti, axe raised high. Kay must have gained leverage during the commotion because he broke away and rushed to their friend. The maniac didn't slow as he plowed Ankti over with a flying tackle. Blinding light exploded, and Phil couldn't tell up from down. He threw his arms out to either side, flailing in an attempt to keep his balance, then landed hard on his butt.

Phil blinked away magenta afterimages and patted the rocky ground trying to locate his knife. Sight returned in a blurry confused jumble. Kay laid atop Ankti, stroking her cheek with the back of his hand and murmuring something too soft for him to catch. Rocks he hadn't noticed jutted from the uneven ground, and Erik and Kasandra were gone—no, that wasn't right. Phil whipped his head around to find a cliff face rising against the starry sky.

"We teleported?" Phil fought down a wave of vertigo, scooped up the knife, and pushed to his feet.

Moonlight glinted off Ankti's eyes, but she closed them again and rubbed her cheek against Kay's hand. Something had been brewing between those two for a while now, but this wasn't the time. Phil cleared his throat, softly at first and then more pointedly. Kay shot him a glare, but Ankti had the decency to open her eyes and wiggle out from under the man.

"How?" She sat up, took in their surroundings, and jumped to her feet. "We left the others!"

"Last I saw, everyone tore off toward the interstate, but Kasandra and Erik…" Phil let the thought trail off. Kasandra was a hunter and Erik something else; mere humans wouldn't stand a chance.

"Do not fear for your friends." Kay stood, stretched with languid ease, and lifted the flute from his belt. "Our lovely Hopi flower has well and truly angered that pair. Erik will not waste time on the scattered players."

Ankti blushed deeply enough to be seen under the pale moonlight, which only caused Kay's insufferable grin to widen. Had they already… No, the two hadn't spent more than a few minutes alone since Kay recovered from his burns—a surprisingly speedy recovery, even given Ankti's healing salve. That nasty knot behind his right ear had shrunk by half too, though it still raised the fine hairs into a lustrous little tuft. Judging by the googly eyes they made at each other standing there under the stars, it would take effort to keep them both on task. And if the angry beings behind the Red Scarfs were no longer after the tribes…

"They're coming for us!" Phil gripped his knife and whipped around trying to look in all directions at once. "We've got to hide."

But where? Whatever had magicked them away also stranded them at the base of a cliff in the middle of nowhere without a car. *And not just any cliff.*

They stood under the mesa Kay kept coming back to. Phil had assumed Ankti used another magic device to transport them, but landing here had to be Kay's doing. They could hide out of sight in those odd shallow depressions along the cliff wall, but that would leave them cornered.

"First, we need a fire." Kay headed for the makeshift fire ring and pile of deadwood he'd gathered on his prior visits.

"Why'd you run?" It was an unkind question, but Phil needed to get into the man's head, needed to know he wouldn't abandon them again. "You could have stayed to fight. And what was that little show all about down at the real ceremony?"

Kay paused with an armload of branches, bouncing a stubby log against his chest in thought.

"It is difficult to explain. Something…pulled me. It was where I needed to be." He shrugged and went back to building his fire, effectively ending the discussion.

* * *

"He's special," Ankti whispered over-top the quiet music drifting from the flute.

Kay sat cross-legged in front of the small fire he'd built, playing haunting music that—while truly beautiful—could only attract the attention of anyone searching for them. The teepee of logs burned hot and bright. He'd been at it for a couple of hours, longer than the scant pile of wood should have lasted. Ankti and Kay had been adamant, so they'd stayed put against Phil's better judgement.

"Yeah, special in the head." He regretted the muttered statement immediately and wilted under Ankti's angry glare. "Listen, sunrise isn't far off. We can follow the ravine down to Salt River, head west, and be back to civilization before lunch."

"Then what?" She seemed to consider his idea for a moment, then shook her head. "Going back won't help. These are powerful beings that aren't just going to give up. Grandmother might have more ideas, but I fear she's already given us as much help as she can."

"Did she give you that magic hand grenade that took out the Red scarfs?" Of course she had; Phil pressed on without waiting for an answer. "You never know, Wikiwi may have more tricks up her sleeve or know other elders who can fight these monsters. Getting to them needs to be our top priority."

"Remember the creature that came to Grandmother's house. We'll put anyone we talk to in danger." Anguish colored her voice, but she sighed as if gathering resolve. "They've been hunting Kay all along, from that very first night we found him. Grandmother sees something special in him. I sense it too, but he's *so hard* to read. His aura is shrouded, maybe by that flute, which is a powerful artifact. But I—" she threw up her hands in frustration. "That's all I know. And now Erik's after me too. You're right, we can't stay out here without so much as a bottle of water. At first light we'll talk it over with Kay and decide."

It was a hollow victory that sat sour in Phil's stomach, especially when Ankti made a point of turning away and taking a seat near Kay to wait. Phil sighed and lowered himself onto a rock opposite the pair, thankful for the warmth that beat back the crisp night air.

At least the arrangement let them keep an eye on all approaches, although Ankti mostly just stared at the shadowed cliff face. And Kay simply gazed into the flames as he played on, intent on something among the glowing embers the other two couldn't see.

Those early morning hours became a waiting game. Between the crackling warmth and lilting music, Phil found himself nodding off. Gangsters with flaming hair, cartoon wizards, and a multi-colored talking buffalo vied for dominance in fragmented dreams. The latter appeared in a surreal office scene where the buffalo sipped a cocktail while asking probing questions about Phil's childhood and feelings toward his mother.

He jerked awake, relieved to find everyone in their places around the fire. The stacked logs within the fire ring hadn't shifted or burned down so he couldn't have been out for long. Yet a distinct glow painted the horizon to the east. Sunrise was only an hour or two off—they'd soon have to decide on a course of action.

Unfortunately, fate forced their hand.

Erik and Kasandra arrived before dawn, stepping quietly off the trail from the road as though materializing from thin air, which they likely did. The red-haired giant still carried the massive black axe that had so easily dispatched Wikiwi's magic. The weapon's edge gleamed darkly in the firelight as if absorbing rather than reflecting the flames.

Kasandra had changed more than just her clothes. She now wore a smart blue business suit pinstriped with narrow lines accentuating her athletic form and drawing the eye down to fashionable high-heeled sandals, an impractical outfit for traipsing through the rocky landscape. A dozen small talismans of fur, feather, and leather dangled from a silver link belt at her waist. All vestiges of the half-beast she'd become were gone, her features again elegant with hair pulled back from intense orange eyes, narrow nose, and sensuous lips. She moved with languid grace that now seemed more hypnotic than predatory, the amulets at her waist swaying in time with her movements.

Ankti must have heard his gasp because she spun around as the newcomers approached. Kay played on, finishing a gentle flourish of notes before lowering the instrument and turning with a resigned air as though expecting the intrusion.

"What is it that you want?" Kay asked, not bothering to rise.

"Why, you, old man." Erik chuckled and shifted the axe to his left hand so he could jab a finger at Kay. "And to put a stop to your meddling."

"I've done nothing to you and yours. We've never even met before." Kay stood slowly and rubbed the lump behind his ear as if baffled by his own words. *Poor addled bastard.*

Kasandra's eyes gleamed, her expression anything but sympathetic. "The fates have delivered us a delicious opportunity."

She drew her arm back and flung it forward, throwing a glowing rope of red power at Kay. The whip of energy coiled around Kay from neck to knees like a python, drawing tighter the more he struggled. Those bulging biceps and rippling shoulders were useless against the magic. He still gripped his flute, but it was pinned at his thigh. The energy cords jerked away from the instrument, avoiding the gleaming wood as Kay thrashed and cursed. Within moments he stood tightly bound, unable to even shuffle away because Kasandra still held the other end of the spell like a leash. The magical bonds settled in an uneven corkscrew so they never came in contact with the man's flute.

"Never met?" Erik strode close, getting right up in Kay's face. "Trickster, you've led us a merry chase. Even if you've given up on directly interfering with our plans, what you do here remains unacceptable. The Neutral Council doesn't condone your actions. They prefer things take their natural course. You think yourself high and mighty and exploit loopholes!" Spittle flew from his mouth now as he yelled. "Accept that humanity's time is at an end. The Dark Court will see to it that your pitiful efforts make no difference. *I* will put an end to your meddling."

"Leave him alone!" Ankti lunged as if to push the giant away.

Kay twisted in his bonds to block her with a shoulder. The flute swung wide, and Erik jumped back with a hiss as it grazed his leather trousers. Pain flitted across the giant's face, though he compressed his lips and tried to hide the fact behind a scowl.

Grandmother Wikiwi was right, there was something special about that flute. It had to be the key to getting out of this mess! That hunk of wood could certainly do more than the small knife he still clutched.

Erik recovered quickly, yet made no attempt to push past Kay as he turned his wrath on Ankti and growled under his breath. "As for you, human, don't think that your parlor tricks will do any good. I will deal with you after the trickster."

Erik reached out his free hand with fingers spread wide as if to again grab her by the chin. Although she was beyond his reach, the bruising prints on her skin pulsed and darkened, and Ankti sucked in a sharp breath. Kay flailed against the spell, throwing his shoulders left and right so that Kasandra had to grip the leash with both hands.

The flute swung wildly, never close enough to again touch Erik. The cords of power snaked and flowed, retreating from the flute's touch until Kay grew still.

"Parlor tricks; is that what you think?" Phil scoffed, drawing everyone's attention and barking out a laugh. "She sent your minions back to hell, or wherever they came from." He edged around the fire, moving closer to Kay, but also into easy striking distance of that long-handled axe. Phil held Erik's angry gaze and willed Kay to see what he was up to. "Seriously, your roadblocks were a joke that barely stopped anyone. Then you concentrate all your resources on the wrong location. And when you finally figure things out, your creatures are bested by an old woman's spell. Seems to me like you're the ones wielding parlor tricks."

Phil refused to look away despite menace and literal fire burning in Erik's eyes. He stood by Kay with chin held high, a puny human daring this monster to make a move. He slipped his right hand behind Kay and felt about blindly. Sharp pain seared his forearm where it touched the bonds, but his fingers worked along the man's belt until their hands met and his fingers grazed wood. Kay pushed the flute into Phil's palm. *Just a few more inches.*

Electric jolts from the spell around Kay made the muscles of his forearm dance as nerves misfired, and numb fingers refused to close. Phil's head spun with the effort of holding Erik's gaze, but he mustered the will to throw out one final insult. "Maybe you're the one who should go sit down with Grandmother to learn a few things."

From the corner of his eye, Phil saw Ankti shaking her head and mouthing the word "no." Mentioning Wikiwi may have been a mistake. The last thing he wanted to do was put the old woman in further danger, though so far she'd proved more than capable of—

Phil's teeth slammed together, and he blinked up in confusion from the ground. He struggled to suck in a breath through aching lungs. Then the pain hit: clenching tightness in the center of his chest and a dull, distant ache from his tailbone where he'd landed hard on the ground behind Kay. He hadn't seen the blow coming, just Erik's flaming eyes and then a blurred impression of the axe handle jabbing out to slam him in the chest.

He'd gone down like a slaughtered cow and still gaped like a beached fish unable to draw breath. In a moment of true panic, Phil worried he'd had more than the wind knocked out of him and would suffocate under some sinister spell. But the pressure eased just enough to draw a sip of air, which brought new agony down his left side. *Broken ribs.*

They weren't done yet. Shallow panting breaths needled his lungs as Phil sat up with his left palm flat on the ground and the right clutching his prize. He pushed to his feet and stood swaying behind Kay.

"So much fight for such an insignificant creature." Erik dropped the hand threatening Ankti so he could grasp his weapon with both hands.

The axe blade gleamed darkly as the sun crested the distant hills. This would be no glancing blow, no incapacitating poke. Erik meant to cleave him in two. As the axe arced down, Phil swept the flute up along the back of Kay's legs. The strange power of the instrument sliced through the magical bonds from knees to shoulder, freeing his friend.

Friend—a strange sentiment for his final thought, but they'd been through a lot in the past few days. Despite the man's annoying habits, mysterious past, and infatuation with Ankti, it felt right to consider Kay a true friend. Phil willed Kay to grab the girl and run as death sliced down and…stopped a handbreadth from his head.

Erik's face twisted in rage, and the muscles in his arms and shoulders creaked as he tried to complete the strike. Kay held his right hand high with fingers curled as if holding the weapon at bay without touching. His black pupils glinted within a fierce mask of determination. He pushed Phil back and beckoned for the flute with his free hand. Electric zapped up Phil's arm as he handed over the instrument.

"You wanted me to remember." Kay struggled to speak, his words grating like rusty hinges on an ancient door. "To remember what I've done, to remember you and yours. I see darkness and cruelty and a misguided notion that you must destroy what sustains you. I recall arrogance and pettiness from cowards who know better but refuse to help." As he spoke Kay seemed to grow in stature and determination.

Kasandra unleashed a feral scream and flung out another sizzling whip of power. Kay's stance hardened into defiance that exploded into a primal force as he batted her attack aside with the flute, which had grown into a thick staff with animal carvings and symbols glowing along its length.

Kay backed him and Ankti to the cliff. They stood with backs to the squared-off shallow depression Kay had rushed into that very first visit—trapped. He lowered the staff, its glow fading along with whatever memories Erik's words had revived. Comprehension fled, leaving Kay blinking down at the dark wood.

Erik roared, and the power holding him shattered. They sensed Kay's weakness. Both gathered energies that even Phil could see. Ankti raised both hands and chanted under her breath, perhaps in an attempt to call up protection. A moment ago Kay had looked radiant, invincible as the flute lent him power. Now, he was just a man, a determined man who raised the staff like a baseball bat as the enemy closed.

Phil gripped the knife in his right hand and hugged his aching ribs with his left arm, reverse pressure easing the pain. It wouldn't be much of a fight, but they had to try.

A massive green claw shot from the darkness behind them, scaled digits with talons the length of Phil's forearm encircling Kay in much the same way the magical bonds had. He kicked and struggled, but was yanked back into the recess and disappeared. Ankti yelped as she too flew backwards into the shadows and vanished.

16. Old as Dirt

P HIL BLINKED at the empty space where his friends had just been, then turned to face the enemy alone. Erik stepped forward, and the whites around Kasandra's eyes shone red. She grabbed a foot-long strip from her belt and traced a finger along bold black patterns decorating the pebbly tan skin.

Erik likely posed the most immediate danger, but he couldn't look away from the woman. Her eyes shifted, orange irises expanding to replace the red and pupils narrowing to vertical slits as her neck and body stretched impossibly long. Kasandra's face flattened, ears and hair melting into the scaly head of a huge snake.

Phil jumped as something touched his elbow. A tiny alabaster hand—the hand of a child—reached from the shallow alcove, took him by the wrist and yanked him into the recess. He crossed into shadows cool as night and found himself falling through gray mist filled with half-glimpsed secrets and possibilities.

A wrenching across his shoulders like a roller-coaster harness pulling tight before the big drop sent new spears of agony through his ribs. The pressure vanished, and he fell. But only for a moment before his feet hit soft sand, knees buckling under a blazing azure sky that was too blue, its sun a little too white.

That sun blazed high overhead while soft burning sand trickled into the back of his shoes, more evidence that it was much later in the day than it had been moments ago.

It was funny how his mind latched onto such things: the sun, the sand, the network of adobe structures stacked high on the cliff face behind him like ancient apartments. He found it easier to focus on trivial details than the figures before him.

Ankti and Kay stood off to his left. Kay's glowing staff was gone, replaced by the wooden flute. The instrument again hung from the man's belt, a wide leather belt with an ornate buckle below his white buckskin tunic. How had he managed to change clothes again?

Phil would have run to them if not for the impossible creature towering over Kay. There was no mistaking it for anything other than a dragon with iridescent green scales, horns sweeping up from each side of a massive lizard head, and a pulsing red gem glowing from high on its plated forehead. Kay stood bracketed by powerful forelegs and stared up into a gaping maw. Water streamed from the monster's open mouth, dripping off ridiculously long teeth as it drooled over its bite-sized human meal.

Phil took a half-step forward, uncertain what he could possibly do, but knowing he had to try. The tiny hand on his arm tightened, holding him in place. Pain lanced through his left side.

"Not to worry," the small woman holding him back said in lilting soprano, but her face grew concerned as she studied him. "Oh, honey, you're hurt."

Without even asking permission, she ran her tiny hands up under his shirt, tickling his injured ribs. An involuntary laugh filled his lung with knives. But the feathery touch grew hot, and warmth flowed under his skin. Phil's breath caught as something crunched deep in his side. He drew a hesitant lungful of hot desert air. The pain was gone!

"There, all fixed." She grabbed his arm again—a not-too-gentle-reminder to stay put—and jerked her chin to where the monster confronted Kay. "Believe it or not, they're friends…after a fashion."

She sounded none too certain of that assertion, but Phil found himself nodding as she looked up with innocent emerald-green eyes. Flowing blond hair framed her porcelain cheeks and pert little nose. She only came up to his waist, yet this was no child. The little woman was perfectly proportioned—if not a bit buxom—and adorable, and incredibly strong. Phil stopped struggling.

"My name's Pina." She released his arm, put a tiny fist on each hip, and glared up at him. "It's not polite to stare, and I can see you're just dying to know. I'm a forest sprite. Hush now!" She held up a finger to stop the questions forming on his lips.

"Old fool!" The accusation rained down on Kay along with gallons of saliva as the dragon ripped giant clawfuls of sandy dirt from the ground to either side of the man.

So dragons talk. Fifty feet away, the spiked tip of the thick green tail lashed back and forth like that of an agitated cat.

To his credit, Kay didn't even flinch, whereas Phil would have needed a change of pants. In fact, the water cascading down with the creature's words didn't touch their friend. Maybe flute magic kept Kay dry as he blinked up in confusion at the giant reptile.

The dragon looked to the sky, roared, and shook its massive head. Its wicked horns whistled as they sliced the air. "You cannot go off and confront Erik the Red on your own, especially when that skinwalker is helping him."

"He's lost his memory!" Ankti shouted and stepped in front of Kay, putting herself between man and beast. "Stop badgering him and just back the hell off!"

The dragon sputtered, water bubbling out between indignant half-formed protests and unfortunately drenching Ankti who lacked the flute's magical protection.

"Oh, I like *her*," Pina said under her breath and gave Phil's hand a squeeze.

What on Earth did you do in a situation like that? Phil felt he should rush forward to offer a unified front, but had little desire to make the same mistake as the others by stepping beneath the monster. Then of course there was the little woman...err...sprite. Pina hauled him back by the hand every time he took an involuntary step forward.

The sly smile that Phil had developed a love-hate relationship with blossomed on Kay's face as Ankti scowled up at the dragon, and he slid an arm around the woman's shoulders.

"Thank you so much, my dear, for coming to my rescue. Slaying such a fearsome beast with mere words in no mean feat." He led Ankti away from the dragon as though turning from a casual exchange. "I'm fortunate to have such a lovely creature as you join my dreams."

The dragon blinked its golden headlight eyes and stuttered all the harder, clearly indignant. "Do not walk away from *me* Kokopelli!" The creature crouched low, its breath a hot wind that blew Ankti's hair forward as the pair strolled toward him.

Can this all be a dream?

The thought was a lifeline. How easy it would be to simply wake and find this insanity a fabrication of the subconscious. But if this was Kay's dream, what would that mean for Phil, a dream within a dream? Could they all wake to find there was no Red Scarf threat, or even better that the entire C-12 virus never happened? Dreams of a "normal" world were the best, the kind of place depicted in old movies and news programs.

"And here's that young man you've been working with, another sight for sore eyes." Kay grinned, black eyes shining with mischief as he winked down at Pina.

"Oh, big faker," Pina muttered and wagged her index finger to show her disapproval.

"Kokopelli!" The dragon's voice held anguish. If it was possible for a reptilian face to plead, his did so now. "What could they have done to make you forget yourself so completely here in your own lands, here where you should be fully restored?"

Kay flipped a hand back over his shoulder in offhanded dismissal. "Begone, foul dragon, for my George has come." He slipped an arm through Ankti's and hugged the woman to his side, bringing a distinct blush to her cheeks.

The beast gaped and gurgled, struggling for words. Pina's expression shifted from startled comprehension to annoyance. She released Phil's hand and stepped in front of Kay and Ankti to keep the pair from sauntering past.

"Ignoring the horned serpent is one thing." Her wagging finger now jabbed in accusation. "But we *both* went to a lot of trouble to track you down and bring you home. I deserve to know if you are fully yourself, fully healed…my lord." She added the honorific as an afterthought.

"Peace, Brightness." Kay's mischievous grin softened to a fond smile as he looked down on the small woman, knelt, and took her tiny hand in both of his. "I am here. Thank you deeply for your concern and help."

The sprite's outrage dropped away, and her face brightened into a radiant smile as Kay kissed her hand. Pina preened under the praise and gazed on the man with such adoration that Phil nearly laughed.

"And you too, old friend!" Kay called back to the dragon. "I was certainly in need of both your help, and your timing was impeccable."

The dragon stomped forward, shaking the ground and letting loose with a gust of air that would have swept away the tents at the camping grounds.

"You infuriate me, old man. I don't know whether to curse your games or praise the fact you are again whole and back with us."

"Indeed." Kay rubbed at the back of his head where the lump left by his injuries usually lifted the hairline, but the reminder of his amnesia was gone, as was the last bit of burn scarring along his collar. "But I make no apologies. You know my nature."

"Yes, old man, your tricks are part of what makes you so very uniquely…you." The dragon's words held grudging respect. "But the courts and the Neutral Council again clash in your absence, and there is news you should hear."

"Likewise, there are events in the mortal plane I would speak of with you also, old lizard." Kay's eyes twinkled at the affable insult as he turned to Ankti and gave a shallow bow. "If you will excuse us, I will return shortly. Pina will see to your needs. That is if you don't mind, Brightness?"

"Of course, my lord." Pina beamed, took Phil and Ankti by the hand, and led them through a ground-level door into the adobe dwelling along the cliff.

The dragon and the man he'd known as Kay settled down to their discussion. Though their words grew indistinct, the exchange quickly took on the tone of an old married couple squabbling and relishing in their escalating banter.

They stepped into an austere common room with a rudimentary kitchen off to the right, simple wooden table and chairs in the center, and a few scattered cabinets. Pina set fruit and a round of nutty bread on the table.

"What the hell is going on?" Phil asked as Pina busied herself pouring out three cups of a clear pink juice.

"First off, I don't think we're on Earth anymore." Ankti hunted for more words, looking as confused as he felt. "And Kay…well, he's not what we thought either."

"We traveled to another world in just a few seconds?" Phil knew that was impossible, but the sun and sky color supported the idea.

Pina passed out the drinks, sat opposite them, and grabbed a handful of berries, which in her case amounted to about four. Phil sipped his own drink to ease a suddenly dry throat. The sweet liquid tasted of ginger and nectar.

"More like another plane of existence than anything out of science fiction. I don't understand exactly how, but this all centers around Kay." Ankti looked at Pina. "And we just happen to have someone here who probably knows more."

The little woman—the sprite—swallowed her mouthful of berries and sighed. "I've heard you call my lord Kay. I like the name, but you are right. He isn't what he seems—he's never what he seems." She spoke that last bit quietly as if to herself, then brightened. "My lord Kokopelli is quite the trickster, but such a good spirit."

"Kokopelli." Ankti repeated the name and swallowed hard. "As in our god of fertility, music, and dance?"

"Yes, among other things." Pina nodded and slurped her drink. "I'm so happy he found nice friends like you in the human world. Thank you for taking care of him." Her eyes grew sad, and her breath caught as she continued on the verge of tears. "I just wish he had called on me for help."

Ankti scooted to the other side of the table and wrapped an arm around Pina's shoulders. "It's okay, honey. He didn't ignore you on purpose. A hard clonk to the head scrambled his memories. That's why we call him Kay. It was the only letter he could get out—the only part of his name he could recall—the night we found him. We found him nearly two weeks ago after our last ceremony, and he'd been hurt. His head injury caused amnesia to the point he didn't remember much at all about his prior life. But there's something about this place. He's better now."

"That explains a lot." Pina nodded and leaned into the other woman as if thankful for her support and explanation. "This is Kokopelli's domain. He crafted this world and has resided here forever. The land is a part of him, and bringing him home has made him whole." Sadness again washed across the sprite's face. "I just wish there was more I could do to keep him safe from his enemies. He walks a path that few agree with. It leaves him isolated and vulnerable."

"Figured people are after him." Phil said. "We've already had run-ins with Erik and Kasandra. Are there others we should know about?"

Pina's eyes grew wide at his mention of the Red Scarf leaders. "I've already said too much. He must be the one to tell you." She picked up another berry. "Let's just enjoy the food. Oh, maybe I can give you a tour. The horned serpent likes to hear himself talk, so it will be a while before they finish."

"Okay, if we can't talk about Kokopelli, how about a little info on the great green one," Phil pressed.

Pina tittered, a tinkling laugh like crystal wind chimes. "Uktena is the great horned serpent, the one and only, despite the myths. Uktena is a mighty and ancient spirit. He and my lord go way back with a kind of on and off relationship. He won't lift a claw to help Kokopelli with the humans, but was worried enough about him to help me find you all and bring you across the barrier. To be perfectly honest, Uktena often rubs me the wrong way, but I do my best to keep him in line."

Phil smiled at the thought of this tiny woman scolding the massive beast, but then, she'd backed Kay down and made him admit he'd regained his memory. The small sprite might be a force of nature when riled, and he decided to stay on her good side if at all possible.

"You keep saying the horned serpent, but, Pina, that's a dragon out there." Phil pointed through the doorway.

"Many great spirits take on different forms," Pina said. "Uktena's natural form is the snake, but he can also appear as the dragon or any combination of the two. Each has its own abilities and advantages. But I do agree he spends an awful lot of time as the dragon. I think he likes flying and spreading fear more than venom and hypnosis."

"So all the creatures out here in this world can shift?" Ankti frowned, worry lines creasing her forehead as her voice took on a hard edge. "Everyone can make themselves look like something they aren't?"

"Not entirely," Pina hedged, suddenly defensive.

"Go on," Phil said as the tense silence stretched. He was missing some nuance of the exchange that apparently was obvious to both women.

"The form would have to be natural to them in some way, and we're only talking greater spirits, not little sprites like me. There are a few powerful evil entities that can steal shapes from others. You've met Kasandra the skinwalker."

"What's a skinwalker?" Phil asked. "At first she turned into some kind of half-human predator, super strong and fast, but I swear she changed into a giant cobra just before you pulled me through to this place."

"Skinwalkers are super bad news." Ankti answered for Pina. "The tribes have many legends, but basically they started as medicine people who were never satisfied. In their pursuit of ever greater power they turn to the dark paths, breaking tribal mores and taboos.

"Most lore agrees there is usually a single horrific act that tips the scales and plunges a skinwalker into true darkness from which their spirit can never return. But they gain power and the ability to change into different animals and sometimes even mythical creatures."

157

"Old ones hold greater power and can assume more shapes." Pina nodded in agreement. "They are much more dangerous than simple shapeshifters. Kasandra is ancient and has butted heads with Kokopelli forever. She and Erik align with the Dark Court, which generally are at odds with all you might consider good and just. But Kokopelli isn't terribly happy with the Light Court either, so circumstances around him tend to get confusing."

"Shapeshifting!" Phil blurted out, thinking of Kay dancing from behind the fire that very first night and then again last night. There hadn't been time for the guy to ditch his costume on either occasion. "A hunchbacked old man, that's what Kay really looks like. Isn't it?"

Pina's green eyes flashed, and she stared daggers at him for some reason. Her gaze swept left and right as if looking for an escape route, but her shoulders slumped. "It's not for me to say what my lord truly looks like. I can only offer some insight. How he appears to you is his true form at that moment in time. Please believe me." Pina's eyes slid toward Ankti, and she gave the woman an apologetic smile.

Phil cursed himself as a fool. Kay and Ankti were hot for each other, and he'd just shined a spotlight on the elephant he hadn't seen standing on the table. Instead of a young beefcake, Ankti had been ogling an old cripple—really old, like literally old as dirt.

17. Return

ANKTI'S CHEST pulled tight. The air turned thick and stifling. She'd fallen for an old man. No, not old—ancient, an ancient spirit. She drew a ragged breath and studied the rough wood tabletop, unable to bear Pina's sad green eyes, the weight of her pity.

Meeting Phil's gaze was just as hard. For a while she'd imagined he'd been romantically interested in her, which had been flattering. She hadn't been in a real relationship since leaving California. But sweet as he was, Phil didn't raise her blood pressure, which was just as well since he had his Simone back home.

Kay—no, Kokopelli—was a different story. If Ankti was being honest, there'd been sparking attraction there from day one when he had lain burnt and confused in Phil's spare room. The man had been so vulnerable and beautiful. But that was all a lie.

Moving into Phil's townhouse had been impulsive, and a wave of shame washed over her as she admitted the reason for the rash decision. Being near Kay grew intoxicating so damn quickly. She'd been certain he felt the same, but now wasn't so sure. How could a god of her people hold any feelings other than pity for a mere human? Or maybe he viewed her fondly, like a loyal pet.

Phil cleared his throat in the cute little way he did when nervous. Ankti sighed, knowing she had to face her own stupidity at some point. She plastered on a wry smile and looked up, striving to embrace the irony of falling for the very being their ceremonies had summoned to help.

A great crash rocked the building, sending chunks of ceiling crashing to the floor and sparing Ankti from spouting inane platitudes at odds with the ache in her chest.

All three surged to their feet and rushed outside to find the dragon piling massive boulders in front of the doorway they'd been pulled through. He worked a third onto the top of two already resting against the entrance and headed off for more.

"You know as well as I that achieves nothing," Kokopelli called after him, a bemused smile stretching his beautiful face. "Pathways to the realms are not physical."

Ankti cursed herself for being relieved he still looked like Kay.

"It does achieve something, old man." Uktena huffed around a mouthful of wood as he returned and dropped a dead log the size of a mature oak trunk onto his blockade. "It emphasizes my point. Nothing good can come from returning to confront Erik."

"Your concern is touching, but if I don't, there will be—" he broke off mid-sentence, noticing the three of them standing outside the far dwelling. "— unfortunate ramifications."

His black eyes shone with regret as he held her gaze. When not suffering from amnesia, Ankti doubted much escaped Kokopelli's notice, so he'd meant for them to hear his statement. She was equally certain he knew they'd been speaking of him inside, that he understood his deception weighed heavy on her heart. And yet, when he smiled her stupid heart fluttered—*so not quite thoroughly crushed.*

"Ankti, I would speak to you for a moment." Kokopelli strode over with an arm outstretched to usher her back inside, and the flutter grew to hammering wings. "Phil, please join us."

Oh.

"Mark my words—" the dragon began.

"Yes, yes." Pina cut the beast short and did her own bit of ushering—perhaps accompanied by some mollifying magic—to back the indignant creature away. "My lord has noted your concern and values your insights. Let the humans hear what he must say. You must be famished after lifting those heavy rocks. Kokopelli has an excellent herd of antelope that I'm sure are quite delicious."

Back inside Kokopelli took a seat next to her at the table, while Phil sat opposite.

"By now I am sure you've come to understand the mess we're in," Kokopelli said.

"Sure, the Red Scarfs are going to keep harassing the tribes until they shut down the ceremonies for good." Phil jumped right in, giving Ankti time to regain her bearings and work to slow her thundering pulse.

Why must he sit so close?

"More than that, my friend." Kokopelli shook his head and patted Ankti's hand. "Erik has been affronted and seeks retribution."

"I don't matter." Ankti knew she should pull her hand off the table and out from under the warm pressure of his palm, but couldn't bring herself to move. "But the rituals must continue. The tribes need your help." She swallowed hard, forcing the next sentence out. "Help from all the gods of prosperity."

"As Pina may have told you, others do not share my concern. The Dark Court would let a few upstarts bring about humanity's demise without a second thought. They thrive on the pain and suffering but can't see past tomorrow when there will be none left to suffer, and their powers will wane for good."

"And those of the light?" Ankti asked.

"Remain too self-absorbed to care or think things through to a logical conclusion. I fear it is I alone who have been answering the calls of your people, but I can do nothing more to hold back the sickness that runs through them. Even with more prayers and offerings, the indigenous peoples will soon share the same fate as all the nations of your world. I am truly sorry."

"So we just give up, let the virus win?" Phil didn't quite manage to keep a whine out of his tone. "I mean, we've got scientists working across the globe trying to reverse their mistake. Those idiots back at the turn of the century spliced their little contraceptive payload to the wrong bug. The virus mutates too damned fast for traditional meds to control. And once the 'medicine' went airborne…well, that was the big game changer. Synthetic polynomial antivirals could hold the answer and change alongside the C-12 target to suppress it—theoretically. I'm no expert. A breakthrough might not be imminent, but it's possible."

"Mankind remains as resourceful as ever." Kokopelli's nod was anything but encouraging. "I strive not to underestimate your kind, but they were not alone in creating this problem. A few like Erik nudged their hand, encouraged key mistakes, and will do all they can to ensure your C-12 virus remains virulent. It will be what it will be.

"In the meantime, there are more pressing concerns. Erik will assume I still shelter the people and help them thrive. He will not rest without crushing their ability to call upon the spirits."

"We have to fight," Ankti said.

"Just so." Kokopelli gave her hand a squeeze. "But killing a god is no easy task, and Kasandra is an ancient power to be reckoned with. We may be better served teaching your elders protections so they may keep the people safe when I depart."

She pulled her hand away as the statement frosted the warmth between them. There it was, bold as day: he planned on leaving her. She tried to focus on the positive. Grandmother would know how best to use any knowledge Kokopelli shared. She could take point on the coming conflict. Ankti just wanted to go back to being a follower.

She lurched to her feet, kicking the bench back and nearly unseating the startled man who'd crashed into her once-simple life. Kokopelli raised a questioning eyebrow, but she no longer felt like talking.

"Let's get to it then." Ankti stormed out, feeling foolish, knowing her anger was rightly justified, and cursing the maelstrom of mixed emotions that demanded fresh air to keep her from screaming.

Preparations to return did not take long and mostly consisted of waiting for Pina, who left to retrieve a handful of talismans. A few looked like the prayer bundles Grandmother had given them, but they glowed with subtle auras, seeming to draw energy from the land around them.

"My people make these a little differently than yours," Pina said when she saw Ankti trying to work out the bundles. "These are just examples you and Kokopelli can use as teaching aids. The goal is to call on your source of power, be it a spirit of nature or other entity, in such a way that the call cannot be ignored. The correct combination of sacred materials and supporting prayers during construction are key to making them self-sustaining. This one here draws power from my lord's domain." Pina held up a blue scrap of cloth tied with red beaded string. "He won't even be aware of the energy drain, unless of course there are many others doing the same. We have time to walk through the basics before you leave."

"You aren't coming with us?" Kokopelli would know the specifics, but Ankti didn't want to be the only other person carrying back such important information.

"I'm afraid not." Pina did not look happy about her answer. "We can't risk too much exposure to…well, what you might call the supernatural. I could easily use a glamour to appear like one of you, but my lord feels it's too risky." Her voice took on a hard edge. "I should be there to watch my lord's back, and the great serpent won't help at all. Promise me you'll look after him."

The speed with which the small being went from loving descriptions of the talisman to fierce protectiveness made Ankti think there might be other reasons for keeping Pina from returning with them. If Erik or Kasandra came hunting, the sprite clearly wouldn't hesitate to engage. Kokopelli probably left her behind for her own protection.

Love and respect ran deeply between those two. The simple realization tugged at Ankti's heart, another crack in the impersonal mask she saw as Kokopelli's persona. Perhaps the god had a heart after all.

In addition to the prayer bundles, which simply provided shielding, protection, and in one case, good fortune, two other items proved to be more like weapons. Apparently nothing they could put in the hands of humans had a chance of countering direct attacks from greater spirits like Erik, but minions could be readily handled if push came to shove. Again the spritely ways of making the small devices called on the cleansing powers of nature. They might not be any more powerful than the weapon Grandmother had provided, but one person could make many without begin depleted. If all went well, the tribes would have a respectable arsenal with minimal effort.

Phil drifted in and out of sight, taking passing interest in Pina's lessons. But unable to see or even sense the magical flows left him looking confused to the point that he always ended up wandering off again. About the time Pina finished, Kokopelli announced the time had come to depart.

"I cannot join you!" Uktena liked to boom out statements, making himself seem quite the drama queen.

"No, old lizard." Kokopelli shook his head, luxurious dark hair flowing with the movement. "You *choose* not to help."

* * *

Phil's stomach dropped as they again passed through the strange gray mist between worlds, and he clenched his jaw trying not to be sick. With Kokopelli's memory and powers intact, they stepped from the portal he created onto the hard-packed parking lot right next to Ankti's car.

The Mount Phoenix ceremonial grounds stood quiet under the blazing Arizona sun. A good half dozen other cars remained from last night, and Phil prayed their owners hadn't been too badly hurt.

"Freeze!" The command boomed from the announcing system, and a pair of guns trained on them from the rocks near the road. "Hands in the air and no sudden moves."

Phil and Ankti lifted their arms, showing empty hands. Kokopelli—Kay, damn that was hard to keep straight—looked about, bemused. The speaker kept out of sight, but that voice was familiar.

"Knock it off, Tommy!" Ankti yelled back. "You know us, Ankti Naatoqa with Phil and Kay."

Both Kokopelli and Pina insisted they refer to the god only by the name he'd given when found. If the tribes discovered Kokopelli walked among them, the knowledge would apparently rip a hole in the space-time continuum or something. Phil doubted the consequences of a name slip would be all that drastic, but standing under the alien sky of another world had forced him to admit that he might not know everything.

"You could have been those Red Scarfs in disguise." The hidden speaker sounded petulant, but the gun barrels slid out of sight and the door to the equipment building swung open. "Party's over."

"Is everyone all right? Are you okay?" Ankti rushed to meet Tommy as he limped down the three steps.

Phil was pleased to see that for once the man didn't have a beer in his hand, but judging by the dark rings under his eyes and haggard expression, Tommy hadn't slept much. Who would after being confronted by a horde of demons? Now that he thought of it, Phil felt oddly refreshed given he and Ankti hadn't slept either—another magical benefit of the land they'd visited.

Magic, a concept that had grown from impossible to familiar in just a few short days. When he got home Simone would think him crazy, but the evidence was irrefutable. He certainly wouldn't try to weave tales of godly protection into his official reports, but his exploits were too fantastic to keep from his fiancé. How to broach the topic remained a puzzle for another day. Right now they had to focus on ensuring Ankti and the others were safe.

"Okay?" Tommy leaned heavily on the fence in front of his building and waved off Ankti's help. "No, but at least no one died. I'm just tired, and my trick knee went out while we cleaned up the mess those bastards left behind. You can bet I gave Jack's folks an earful about not listening to old Tommy Roundbush when they had the chance." An odd sort of pride glowed in the man's eyes; he'd been vindicated. "Of course they took anyone with more than scrapes and sprains down to the hospital. The rest are holed up with Jack and what's left of security. Tribal counsel's finally gotten engaged and been busy consulting with elders near and far for ideas to keep everyone safe."

"So you're in charge of the rear guard?" Phil asked.

"More like I *am* the rear guard." He whipped out what looked like a garage door opener and pressed one of its buttons. The guns swung back into place along the rocks with a skittering of metal on stone. "Just old pipe with no firepower, but I went for the intimidation factor."

"Ingenious." Kay's compliment had Tommy nodding and grinning from ear to ear.

"I've got a few more tricks, but the demons seem to have given up on this place. Haven't seen hide nor hair of 'em since the fight, but no way was I leaving my gear. Camping grounds are a different story. Bad dust-up near dawn, but most folks had already moved out, so Jack's people took the brunt of things. Heard over the radio that it was just more flaming heads. The two that are really bad news must be off looking for something."

"We've got to get to Grandmother." Ankti jangled her car keys for emphasis.

"You'll find Wikiwi up at her house," Tommy said. "Jack's men reported demon activity up near there, but she refuses to leave. Old biddy is just too damned stubborn."

Ankti raised an eyebrow at the old quartermaster, extending the look to his treasured storage building that demons weren't likely to care about and the shattered gates to the already desecrated ceremonial grounds. The irony of the situation was lost on Tommy. He simply waited, oblivious to the sarcasm and question in her gaze.

"We better get going then." Ankti sighed and waved them to her car. "Tommy, be careful down here."

"Wait, before you go." Tommy shuffled up the stairs, disappeared inside, and returned a minute later carrying a pump-action shotgun and an insulated shoulder bag. "You need a weapon. Plenty of shells loaded with rock salt in the bag along with some sandwiches and drinks. Now, don't look at me like that. I've got plenty here and can't figure a good way to rig the extra gun to fire. My decoys are enough."

Phil took the gun, and Ankti gave the old man a hug.

The drive went smoothly, and they soon pulled onto a familiar street, which thankfully wasn't cordoned off by a Red Scarf roadblock this time. Even before hitting the abandoned section, the streets had been too quiet, as though those not involved in tribal problems sensed danger and opted to lay low.

Four cars parked haphazardly in a loose circle around Wikiwi's home. Ankti slowed to a crawl and stopped well short of the house.

"I don't recognize any of those," she said, turning off the ignition. "Let me go first and keep your eyes open for anything suspicious."

"Like that?" Phil grabbed her arm to keep Ankti from opening her door as a hundred pounds of angry black devil raced from between the parked cars and streaked toward them.

It leapt onto the hood, claws raking the paint as it snapped at the windshield and let out a growl. Half dog, half cat, the creature lacked the hellfire flames so must've been of the variety that had disrupted Jack's ambush at Mount Phoenix.

"Kay," Phil whispered, not taking his eyes off the creature as he reached blindly into the back seat. "The shotgun."

"I doubt that's needed."

"Just give me the damned gun!" If he rolled out his door quickly, he could catch it by surprise and get off a clean shot.

"Be careful," Ankti said. "Our talismans will keep us safe, but we can't leave that thing loose to wander into the village.

Phil wrapped his hand around the barrel, heaved the gun into his lap, and eased his door open. The animal's ears pricked up at the creak of the hinge, and its head swiveled to watch him slide out. *So much for the element of surprise.*

Phil poked the barrel through the hinged opening, using the door as a shield, and fired. But the thing leapt just as he pulled the trigger and landed on the far side of the car. High-velocity-salt blasted the dark blue paint, exposing bright metal in a vee across the hood.

It ignored Phil, rose on its hind legs, and clawed at Ankti's window. Phil pumped another shell into the chamber. Unable to shoot back through the car, he dashed around the front and fired down the side. Again, it was too fast, disappearing underneath just as Phil blasted the left side-mirror into scrap. He got another bead on it as it shot out from under the back bumper, but the gun merely clanked when he pulled the trigger. *Damn!*

Phil fumbled to pull spare shells from his pocket as the creature stalked close. The first shell slid smoothly into the magazine. He cupped the others in his hand, pumped to load, and brought the barrel up just as the monster plopped its butt down in the dirt and stared with wide unblinking eyes as if daring him to take the shot.

"Stop shooting at Deedee!" A woman yelled from behind him.

Phil half turned to keep his eyes on the creature. Someone stormed from the house and headed for their car.

"Grandmother?" Ankti leaned to her right to call out the open door. "Stay back! It's one of the demon animals."

But the old woman stormed on, kicking up dust and bearing down on Phil. She grabbed his gun barrel, pushed it down, and was past him before he could think to stop her.

"Grandmother, no!" Ankti flung her door open just as the woman reached the demon and…placed a hand on its leathery head.

The demon leaned against the old woman, pushing into her palm as Wikiwi scratched between pointed ear and sweeping horn. The glowing amber eyes closed in contentment, and it let out a rumbling low growl like boulders crashing downhill—no, it purred. *What the hell?*

"Oh, hush now." Grandmother turned with a doting smile. "You remember Deedee. I got her on your last visit."

Ankti's jaw dropped open. "Yeah, when it attacked."

"*That* was a misunderstanding. She had bad owners. Poor dear had to lose her flames, but we've straightened all that out now. Haven't we, girl?" The last was directed at the cat-thing, which now tried to weave between the old woman's legs, but instead ended up simply pushing her to the side several steps.

Wikiwi pulled a strip of raw meat about a foot long from her belt pouch and held it up. A paw swiped out like lightning, razor claws snagging the morsel. The meat disappeared in a single bite, leaving

Deedee to primly groom her foreclaws as the woman resumed scratching and the avalanche purring resumed.

"Um." Phil cleared his throat. "You gave it a name?"

"Stands for demon dog. She does quite a good job of patrolling and keeping the occasional bad demons away."

"What's with all the cars?" Ankti asked. "We've got something to show you that may help. Kay's worked out improved prayer bundles and talismans to help control the Red Scarfs."

Ankti brought out a folded blue towel and flipped back the material to expose Pina's samples. Wikiwi's hand hovered above the innocuous array of handcrafted items. She closed her eyes for a moment, then nodded.

"You have indeed." The old woman looked Kay up and down. "I see you have found something else also." She studied his face for a moment more. "Yourself, perhaps? Well, time to speak of that later." She waved them toward the front door. "Let's go in."

The supernatural cat trailed them to the house, but stopped short of the doorway and watched them enter, tail twitching. Phil went in last. As he stepped across the threshold, Deedee gave a long luxurious stretch, her front paws kneading and tearing great clumps from the hard-packed path. Phil swallowed hard. But the cat-thing's eyes dropped to a lazy half-mast, and it padded off, presumably resuming its patrol and looking relaxed—as if Phil and the others had been weighed and deemed Grandmother's friends.

Inside they found six exhausted women hard at work. Three were elders like Wikiwi. A teenager and two women in their late twenties rounded out the group. Dark hair and classic features marked each as Native American, but were insufficient for Phil to guess from which tribes.

Patches of material, twine, and ingredients like sticks, stones, and seeds were scattered around the room in plastic trays that provided a kind of rough organization. Dust motes danced in bands of sunshine angling through the front windows, and spicy floral scents told of other ingredients. A handful of small cloth bundles were already piled on the corner of the dining room table along with a simple dreamcatcher and a small wooden cylinder much like the one Ankti had used against the demons.

"You're already working on defensive charms," Ankti said as she surveyed the loose production line.

"Been working all night, child." The plump elderly woman sitting by the kitchen door nodded wearily. "We could certainly use an extra pair of hands. Wikiwi speaks of you often, and your power will help."

"Give the girl a moment, Vivian." Wikiwi made shooing motions at the other woman. "Introductions first, then my granddaughter is going to show you ladies how to step things up a notch."

The three older women turned out to be elders from nearby villages. They'd each brought an apprentice, and all had been busy making more prayer bundles. With introductions complete, Ankti pulled out her stash.

"We're going to show you how to make these." Ankti unwrapped the items from Kokopelli's realm, and Kay stepped forward to hold each out for inspection.

"You'll notice how this is attuned to the land," Kay said as he fingered a red patchwork prayer bundle. "With proper preparation, you'll learn techniques requiring very little personal energies, just your expertise and craftsmanship. We will send up prayers to the land, sky, river, and more, asking for the power to protect nature's balance."

"You'll teach us yourself?" Dianne, the oldest of the apprentices, asked in a breathy purr as she leaned in close.

"It will be my privilege to personally provide lovely, intelligent creatures such as yourselves with as much attention and instruction as you each require. I am certain you will all rise to the occasion." A sort of inspiring energy flowed out with his words.

Kay's tunic had come undone, so that it hung open exposing his sculpted bronze chest and abs, both of which drew as many stares as the magic talismans he went on to describe. The women certainly didn't seem to mind the defective buttons, and quite a few hands "accidentally" brushed the man in borderline-inappropriate places, though he seemed not to notice.

By the time Kay opened the first bundle to catalogue its contents, the women's tired eyes were alight with an intense fire and hunger, all traces of their prior weariness gone. Clearly the hunger wasn't all for knowledge, but Phil supposed that might be the norm when dealing with the embodiment of fertility, especially when he looked like…well, like a god. Still, he kept his eye on Ankti to make sure his friend was okay with the many flirtatious comments that wound their way into the discussion. But despite a few initial sideways glances, she seemed not to mind.

The women gathered close to ooh and aah when Ankti took over, comparing the open bundle with an intact magenta one and reciting what Pina had taught her of its construction. Two of the women worked fingers through the air as if tracing patterns extending from the devices. Whatever they saw was more than Phil could sense. He'd been bored out of his skull while Pina and Ankti worked, and it looked like he was in for another long yawn-fest.

The sun set while Phil did his best to stay interested and, failing that, to stay out of the way. As the first experimental bundles were built under Kay's watchful eye, Phil caught himself nodding off. When he asked for strong coffee, Wikiwi directed him to a pot of bittersweet tea she'd made from bark shavings and herbs. It wasn't half bad, but did little to stave off sleep.

Phil jerked awake at a scratching sound outside the back door. He lifted his head from the kitchen table where he'd used crossed arms and a dishtowel for a pillow. The crick in his neck had him checking the time, well past midnight. *Definitely no caffeine.*

Another scratch like nails on wood preceded a heavy thump—as if someone had thrown a big old Sunday newspaper onto the back porch. A peek into the front room showed the ladies still hard at work. The pile of bundles had tripled, and they were definitely in the flow. The women worked diligently but still managed to spare comely smiles and appraising glances for Kay, who at the moment gave a bit of individual advice to Megan, the Apache elder with hair down to the middle of her back and rosy cheeks. The woman was all too happy to have Kay guide her hands in tying off an intricate knot. The way she pressed up against him and sighed you'd think she was a schoolgirl swooning over the star quarterback—if schools actually ran sports programs anymore.

Phil left them to it, grabbed his shotgun, and crept out the back to investigate. It didn't take long to find the source of the odd sounds. A dead animal lay to the left of the door, its torn-out belly glistening darkly in the pale moonlight. Whitetail deer was Phil's first thought, but the stubby antlers and rounded snout looked off. The light from his phone fell across white horizontal stripes on the ruined neck and a comically large black nose designed for sucking up tons of oxygen while on the run—pronghorn antelope.

Phil jumped as another carcass thumped down behind him, and turned to find Deedee daintily licking her front left paw and wearing a satisfied look-what-I-brought-you expression. *Definitely more cat than dog.* But he had to admit Deecee didn't have the same ring.

What on Earth was the demon creature thinking? Was it trying to feed them for a month? Each carcass had to weigh nearly a hundred pounds and, by the looks of things, had been killed brutally.

Phil knelt to examine the new carcass. The antelope's throat was torn out, but a knife had neatly sliced open and emptied the poor animal's abdomen. Unless Deedee had a couple of hidden opposable thumbs, that certainly wasn't her handiwork. Plus, blackened fur along its back fell away in charred bits. Despite looking freshly slaughtered, the scent of rot rose from the dead animal. Nothing would eat these things.

18. Haven

"RITUAL SLAYING." Kay dusted off his hands and sparks of energy fell onto the dead antelope, which immediately burst into flames. He turned and did the same to the second. They burned like flares, blinding and hot until nothing remained except an outline. Even the stench was gone.

"Erik's doing?" Phil asked.

He'd grabbed Kay, literally dragging him away from his adoring pupils. Ankti and her grandmother had followed, and the four stood behind the house staring at the charred outlines and self-satisfied demon the old woman had made her pet.

"Not personally, but this is the work of his Red Scarfs, lesser creatures who pull life energy from the suffering they inflict. It's a pale imitation of their master's manipulation of humanity and other races, but serves to gain them a measure of power."

"This means the village isn't safe." Ankti turned to Wikiwi. "You need to come with us."

"Child, I'm as safe here as anywhere." Wikiwi shook her head, a stubborn glint in her eye. "If I run off, there will be none to protect the others. You bring new knowledge for which I am grateful. I will stay here and use it."

"I think Grandmother may be correct." Kay seemed to be treading lightly and gauging Ankti's expression as he reached out and brazenly petted the demon animal's head—but then a god probably didn't have to worry about his hand getting bitten off. "And Deedee adds yet another layer of protection. By stealing these before they could be consumed, she's kept the power from the Red Scarfs. The prayer bundles and soul-catchers will be more than enough to keep things stable here. Our focus needs to be getting similar help distributed to others and finding Erik."

"My women will carry the charms and knowledge of their making back to their villages," Wikiwi said. "We will keep the people safe at home, but those still gathered need your help."

"We can head down to the camping grounds with enough bundles to establish a decent defense." Ankti nodded under the pale light. "Between those and security we ought to be able to keep everyone safe until…" She trailed off and looked to Kay. "Until what? We don't have weapons to take on Erik and Kasandra—unless you know how to handle them."

"I have an idea for that pair." A Cheshire Cat grin spread across Kay's face. "A little game of cat and mouse, but I'll need your help to flush them out, my dear."

His words sent a chill down Phil's spine. Erik and Kasandra didn't seem like the mouse type.

The women worked on tirelessly, amassing several hundred bundles, a dozen of the small wooden cylinders he'd come to think of as flash grenades, and three intricate little dreamcatchers the size of his palm. If anything, the women drew strength from Kay's presence and constant flirting—to the point that all looked fresh as daisies by mid-morning when Kay declared they had better move out.

After a round of teary goodbyes and hearty hugs—a few of which left Phil red-faced and crushed up for way too long against unfamiliar bosoms—everyone loaded up the cars and took off on their respective assignments.

They arrived at the camping grounds at noon after an uneventful ride only to find most of the tents had been torn down.

"Where is everybody?" Phil asked as the three prowled between the handful of empty tents left behind.

There wasn't a car in the lot, and all but one of the little white security trailers had been hauled off. They converged on that and saw its dry-rotted tires had split open along the sidewalls when someone tried to move it. Ankti pulled open the door and hopped up the two steps.

"Jack led our planning sessions here," she said as Phil and Kay joined her inside. "Without that big tan tent out front, I didn't recognize it. See the cork boards?"

The maps and notes had been stripped off, leaving an artistic array of colored pushpins jutting from the three aluminum framed panels lining one wall. The desk had been similarly cleared, but the bank of chargers bolted to the front wall remained, along with one lone radio flashing green with a full charge.

"They burned everything." Ankti lifted a basket of charred remains from behind the desk and poked at it with a ruler as Phil plucked up the little handheld radio. "Wait, here's something."

She pulled out a charred bit of map, the one they'd used to lay down the backroad route to Thursday night's ceremony. A fresh red line ran down to a highlighted area along the Salt River.

"Bet we'll find them down there." Phil held up the handheld radio, raised an eyebrow, and keyed the mic at Ankti's nod. "This is Phil Johnson calling tribal security. Do any of Jack Fletcher's people copy? Over."

Silence. He tried again and was about to slip the radio into his pocket when static burst from the speaker.

"Challenge phrase sky totem seven four." The female voice came in clear on the heels of the burst. "Please authenticate."

Just great!

"Do we have an authentication password?" Phil asked the other two.

Kay snorted and shrugged. Ankti shook her head, frowning, but then brightened.

"That's Susan Skydance." She waved for the radio, and Phil handed the device over. "Sue, this is Ankle Biter and those cookies are mine. Over." She released the transmit button and explained. "I was an annoying kid and on the small side. Susan's big sister was a real pain in the ass and called me Ankti Ankle Biter until I was big enough to knock her on her ass. The cookie story is too long to get into, but not something anyone else would know about."

They waited a good thirty seconds, hardly breathing.

"Well, I guess that'll do. Where the hell have you been, Ankti? Jack threw a fit when he couldn't find you two after the ceremony, and witnesses gave us everything from 'you'd run off into the night' to 'the demons dragged you away.'"

A few minutes of back and forth filled in details. After more Red Scarfs came calling on camp, Jack decided a move was necessary. Since salt loads still proved effective, he reasoned the demons wouldn't be able to cross the Salt River. They'd originally headed for the spot on the map, but had moved to a horseshoe bend in the river that offered protection on three sides.

Ankti told her they were inbound with a few more surprises to keep the Red Scarfs at bay. She also promised to meet with Jack and work out the safest way to escort people home so they didn't present such a big fat target. Phil nodded. They might be able to drive off normal Red Scarfs, but Erik and Kasandra were an entirely different story. They needed people out of the line of fire.

"Okay, we'll watch for your car," Susan said as she signed off. "Monitor this channel, and if you lose comms, change down to channel twenty-two. We'll see you soon. River Basin, out."

* * *

"So what exactly is the plan after we clear everyone out?" Phil asked as they rode down the dusty road toward the river.

They planned to distribute prayer bundles to drivers that could deliver folks back to their home reservations. The exodus had to be metered to give Grandmother Wikiwi's network of medicine women time to get the various regions under adequate protection. Aside from that, Phil only had a vague notion of how they would find and deal with the ringleaders.

"I have a little surprise in store for Erik and Kasandra," Kay said from the back seat. "Something I hope will convince them to leave Ankti and the tribes alone."

Kay patted Ankti's shoulder and left his hand resting lightly against her collarbone. Phil sighed, admitting to himself that he didn't understand this pair. In Kay's adobe domain, Ankti looked to be fed up with the man's overtures. But now, seeing how she leaned into the contact, he wasn't so sure. It shouldn't matter, but he didn't want to see her hurt. And knowing where Kay stood might be important in the coming conflict.

"We don't even know where those two are," Phil complained. "No one does. Jack's people only have vague reports of them flitting in here and there, leaving flaming Red Scarfs to do their dirty work."

"They're searching," Kay said. "Looking for me, and probably Ankti too—a futile effort now that my powers are returned. When we are ready, I'll let the wards keeping us hidden slip. Have no fear, once they sense us, they will come."

That was exactly what he *did* worry about. "And you're strong enough now to ensure she's safe?"

179

"*She's* right here, slick, so cool your jets." Ankti shot him a quick glare then scowled at the road ahead. "No doubt it'll be risky, but we've got to get these goons off our backs for good."

"I have something they want far more than simple revenge." Kay again laid his hand on her shoulder. "Their greed should keep them in line."

The sun blazed high overhead by the time they arrived at the barricade by the river. Jack's people had stacked cars and trailers across the narrow entrance to a spit of flatland ringed by the sandy shores of Salt River. The opposite side had been undercut by water, leaving jagged rocks that would make it difficult to enter the water unseen. And of course the salt water should deter the demons. A white shuttle bus with skirting tacked on its sides to cover wheels and undercarriage acted as a simple gate and rolled aside when the posted guards spotted them.

"Welcome to our little oasis." Jack strode over with Susan Skydance in tow as they spilled from the car.

"You've done well to put the river to your backs." Kay nodded in approval at the defensive ring.

Rather than their prior scattered arrangement, tents had been set up in a neat grid with fire rings near the corners. In addition to the gate guards, men and women with shotguns stood atop several trailers and scanned the road and ravine that would funnel any intruders down to camp. Two others faced the river, studying the lazy waters and far bank through binoculars.

"It's Kay, right?" Jack asked and continued at the man's nod. "Took us a bit to get the field of views and defenses dialed in. A couple of demons came poking around, and we even had one of those devil hounds slip in under the blockade before I thought to add skirting. Shotguns are still effective, but sooner or later we're going to run out of rock salt."

"We have something to help." Ankti popped the rear hatch open and pulled out her cardboard box of prayer bundles. "Put one in each car along the perimeter. Grandmother helped make them even more powerful than the ones we used before. She's also mobilized the women's circle and will let us know when it's safe for people to return home starting with the lower Hopi reservation near Cave Creek." She counted the cars and bundles. "You can run up to ten drivers and still have a couple of spare prayer bundles in case of emergency."

Phil found it interesting she didn't mention Kay's part, but then again, the security crew didn't see him as anything special—just an extra pair of hands, which was probably for the best. It was hard to imagine people back home taking supernatural enemies in stride like the tribes had, but who knew how Jack's crew would react if they knew a god incarnate walked among them—a god who was currently giving Susan a toothy smile that had the woman batting her eyes and turning crimson even as he slipped an arm around Ankti's waist.

"Turn down the charm a notch, cowboy." Phil's whisper made Kay's grin stretch wider, but with a little nod the sexual pressure resonating between both women and Kay dissipated.

The discussion turned businesslike, and in short order three drivers set out with the first crew of refugees heading up to Cave Creek. Jack dug up half a dozen radios for Wikiwi to distribute. Only about one in a hundred calls went through, so the Red Scarfs must have still controlled the cell towers. The handhelds used a reserved satellite frequency and would provide enough communication to orchestrate getting people home safely.

The entire process took three days, with cars rolling out at all hours in response to calls confirming various villages and areas had been made safe with the new charms. Jack used the spare bundles to position road guides along the ravine. Those assured a safe corridor out to the larger roads where it would be harder for the Red Scarfs to manage an ambush.

The bundles worked well, or perhaps the monsters had lost interest in the group. Either way, no one spotted a flaming skull or skulking demon animal along the road out. A few reports of Red Scarfs did come in over the radio, but never close enough to hurt anyone, so again the bundles were doing the trick.

A good number of the demons had been dispatched that first night by Ankti's glowing vines, but Phil worried the stragglers might be biding their time before making some big play. The security force that had started at about two dozen was down to four plus Jack. The rest returned to their home villages to beef up their defenses, which made sense since there was no one left to guard at the river camp.

"Now what?" Jack asked as the last carload rolled through the gate and disappeared into the long morning shadows.

19. The Setup

P HIL HELPED Jack's people rearrange the remaining vehicles. They formed a small corral where the humans could defend themselves. Several cars were seeded with the remaining prayer bundles, and two trailers provided ample height to watch their surroundings.

The arrangements left the road into camp unguarded. Kay pointed out that Erik and Kasandra crossing the defensive line would overload the bundles, rendering them useless. So they were put to better use protecting Phil and the others. Ankti would be out in the open with Kay, awaiting those who hunted them.

"That about does it," Susan said as she drove the final screw home to secure the trailer skirting Phil and Jack had been holding in place. "Only easy way in is through the mobile office here. Ladders inside the ring will let us get onto the roof quickly. Do we set watches right away or wait?"

"You know what's going on better than we do." Jack gave his end of the sheet metal an experimental pull and looked to Phil.

Getting the defensive position set up was the priority. After the others were safely behind the new walls, Kay would bait his trap and they'd wait. Jack passed a sack of supplies up to a thin man standing on the roof of a minivan that butted up against the trailer. They'd used the tallest vehicles but were relying on the bundles and guns to keep demons out.

"I know they want this done before dark." Phil looked out into the horseshoe of land. Kay sat before a teepee of burning logs. Ankti stood over him. "A few hours 'till dusk still. Let me go see what the plan is."

Phil walked slowly so they'd have time to notice him. He couldn't make out what they said, but judging by Ankti's curt hand gestures, she was angry. Kay nodded occasionally and kept feeding sticks into the fire. God or not, the guy was a classic pyro.

Phil took two more steps and staggered. The ground shook and leapt under his feet. The inbound road off to his right heaved and split, and a jagged crack shot across the entrance to the flats. The rock surface snapped in rapid succession, gunshots as the fissure widened to ten feet across, cutting off their spit of land.

Shouts rose from behind as two people on car roofs fought to keep from being thrown. One of the remaining trailers they hadn't needed to use in their new fence line sat too close to the road. It rocked and swayed as the ground opened up. The wheels jumped their chocks, and the trailer lurched forward into the gap, twisting as it fell to crunch against the far side like a derailed model train. If they'd left the original blockade in place, most of the cars would have been swallowed.

Phil hurried the last few yards to Ankti. Kay stared into his little fire as if waiting for someone to pass the marshmallows. At least he wasn't wearing that infuriating smile. But neither did he seem annoyed despite the woman yelling at him.

"I *told* you it was too soon!" She jabbed a finger at Kay and waved at his fire.

"Peace, Ankti. This will be what it is." No smile, but infuriatingly placid given flaming heads rose within the trench as Red Scarfs marched up from the depths.

There must be a ladder or ramp inside the fissure—assuming they hadn't been lifted by magic. A dozen of the black creatures spilled onto their side of the chasm. Not as many as Phil had feared, but who knew what else was coming for them? Jack's people had already hurried into position.

"I assume your wards are down?" Phil didn't really need an answer. "A little warning would have been nice."

"Take this and get back with the others." Ankti pressed one of the little wooden grenades—soul catchers, Kay had called them—into his hand and kept one for herself.

"Like hell." Phil hated the thought of leaving Ankti out in the open, even under Kay's protection.

Ankti's anger shifted from Kay to Phil. "Get your ass out of here!"

"Do not move," Kay commanded, and Phil didn't think he could have stepped away if he wanted to because the power in those words settled over his legs, rooting him in place.

High pitched hissing like escaping steam or a punctured propane tank rose from the chasm, followed by a long, grinding scrape. A claw big enough to carry off a German Shepherd rose from the opening and slammed down on the rocky ground, fresh billows of dust making the flames dance over the skeletal heads of the waiting Red Scarfs. A massive green snout and body followed, hugging the ground as it rose from the depths.

Uktena had come to join the fight after all—but no, as it slithered forth, Phil saw the color was a dark mottled green, ugly compared to the great serpent's iridescent plates. And this monster wore a dull pebbly hide instead of shining scales. Its ropy black tongue shot forth to taste the air before retracting through needle teeth that slanted back into the cavernous mouth. The squat fat creature emerged on stubby legs like an overgrown monitor lizard stretching only half the length of the dragon, but still more than formidable.

"If you run, instinct will take over." Kay waved a hand, and Phil found himself again able to move. "And to answer your question, no, the wards are still up. I'm dropping them now, but this may get messy."

"You could not hide forever, old man." The words slid forth in a rich female alto out of synch with the movements of the blocky muscular jaw, like poorly dubbed dialogue in a foreign film.

The lizard cocked its head, the vertical black pupil of its near eye swiveling to focus on them. It looked more like a snake than a lizard eye, more like the eyes he'd glimpsed on Kasandra just before Pina had yanked him through the gate between worlds.

"Impatient as always, Kasandra. Shouldn't you wait for your master?" Kay's question drew a hiss from the monster, from the woman.

Even though Ankti had explained that the skinwalker could shift forms, what about conservation of mass? That alone should keep her from becoming something this big.

"Erik is no master of mine!" Kasandra hissed then seemed to recover her poise—or as much poise as a two-ton lizard could muster—and her voice softened to a purring threat. "Even when not yourself, you get under my skin. This will be fun. I knew you couldn't keep away from the people. All I had to do was wait."

"Monster, what *are* you, and what do you want?" Kay shook his head, looking convincingly perplexed.

"How delightful." Rich female laughter echoed from deep in the thing's gullet. "You still don't remember. We go way back, and every time our paths cross, you seem to be in my way. Erik is even more angry about it than I."

"So you want revenge," Kay said.

"Erik does love payback, and we both need you out from underfoot." Her voice turned silky, almost lustful, which left Phil queasy as he gaped at the hulking lizard. "But he need never know you returned. I could simply leave and forget about you and your friends."

What was this? It had to be a trick, but Kay leaned forward, clearly intrigued. In his eagerness, the fringes of his tunic swept close to the flames of his little fire.

"Why would you do that?" Ankti stepped into the conversation, her tone sharp. "You and your minions attack us, and you chase down poor Kay like a fugitive. Not exactly the actions of someone willing to walk away. What do you want?"

"So it's Kay now. How quaint." Kasandra stepped closer so her snout hovered twenty feet from the fire. Although Ankti had asked the question, the lizard focused on the man sitting placidly before the burning logs. "As you can see, I am a hunter. The fun was in the chase, but now I grow bored. Give me a small token so I may show I bested you. That bauble on your belt would do nicely."

Oh crap, she wants the flute!

Ankti gasped, apparently reaching the same conclusion. She took a step back and bumped into him as the monster leered and a great slinger of drool slipped from the corner of its mouth.

Even when Kay had no idea who he was, the instrument worked to keep him out of harm's way. Ankti said it was a potent artifact. Not necessarily the source of the god's power, but the world wouldn't be safe for any of them if something as evil as this skinwalker commanded the flute's magic.

"Ah, you want this." Kay dropped a hand to his waist, but instead of touching the flute, his fingers ran over the shimmering triangle holding his belt together.

"Yeeesssss!" Flecks of spittle rode the eager word, some even reaching the fire and landing with an angry hiss.

She wants his belt buckle?

Kay nodded in understanding, but Phil didn't get it. Sure, it was big and pretty, a gaudy hammered concho inlaid with green stone, probably semi-precious but nothing to rival the value of that flute. The stone reminded him of polished abalone shell, iridescent and shimmering through shades of green instead of pearl and blue. He'd seen similar colors somewhere recently…under the blazing sky of Kokopelli's domain.

"That's one of Uktena's scales," Phil whispered to Ankti. "What the hell does she want with *that*?"

"But what would hold my pants up?" Kay actually smiled at his little joke. "And why on Earth would you want this?"

"Just a trophy to prove I bested you, old man." Kasandra drew a step nearer.

"Like hell." Ankti gripped Phil's forearm, her whisper hard and brittle. "She could use that to change, to become the great serpent."

"No, I better keep the wardrobe together."

Kay's mild reply caught the monster off-guard. She took another step but paused with foreleg raised. The giant head swayed in agitation. Kasandra finally drew in a great breath and let it hiss back out as a massive sigh.

"Then I guess we do this the hard way." Kasandra flicked her front right claw, sending out a cord of energy like the whip she'd used to bind Kay last time.

He'd need the flute to block the blow. But instead of reaching for the instrument, Kay simply raised his left hand, caught the whip, and yanked it from the lizard's claw. The length of the cord exploded in a shower of gold sparks and was gone.

"Impossible!" The monster lashed out again, looking clumsy as she used the giant claw for a task better suited to human hands.

The spell that sizzled toward them was more powerful and spread wide to snare all three. Kay clapped his hands over his head, sending out a wave of blue-white energy that blew the net to pieces.

"Wenona Kasa Kakawangwa, I said no." Kay wagged a finger at the beast.

"You know my full name. You block my spells." Kasandra glared and flexed her claw as if working feeling back into it. "Faker!"

"Trickster *is* my nature." He stood and gave a shallow bow, acknowledging her conclusion. "But you are correct, I have fully recovered. So perhaps—"

The monster lurched sideways, spun away, and smashed her tail into one of the abandoned vehicles, launching the small blue car at them like a lopsided bowling ball. It came on with screeching metal and shattering glass and would have flattened them all if Kay hadn't drawn his flute. With a wave of the instrument, the wreck bounced left at the last moment, but fiberglass shrapnel pelted Phil and Ankti.

The lizard came hard on the car's heels, snapping at Kay. The fire flared as he reversed his swing and the flute lengthened into a staff, catching Kasandra on the jaw. Power flashed where teeth raked the magical barrier separating lizard from prey. Kay drove the staff up under the massive creature's chin, flipping her over sideways so that she landed on her back with a mighty crash. The effort left Kay panting over his fire, which had blazed high during the exchange before dropping back to a cheery little blaze.

Kasandra thrashed, her tail whipping the ground until she managed to roll herself upright. Dark ichor dripped from a jagged hole in the hide under her jaw, and her orange eyes glowed with hatred.

Phil shielded his own eyes as a sizzling bolt of dark energy slammed to the ground between them and Kasandra. It hit with a deafening crack, leaving magenta afterimages. Erik stood tall in his shining leather armor amid a circle of molten sand, axe held loosely in his left hand and a smile pulling his beard and mustache wide.

"You could not hide forever," Erik said as he took in the scene. "Huddling with your friends behind crude talismans worked for a while, but your time is up."

"Take him now, Erik, while he is weak." Kasandra flicked her tongue at Kay, then swabbed it across her bloody chin.

"You hunt well in that form." Erik looked the lizard up and down with a frown. "His pitiful wards fell just moments ago, so how is it I find you already here and making a mess of things?" He pointed the axe at her wound, but shrugged and turned back to Kay. "No matter. The time has come."

Erik roared as he charged, axe lifted high and clearly meaning to cleave Kay from the world. The fighting style telegraphed his intentions. Kay had no problem bringing his staff up to intercept the blow even as Erik grinned in triumph. But the Viking's eyes went round when blade met wood with a mighty flash of power. He staggered back and gaped at a glowing half circle where a chunk of the blade had been blasted away.

This time Erik came on slow and deliberate, pacing around Kay in a wary circle and making the man twist to stay face to face. Erik lunged with an underhand thrust meant to hook the staff and sweep it from Kay's hands. As the shafts of the weapons met, Kay grunted and the fire flared high. The two struggled for control, each trying to pull his opponent's weapon free. Neither saw the lizard dart close.

Kasandra's tongue shot out and the forked tip wrapped around the dragon scale at Kay's belt. He glanced down just as the scale tore free. The muscles along his shoulders rippled and with a mighty heave, Kay yanked the axe from Erik's hands and with a sweep of the staff cut his legs out from under him.

Erik landed hard in the dirt. Kay stood over him with staff in one hand, dark axe in the other. He cast a furtive glance at the retreating lizard, but couldn't afford to turn his back on his opponent. Kasandra headed for the chasm, intent on deserting her comrade and fleeing with her prize.

Phil clutched the grenade Ankti had given him. These were made to counter Red Scarfs, not the skinwalker. But the lizard was already disappearing into the gap.

"Hey, Godzilla!" Phil yelled and ran for the trailer spanning the far end of the fissure.

As Kay had warned, the movement triggered some primal hunting urge. The massive head jerked in his direction. Kasandra climbed from the crevice and came for him—slowly at first, but building speed as all four feet hit the ground. Her tongue still dangled from the left side of her mouth, clutching Uktena's scale. The lizard wouldn't be able to chomp him without biting off her own tongue, but those claws gouging furrows in the rocky ground were another thing entirely.

The roof of the toppled trailer sat just below the near side of the fissure. If this didn't work, he might be able to scramble across and drop to the ground on the far side, but it looked like a mighty unreliable bridge.

Holding the scale meant the lizard had to keep its mouth open, and pitching in high school had given Phil a decent arm. He clamped down on a rising panic, hauled back, and threw. The little wood cylinder tumbled end over end in a flat line drive and disappeared down the thing's gullet.

For a long moment nothing happened. He stepped out onto the makeshift bridge, just as the lizard planted all four feet and skid to a stop in a cloud of dust, head swiveling as if looking for something on the ground. Then she went very still.

A white tendril of light snaked out alongside the black tongue, followed by a second. The trap that pulled the Red Scarfs down had consisted of delicate vines. These were thicker, ending in barbed arrowheads. Kasandra raked at her mouth with a claw as more cords burst forth, their wicked ends twisting and jabbing, looking for purchase. One curled up over her eye ridge, but a massive swipe dislodged it before the tip blinded her. Another speared into the wound Kay had left, and the lizard keened and thrashed as the energy sank in.

Kasandra slammed her head into an outcropping, trying to dislodge the spell and leaving a bloody trail where she scraped along the rocks. The scale flew loose as she thrashed. Phil climbed off the shuddering roof and sprinted for the belt buckle. To his left Kasandra curled in tight on herself, tail and legs blurring into a compact silhouette that rapidly shrank.

He scooped up the scale, its unexpected weight throwing him off balance as he staggered on to Ankti. Though only the size of his hand, the thing had to weigh five pounds. Ankti steadied him as he sucked in a lungful of hot air.

Kay had backed away from Erik, still holding staff and axe but letting the other climb to his feet. Ankti pushed Phil to the right, putting Kay between them and the monsters.

The frantic lizard hisses changed to frustrated growls. Kasandra settled into her human form, spitting out bits of white energy along with her curses. Blood trickled from a puncture on her lily-white throat. She looked disheveled and exhausted, but the wound didn't seem to bother her.

She cast about searching the ground and narrowed her eyes at the scale glittering in Phil's hand. He revised his opinion of her appearance. *Human-ish.* Kasandra wore the angular features of a hunter, perhaps preparing to turn into the loping nightmare from the other night. She took a step forward. Erik blurred into motion, moving faster than should have been possible, and grabbed Kasandra around the throat with a beefy hand.

"You knew!" He lifted the woman off her feet as he yelled in her face. "Setting me against a fully recovered god as a distraction to gain your trinket. You selfish bitch!"

He shook Kasandra like a rag doll and threw her to the ground, hard. She landed in a heap. The attack would have killed a mere human, but the skinwalker climbed to her feet, dusted off her blazer, and turned a sneer on her companion.

"As if you haven't been using me on this inane hunt of yours," Kasandra said. "I don't care one way or the other about the humans and their virus."

Both bristled, and for a moment it seemed they might go at it and spare Kay the trouble. But something unspoken passed between the two. Their postures relaxed—though the look in Erik's flaming eyes promised a future accounting—and they turned to face Kay.

20. The Deal

"**N**OW THAT everyone knows where they stand, we can get on with business." Kay's staff shrank down, becoming the wooden flute. He slipped the instrument into his belt and dropped Erik's axe next to the fire. "You two need to take your minions and leave these people alone."

Erik leaned forward, looking as though he might lunge for his weapon. By now he certainly realized Kay—Kokopelli—was at full strength and not to be trifled with. But the man was by no means cowed. The Red Scarf demons clumped in a tight little group off to their right just beyond shotgun range of Jack's rooftop guards, waiting.

"And why would we do that?" Erik asked. "You can't be everywhere at once."

"Because of this." Kay lifted his right hand, again holding up a staff.

But his flute hung on his belt, and what he brandished was only three feet long, more of a baton. Unlike his crude carved walking staff, this work of art gleamed with polished perfection. The wood formed an elegant spiral that looped gracefully from foot to jeweled head. A smooth knobby lump of turquoise the size of a child's fist sat on top encircled by the spiral as if the mineral had grown within the tree from which it was carved.

"It's a trick," Kasandra shrieked. "How could you have the Staff of Balance?"

"Open your *sight*." Kay held the beautiful object high. "Feel its power and know this is no illusion. You will leave this place in peace, and I will return the staff to the Neutral Council where it will neither benefit nor harm your cause. Defy me, and it goes to the Light Court."

"That power was never meant for the courts," Erik said.

"No, it was not," Kay agreed. "But if you do not leave these people be, I will ensure it makes its way into the hands of one of the more…aggressive lords."

"The potential for destruction would be too great." Erik shook his head, but did not look at all certain. "They wouldn't stop with thwarting our plans for the humans. You wouldn't risk it."

"Do not underestimate my nature." Kay's sly smile returned, the trickster shining in his eyes with fanatic intensity that raised gooseflesh on Phil's arms. None of them knew what the god Kokopelli was truly capable of.

Judging by their sour expressions Erik and Kasandra saw it too.

"Why do you care about them?" Erik's voice broke into a hoarse, demanding whine, as though he just couldn't fathom Kay's motives. "They are mere mortals."

"Hey, we're right here." Phil's face grew hot, but he was sick of always being caught in the crossfire and couldn't seem to stop himself. "You might be stronger than we are and live longer. But you know what, buddy? There's always someone bigger, someone tougher. You aren't exactly at the top of the food chain, so cut the rest of us some frickin' slack!"

That last assertion was a guess based on the cautious way this pair eyed Kay. From the little they'd talked to Pina and what he'd observed, Phil was pretty certain these two fell squarely in the middle of the pack when it came to dark forces. Older, more ancient beings that could use Erik to wipe the floor with one hand tied behind their back had to exist. Still, having said his piece, Phil's stomach clenched and threatened to undermine his brash words. He stepped back and bumped into Ankti.

"*That's* why I like them." Kay beamed at Phil and slipped in a little wink for Ankti. "Well and fearlessly spoken to a being that will outlive him for eons and could crush him in a heartbeat. Humans are a marvel of contradictions and surprises."

Phil sighed. Sometimes Kay just didn't get it, and neither Kasandra nor Erik looked convinced.

"Take some time to decide." Kay swung the staff in a circle as if to encourage them not to take too long. "But I want this business concluded by dark."

With that declaration, the two groups parted. Erik, Kasandra, and their demons moved to the far end of the chasm, while Kay and the humans headed off to join Jack's people within their defensive ring. Kay gratefully accepted Uktena's scale and clipped it back on his belt as they walked. The weight should have dragged the guy's pants down, but of course didn't. Phil just shook his head—magic.

"This is some insane shit," Jack said after maneuvering the gate vehicle back in place and making certain his handful of defenders were in position with sufficient ammunition. "It sounded like you gave them an ultimatum. Any chance they'll leave in peace?"

"Under normal circumstances I wouldn't expect those two to honor *any* agreement." Kay brandished the Staff of Balance and jammed it into the dirt near the fire so that it stood upright, but he never took his hand off it. "I am hoping this will change their minds."

Phil blinked at the cheerily burning teepee of logs. *How the hell did that get inside the enclosure?* He peered through the dusty back windows of an SUV that was part of the barricade. Rocky ground stretched to where the little fire had been just a minute ago. There wasn't even a burnt patch left out there.

"So another powerful artifact as a bargaining chip." Phil kept one eye on Jack to see how the man was coping. His own internal struggle to come to grips with this craziness had left him questioning reality for a time. But as a group the Native Americans proved more resilient and seemed to accept recent events without mind-bending gymnastics. "Still sounds like you're walking a pretty thin line though."

"What is a staff of balance?" Ankti asked. "Its power spirals and pulses in one direction, then reverses—over and over. Very unlike your own energies." She studied Kay's face through narrowed eyes as if daring him to lie. "Tell me you didn't steal it."

"*The* Staff of Balance was forged by Damballa the great creator as a badge of office when the Neutral Council formed. It lends the council power to enforce their misguided notion of balance. Tia, the goddess of peaceful death, chairs that body. She grew tired of the games and back and forth of the courts, a sentiment I wholeheartedly agree with. But the concept of enforcing stagnant détente, with neither side ever gaining clear advantage will have us all dying of boredom. Without the natural ebb and flow of struggles between light and dark, both courts will crumble."

"Why not just make good on your threat then, give the staff to your Light Court buddies, and let them take care of these clowns?" Ankti asked.

"The courts are not easily painted black and white. Neither is fully evil nor good." Kay warmed his hands over the flames. "Your own stories and legends tell of the dangers inherent in the Light Court. Suffice to say that Erik is quite right. If the staff fell into the hands of even one with good intentions the consequences would be unpredictable at best and catastrophic at worst."

The smile was back in Kay's eyes, as if he relished the idea of witnessing such chaos. Friend or not, Phil realized they had no true insight into how far Kay might take things.

"So you steal her badge of office to back down the Red Scarfs." Phil scratched his head as he tried to puzzle out how that could be. "But you've been with us recovering. When did you have time?"

"Time is more fluid than you may imagine." Kay fell silent, looking lost in thought. "But to answer your question, I acquired the staff before we met. I had help from an old friend and had other plans for this beauty." He caressed the turquois insert and raised his other hand to forestall an angry rebuke from Ankti. "It was borrowed, not stolen, but I hate to return it so soon."

"You'll have to in order to keep your end of the bargain." Ankti nodded in satisfaction, apparently keen to see the staff back in the hands of its rightful owner.

"I doubt it," Kay said absently. "Erik will almost certainly betray any agreement. As much as I'd like it to be otherwise, I'll be dealing with him and Kasandra again."

"If this is just a temporary fix, then what's the point?" Phil's head spun trying to find the logic. It was starting to sound like a big game with Ankti and the others as sacrificial pawns. "They'll just blast you out of the sky like last time." Outrage flitted across Kay's face, telling Phil he'd struck a nerve. "Or am I wrong in assuming this pair of lunatics were the ones responsible for your injuries the night we found you burnt and broken?"

It made sense. They'd been hunting him the night of the ceremony and ever since. It had always been about stopping Kokopelli from helping the tribes. Ankti laid a hand on Kay's shoulder, concern furrowing her brow.

"Worry not, my flower." Kay shot an angry glare at Phil. "They had help last time, two hidden allies that struck from the shadows. Who worked with them remains a mystery, but the help doubled their power—that and that alone is the reason I fell." He bristled and nodded as if internally rationalizing that prior defeat. "Kasandra and Erik are formidable, but I am in no danger, especially with this." He gave the Staff of Balance two sharp raps.

What a mess.

"If time's so malleable, maybe you should just jump back and stop all this before it starts," Phil grumbled under his breath.

"There is a certain…inertia to these things," Kay said. "It would once more come down to a bargain unlikely to be honored. With no clear way to avoid it, events would again unfold as they have."

"Can't you—"

"Boss!" Susan called from atop the nearest trailer. "You're going to want to see this."

Jack broke away from the group, and Phil followed. Susan pointed out into the growing shadows of late afternoon. Six figures scrambled across the trailer spanning the chasm. A broad man wearing a khaki uniform led the others to the rolling gate. Phil worried the bedraggled group might be set upon before reaching the enclosure, but the Red Scarfs were nowhere to be seen.

"Brandon, what the devil are you doing out here?" Jack's call brought the procession to a halt and a smile to the haggard face of the man in the lead.

Beneath the grime and matted hair, it was indeed Brandon Owlfeather. The security chief's uniform hadn't fared much better than the clothes of the dark-haired group of men and women he led. The others were dressed in what had once been casual business attire before the desert erased the luster from leather shoes and decorated jackets and skirts with ragged tears.

"Getting our butts handed to us is what we're doing. We followed the smoke in and could really use some help."

"Susan, get this bus out of the way." Jack pitched his voice so the others standing guard could hear. "Stay sharp while we're exposed and sing out if you see any uninvited guests coming our way."

Susan and the skinny young man hurried to roll the gate vehicle back and usher the weary group inside before sealing the gap. Brandon's people were despondent and shuffled inside quietly. The maneuver was completed with a minimum of commotion and no interference from Red Scarfs. But they all breathed easier as the bus rolled back into place.

"Where the hell have you been?" Jack slapped Brandon on the back and grinned broadly. "Thought you'd headed for the hills or worse."

"Long story." Brandon's voice was a dry croak. "These people need water first and food if you have any to spare."

"Is that the missing Navajo delegation?" Ankti asked as the group shuffled after Susan toward the shade of the supply trailer.

There were no smiles or chatter among the weary people. Every head hung low, focusing on the ground as if to ensure they didn't misstep.

"Sure is." Brandon gratefully accepted a bottle of water from the young man and swigged half of it down. "Found them wandering out by Devil's Creek, all turned around. They're a little disoriented and dehydrated. Figured we'd head to the river and work our way west. Smoke from your little blaze brought us along the wash there." He swung the plastic bottle toward the path they'd used. "That's an awfully big crack in the ground. Everyone okay?"

"That's a long story too, but everyone's fine given the circumstances." Jack said. "Glad you got these folks headed in the right direction, but what the devil were you doing out there alone in the first place? You've been gone for days, and we looked everywhere."

"You know, I can't rightly say." The big security chief scratched his matted hair, then grimaced at the dirt caked under his nails. "I went to check on Tommy up at the ceremonial grounds, and the next thing you know, I'm in the middle of nowhere hopping over cacti and looking for familiar landmarks."

Further discussion with Brandon grew frustrating. They discussed what transpired in his absence and filled him in on the organized attacks, how moving the ceremony bought them time to complete the rituals, and the fact they had to evacuate everyone to a safe location in the face of continued Red Scarf raids.

Brandon perked up as the water revived him and asked plenty of questions about how they kept the demons at bay for so long, but in return offered frustratingly scant information about his own circumstances. Several days appeared to have been wiped from the man's memory.

The security chief applauded Ankti's ingenuity in relocating the ceremony. Though no one mentioned how Kay helped improve the defensive prayer bundles and grenades, Brandon nodded in approval of distributing them to protect villages and bolster the ring of cars making up their little enclosure.

"Better than hanging fuzzy dice." Brandon forced out a short barking laugh to accompany the lame joke when he spied the bundles they'd hung from each rearview mirror.

Ankti and Phil left the security chief chatting with his deputy and tried to engage the Navajo delegation. They'd been the last group expected for the ceremony and presumably stopped by Red Scarf roadblocks. Despite food and water, the group remained sullen and disoriented, having apparently suffered more exposure than Brandon.

With many leading questions and a bit of badgering they established the group had entered Phoenix from the north when they pulled up to an unexpected roadblock. Despite complying with the deputy's requests, they found themselves detained. The story unfolded mostly as a series of head nods, grunts, and single word responses.

Even the most talkative of the group, an older man with sunken cheeks and rheumy eyes, refused to say more than that they too had found themselves wandering and lost in the desert.

When Phil and Ankti rejoined the others, Brandon acknowledged the delegation was a sullen lot, made his apologies, and went to speak with them himself.

"So much for minimizing the number of civilians," Ankti said as Brandon sat down with the others. "Kay, if your plan gets Erik to back off for a while, maybe we can load everyone in a car beyond the chasm. Susan said the red van out there is gassed up and ready to go."

"We could ship them off now," Phil said. "There hasn't been anyone out there in hours."

"No." Kay shook his head. "Kasandra and Erik are waiting and hidden. Sending people beyond this enclosure would not be safe."

Time passed in silence as the sun worked its way to the horizon and a night chill forced them all closer to the fire. Brandon's talk revived the others, or maybe the dried beef and trail mix finally hit bottom. Either way, it seemed a good sign that the newcomers began to show interest in their surroundings. With coaxing from the security chief, they moved about the small compound, checking out the defenses. As long as none of them tried to climb out through a car, they were safe enough. Jack's guards still manned the rooftops, though Phil wondered at the effectiveness of that strategy when Erik's voice boomed out of the gloom before security spotted him.

"Old man!" Erik called from beyond the barricade. "We have your answer."

21. Fight or Flight

FLAMING HEADS flickered just beyond the gate as the Red Scarfs fanned out and surrounded the enclosure like an invading army setting up a siege. Kasandra and Erik stood directly across from the gate vehicle, brash and confident again now that they'd had time away from Kay.

"Shall we?" Kay asked, the ghost of his grin returning.

Susan rolled the bus back just enough to let them through before closing the gap, but stayed behind the wheel, ready to let them in on a moment's notice. Phil, Ankti, and Kay strode out to meet the enemy. The rest of Jack's people took their rooftop stations with weapons at the ready and all eyes on their small procession.

They hadn't told the security people much, just to watch and be ready to let them fall back behind the prayer line if things went sideways. Hopefully the Red Scarfs would leave long enough to get the humans to safety, which Kay thought likely—assuming they at least made a show of honoring an agreement concerning the staff.

Kay held the Staff of Balance before him, a reminder of his threat should they fail to cooperate and a warning that he could draw on its power if betrayed. The Red Scarf demons parted to let them through to face the two leaders. No one spoke, and the quiet standoff stretched on uncomfortably.

"We've come to meet," Kay finally said.

Light flickered behind them, reflecting off his lustrous mane of hair. Phil whipped around to find that the stupid fire had again followed and sat burning just ten paces away—another demarcation between themselves and the ring of demons standing sentinel around the enclosure. That cheery little teepee of logs was starting to give him the willies.

"Before any agreement can be struck, we need specifics," Erik said. "Who exactly you will give the staff to if we agree to leave these humans be."

"The artifact belongs to Tia, goddess of peaceful death," Kay said. "Assuming she is not in her alternate incarnation, I will return the staff to her. You can be assured *she* will do all in her power to maintain balance."

"Which includes keeping you from interfering, old man," Kasandra said.

"So it does." Kay shook his head and let out a low chuckle. "As misguided as her actions are, Tia's motives are pure."

"And what of the other magics you've given these people?" Erik pointed his axe at Ankti, having recovered the weapon since Kay disarmed him. Interestingly, the blade was again intact.

"They will keep that small knowledge. It is no more than their ancestors once possessed."

"Unacceptable." Kasandra spat out the word like a curse as she rubbed the wound on her neck and glared at Phil, perhaps remembering the grenade she'd swallowed.

The great beings settled into what amounted to childish banter. They traded off concessions over the next half an hour. Erik vowed the Dark Court would leave the tribes alone, but insisted Ankti be turned over as some sort of sacrifice to appease his damaged honor. Of course Kay vetoed that, which spiraled the discussion into tit-for-tat bickering about allowances that made little sense to Phil.

The three diddled and dithered back and forth over the details of Kay's promise to no longer use his powers to help Native Americans prosper and reproduce, including—but not limited to—a laundry list of dos and don'ts.

Back in Kokopelli's domain, Pina had made quite the sour face when Uktena and Kay entered into discussions. She'd also gone on at length on how great spirits communed for hours, sometimes days, leaving lesser beings chomping at the bit to get on with things.

Night fell in earnest. He and Ankti slumped, exhausted by the day's events and the sheer tedium of listening to bickering and pointless minutiae. But an odd sense of unease crept in with the fatigue. As minutes stretched to hours, Phil became increasingly certain Erik was stalling.

Phil surveyed the landscape, but all seemed in its place. Kay's wandering fire still flickered quietly behind them, and the ring of Red Scarfs burned like sullen matches in the distance. All seemed as it had, except…the flaming skulls were just a few steps from the barricade and on the move, walking with determined strides back toward the negotiations.

Making things out in the gloom was difficult. Phil shielded his eyes against the fire's glare, trying to figure out why the Red Scarfs looked bulky and wrong. Each carried something large.

"What the hell have they done?" Ankti turned to study the approaching figures.

Each demon carried a limp body. The biggest of the bruisers hoisted Jack by his armpits so that the man appeared to be walking in front of the Red Scarf, except Jack was unconscious—hopefully—and dangled like a life-sized doll. The others were all being carried away from the enclosure: Susan, the skinny boy, and the rest.

People walked behind the Red Scarfs, Brandon's large frame most notable among the missing delegation. Further back, the doors to every car making up the enclosure stood open, the avenue by which camp had been compromised. The demons stopped short of Kay's fire, and the individuals trailing them stepped into the light. Brandon's people walked like dazed zombies, with scraps of cloth dangling forgotten from their hands.

"They pulled the prayer bundles apart," Ankti said.

Phil cursed. He'd been so focused, so bored, by the proceedings that he hadn't kept his eyes open. Brandon and the others hadn't been suffering from exposure, they'd been bespelled and taken down the defenses from the inside. They must have overpowered the guards too since no shots had been fired. *Stupid, stupid, stupid!*

Each demon slipped a hand up around the throat of the unconscious person it held. Kay raised the staff a fraction.

"I wouldn't, old man. Try anything and necks snap like popcorn." Kasandra held out a well-manicured hand, victory shining in her snake-eyes. "In fact, why don't you just hand over that staff right now? Then we'll leave you all in peace."

"You know I cannot do that," Kay said.

"Not even for them?" Kasandra looked to the lead Red Scarf and nodded.

Every demon tightened its grip and twisted, bending their respective captive's neck off at an angle that would have been excruciating if they were awake. Phil imagined he could hear spines creak under the pressure. It wouldn't take any effort at all for these inhuman monsters to finish the task and turn those people into a pile of corpses. Ankti sucked in a sharp breath, the sound catching Kay's attention. He studied her sad eyes and furrowed brow—anger and misery warring across her beautiful face.

"But so many more will die," Kay whispered.

"I know"—her breath caught on a sob—"you can't."

Kay's gaze swept from Ankti to the captives and settled on the staff laying in his open hand. Agony etched his rugged features, a raw, palpable anguish. His fist tightened around the wood as if prepared to go on the offensive. But his shoulders slumped, and his grip relaxed. He held out both hands with the staff laying across his open palms, offering up the artifact.

A wicked smile spread across the skinwalker's face, and she snatched the Staff of Balance.

"Yes!" Erik slammed the butt of his axe into the ground. "Kasandra, I had my doubts about your plan. But sending the ensorcelled humans to do our work for us was a stroke of genius. Nothing can stop our plans now."

Kasandra brandished the artifact like a sword, testing its balance with an evil glint in her eyes. Her gaze fell on Kay, who stood blinking at his empty hands as if unable to comprehend what he'd just done.

"You promised not to hurt him." Ankti hurried to Kay's side, wrapped a protective arm around his shoulders, and gently pushed down the open hands he still held forth. "And to let them go." She waved at the Red Scarfs still holding their captives by necks on the verge of breaking.

"They are no longer of consequence." Kasandra lifted her chin, and the Red Scarfs stepped away, letting their prisoners hit the ground like bags of wet cement. "The suffering of your short-lived, inconsequential species will fuel our rise."

Whatever compulsion had been laid on Brandon and the others lifted, and light came back into their eyes. Confusion gave way to horror as they took in the scene and backed away from the flaming demons. Jack's security people lifted groggy heads and scuttled back to join the group forming behind Phil.

"None of it matters." Kay patted Ankti's hand, spoke quietly into her ear, and gently pushed the woman toward Phil before looking up at his antagonist. "How does it feel to win for once, Kasandra?"

The question rose from what sounded like the depths of despair, but an impish grin twitched at the corner of Kay's mouth.

"It feels like the beginning of a new era." Erik answered for his companion. "A future where you and the Light Court dwindle to insignificance."

"And I will lead the forces of darkness," Kasandra crowed as Erik narrowed his eyes at the interruption, his jaw tight. "Gods and goddesses alike will bow before me and…" Kasandra thrust the staff high in triumph, but her words faltered as the wood blurred and shifted. She found herself waving an old style toilet plunger complete with wooden handle and red rubber cup. "What is this?"

"Just something I thought you could use. I found it in one of the trailers." Kay's trickster smile returned with a vengeance. "You should always inspect the goods on an important transaction."

The Staff of Balance—the real one this time, judging by the looks Kasandra and Erik shot Kay—materialized in Kay's right hand.

"Kill the humans!" Kasandra screamed.

The Red Scarfs pivoted to face the people huddled behind Phil. But Ankti's arm flashed out and her last grenade landed amidst the demons. White vines blossomed and spear-tipped leaves impaled black flesh. Erik roared, seemingly on the verge of charging the humans himself.

"If you want this come and take it," Kay taunted them with the staff as he took a step back, spun, and sprinted away.

Kay headed straight for the chasm, and Kasandra's hunting instincts took over. She snarled and flashed after him, her arms and legs lengthening to ghoulish proportions. She fell into a loping trot that ate up the ground. Erik followed close on his heels, looking disgusted but clearly unwilling to lose his prize.

They would have already lost sight of Kay in the gathering gloom if not for the spears of yellow energy the skinwalker threw at his retreating back. He managed to deflect the first few strikes, but the next caught him squarely between the shoulders and he stumbled.

Phil wasn't worried. This was just an act, another of Kay's tricks. But Ankti gasped and clutched his arm. He looked down and saw fear in her eyes. But their friend was a god and had already proven himself more than a match for this pair. At his questioning look, she gazed down at something clutched in her trembling left hand.

"He's vulnerable," Ankti's whispered as she brought Kay's flute into the firelight.

Crap!

Erik and Kasandra closed on their quarry, and crimson balls of fire from the black axe joined the magical attack. Despite his earlier confidence Kay stumbled under the onslaught. It looked like he might simply plunge into the chasm, hoping to take his pursuers with him. But Kay staggered up a slope Phil didn't recall, climbing above ground level.

The scene didn't make sense in the sporadic energy flashes. Kay continued to climb, while his pursuers…didn't. A rapid-fire barrage painted the landscape just as their friend hit the drop-off. There was no hill; Kay raced on a good fifteen feet above the ground. With what looked like a mighty leap, his legs went still, and he zoomed out past the chasm edge still gaining altitude. Kasandra and Erik pushed off at the last possible second, sailed across the gap, and rose into the distance in hot pursuit.

And just like that, Phil and Ankti found themselves alone with the refugees.

"Of course," Phil said into the stunned silence. "Now they fly."

22. Rabbit with a Timepiece

W ELL THAT *didn't go as planned.* Kokopelli zoomed into the night sky, drawing Erik and Kasandra away from the defenseless humans, away from lovely Ankti.

Wind whipped past, growing colder the higher he climbed. The plunging temperature was easier to ignore than the magic pummeling him from behind. Not quite pain, the energy crashed against his defenses like shockwaves from angry surf. Yet it was something he could power through, and the experience made him feel somehow more alive.

Kokopelli slowed, adding a wobble to his trajectory to keep Erik and Kasandra interested. Letting them believe they could bring him down was critical—and more than merely an act. Slipping his flute to Ankti left a void, a hollow weakness that should have brimmed with power. But he couldn't risk leaving her exposed as he fled—her and the other humans, he amended. This adversary had surprised him twice now. He was not willing to be fooled a third time, especially if it put his Hopi flower in danger.

He'd known the pair wouldn't let things go easily but had expected them to strike from the shadows after making their false agreements. He could have paid closer attention, should have seen the trap closing. *Sands through the hourglass at this point.* Any peace would be short-lived at best, so a more permanent solution was needed.

He grunted as another fiery ball slammed into his stomach from below, forcing him to increase his lead or risk taking more punishment. Sometimes those shockwaves *did* hurt.

Despite his limited human perspective, Phil had planted the seed of the answer to their dilemma. His simple idea of jumping back in time came across as laughable at first. Even gods often had the misplaced opinion that time travel could solve all woes. But the practice generally created more problems than it fixed. Going back occasionally led to catastrophic paradoxes, but less dramatic ripple effects were unpredictable and the true issue of concern.

A single jump back in time could have stopped Erik if there had been one pivotal event to redirect. For instance, if they had accidentally stumbled upon a piece of evidence pointing to Kokopelli helping the tribes, he might hide that information or divert attention so that it was never discovered.

But his intervention in human affairs was a long-standing sore spot with the Dark Court. Over the centuries he and Uktena had worked to minimize damage caused by individuals like Erik who sought human suffering to fuel their dark power, and his affinity for the Native American tribes was no secret. He felt deeply for the people of the Southwest in particular because they still spoke of him to their children and prayed for his guidance and support.

In recent years Uktena grew tired of the game, to the point he let Tia court him as a potential recruit for the Neutral Council. Kokopelli chuckled the first time he heard of Tia's efforts. The great serpent was not exactly a joiner. Yet the council's interest provided an opportunity.

It had taken stringent promises that Tia's symbol of power would not be damaged to persuade the lizard to borrow the Staff of Balance for this ploy. How the serpent in turn convinced Tia remained a mystery, but Kokopelli sensed the great lummox had promised a major concession for the favor.

Even though Tia locked away the bulk of its power, the artifact throbbed in his hands. Some of that energy would be needed to complete this gambit. Kokopelli reached beneath the goddess' locks, drawing out threads of power in preparation for what was to come. His own energies shimmered in the air before his outstretched left hand, making it seem as though he flew through cloudy veils despite the previously clear night sky.

He plunged on through the wispy layers, glancing back to ensure Erik and Kasandra followed and allowing the transition to take much longer than necessary. With each passing veil his spell gradually slipped him and his pursuers back through time. Few were as accomplished as the trickster god in traveling the bridge between past and future, but still he took it slow so that Kasandra and Erik didn't notice.

Finally, they emerged under again sparkling skies and a half moon. Nothing could be done about the change in the moon's phase, and he let one of Kasandra's bolts sizzle close, charring his tunic down the left side. Keeping their focus on him was crucial.

He'd brought them across the landscape and time to the night of that first ceremony, the night he'd been struck down. Fire flickered from within the wooden enclosure in the distance, and fireworks blossomed in the sky ahead. Another figure streaked in low from the left, heading for the ceremony in answer to the people's prayers. This would be the tricky part.

Phil's naïve idea of going back to right all wrongs flat out would not work, and his human friend's observation that Erik and Kasandra had already gotten the better of him had grated on Kokopelli's dignity. But the barb had gotten him thinking, trying to recall how exactly he'd been brought down that night.

Phil was right, Erik had indeed been chasing him with help from the skinwalker; he remembered that much clearly. They'd known he would answer the tribal call for aid and had laid an ambush. But that pair didn't wield sufficient power to lay him low.

Battles among gods were usually solitary affairs. Even beings from the same court seldom joined forces against a foe except during all-out war between the courts. Granted, Kokopelli had annoyed a great many over the years, but he thought it unlikely others would rise above their self-centered apathy and expose themselves. Kasandra would be an exception. He and the skinwalker had a long jaded history, and she would have jumped at any opportunity to get the upper hand.

When Uktena and Pina first returned him to his domain, he'd assumed in his confused recovery that Erik had found several willing participants to join the ambush. But there was no evidence of involvement from other major players. He'd scoured his memory, flashing back to take in the flavor and subtle feel of the energies that pummeled him from the sky and knocked him senseless into the ceremonial enclosure that fateful night. He'd experienced the pain and outrage anew as the truth emerged. Erik and Kasandra were his only assailants, but the pair had attacked from opposite directions, impossibly doubling their power. Two Eriks and two skinwalkers attacked him on that night—on this night.

Kokopelli veered right and zoomed lower, keeping the fireworks between him and the waiting ambush. His earlier self, blissfully ignorant of the pain to come, flew into the midst of the display, a flourish of unnecessary bravado he'd been unable to resist at the time.

Kokopelli threw waves of power into his wake like chaff, forcing his pursuers to bob and weave and keeping their full attention while he scanned the sky on the far side of the manmade explosions. *There!* Beyond the blinding starbursts two figures dropped like diving hawks, the earlier versions of Erik and Kasandra closing on their prey.

He came in from the opposite side, trusting the fireworks and his defensive magic to keep his own enemies from spotting the others. Kokopelli gritted his teeth in remembered pain as he looked down upon his own exposed back. *This is going to hurt.*

Of course it would hurt his earlier self, but the memory was a raw wound. The timing would be tricky, but he knew the ploy would work because he'd already done it. It was how he'd been bested in the first place that night. He himself had brought the second pair of attackers to bear.

The pursuit he led was still just out of phase with the attack. One last wispy veil lay ahead separating them from the crucial moment. Kokopelli slowed, drew power from the staff, and blurred his outline. Triumph radiated from the pair behind him as they drew close and readied a massive assault. He passed through the final veil, slipping a few seconds into the future, and stopped cold. The instant deceleration wrenched his innards, trying to turn him inside-out.

Kasandra and Erik flashed past, entering the fateful moment in time and looking down at the earlier version of Kokopelli. They took the bait, releasing their collective power. On the far side of a red-petaled explosion, the other pair did the same. The quadruple blast slammed into the hapless figure below, Erik's flaming sphere striking alongside the energy bolt Kasandra forged into a diving hawk. The massive energies lit up his earlier self like a small sun that tumbled in a smoking arc toward the ceremonial grounds of the people he'd come to help.

Kokopelli triggered the power of the staff, lashing out with one last massive time distortion. The Staff of Balance flared and bucked as Tia's wards tried to clamp down on the energy he drew to complete his casting. The time distortion slammed into the Kasandra and Erik that had followed him here, and the pair winked out of existence. He sagged with exhaustion, but one final task remained.

Those earlier versions of Erik and Kasandra swooped low over the enclosure, searching for the man who would lay dazed and helpless within.

Kokopelli slipped back in time a few minutes and landed quietly on the near side of the fence. As participants streamed from the main entrance and drove off, he snuck around to the back gate where two people would be talking. The fireworks fell silent just before the flaming ball that was his earlier self streaked down from above.

"Rogue firework, something in that last barrage went haywire!" Phil's voice made Kokopelli smile.

He rounded the corner just as Ankti disappeared into the enclosure. Phil jerked his head toward Kokopelli's shadowed nook, shrugged, and hurried to follow. Satisfied, he again launched skyward, letting a trail of sparks trickle in his wake as if he were a not-quite-extinguished log flying over the landscape.

Kasandra, always the hunter, spotted him immediately and pulled Erik into a climb to follow. He zoomed across the desert, away from the ceremonial grounds and the injured man who would be Kay for a few short days.

Kokopelli kept the pursuit on a short leash. When they were well beyond tribal lands he jumped forward to his original timeline, leaving Kasandra and Erik searching the night desert for prey that wasn't there.

23. Reunion

"THINGS ARE getting back to normal," Phil told Ankti as he hung up the phone and reached for his travel bag. Packing his main suitcase would come next. "Brandon and the others are fully recovered, but he's leaving Jack in charge for the time being. Seems pretty embarrassed."

Once the Red Scarfs were gone it had taken a while to ferry everyone back to civilization. They'd had to cross the chasm that Kasandra left behind, but the footing on the trailer spanning the gap proved adequate, even for the dazed people that had been under mind control.

Their major obstacle was simply that most of the cars were trapped. They'd had to send the one working car sitting outside the broken ground off to get help and more vehicles to transport everyone. The lost delegation was treated for exposure, and within two days all were declared fit and found rides home.

Tribal leaders keenly interested in what had transpired out in the wastelands had grilled Ankti, Jack, and Phil. With a bit of fancy footwork, they'd managed to dodge the more pointed questions, and no one went into Kay's role or the fact Erik and Kasandra had been hunting him and Ankti. Whatever Kay had done worked. Cell networks came back online, and demon-based vandalism was nearly nonexistent.

"Jack says they found a couple of the demon animals rooting through trashcans, but aside from that all's been quiet." Phil stuffed his draft report into the front pocket of his carry-on bag. He'd take another stab at it on the flight home.

"And what about…" Ankti wrung her hands and rearranged the first aid supplies in her blue pouch on the sofa for the third time. "Any sign of him?"

"Afraid not." Phil winced as her face fell. "But I'm sure Kay will turn up. The guy's a survivor, that's for sure."

"But they *hurt* him." She fingered Kay's flute, the source of the god's power and protection. "I know he's an ancient spirit and all, but there were two of them. If he doesn't come back, we'll never know what happened. Grandmother's watching too but says she and the elders haven't sensed anything—evil or good."

"Discounting her pet demon, I'm guessing," Phil said, trying to steer to a lighter topic. "How's that going to work anyway? What if Deedee needs a flea dip or something?"

Ankti laughed at the stupid joke, but it came out more like a sob. His friend was having a rough time coping. Still, she managed to blink back the unshed tears and smile.

"Don't worry. Grandmother will make it work. She loves that stupid thing. When something that rare and wonderful wanders into your life, you don't let go." It didn't sound like she was talking about the demon dog, but Phil nodded anyway.

They fell into awkward silence, Ankti brooding as she too packed up her belongings. They both had agreed to stay at Phil's place until things settled down. It was the most likely spot for Kay to find them. But the job in Phoenix was at an end, and Phil needed to head back east—even if the final report remained a bit of a conundrum.

He certainly couldn't attribute the locals' resistance to benevolent gods nor the root of the C-12 virus to evil fairies—or whatever Kasandra and Erik were. But something had to get back to the authorities and scientists.

The fact that the Dark Court had been meddling in human affairs might provide a clue to how the virus could be brought back under control. No, he couldn't put things like that in his official report, but maybe there was a subtler way to spread the information to those who could use it.

Ankti's head whipped up as three sharp knocks sounded at the door, but her hopeful expression melted away when Phil pulled out his wallet and went to answer. They'd ordered Chinese for their last dinner together. Going out felt too much like a celebration, and—although neither said so aloud—a couple more hours at the apartment meant more time for Kay to find them.

Given all the recent problems, Phil took the precaution of peering through the peephole before opening the front door. "This guy must have grown up on the sun or something. He's wearing a fur coat."

Phil couldn't make out much more because the driver held a stack of stapled paper bags in front of his face so that only his eyes showed beneath an old-style hat, a fedora if Phil wasn't mistaken. That wall of bags had to contain more food than the two combos they'd ordered. He was still on per diem, so the price difference wasn't a big deal, but what the heck was he going to do with the leftovers?

"Hope you found us okay." Phil said as he opened the door.

There wasn't a car idling out front. In addition to messing up their order, he must have parked at the wrong apartment.

"Well, it not too hard." The accent was clipped and only vaguely resembled Asian, but then anyone could work in an ethnic restaurant.

"Credit okay?" Phil took the top bag with his right hand and fumbled for his card with the left.

Wideset black eyes peered over the remaining two bags, the skin to either side crinkling in amusement. No way had they ordered that much.

"I'd rather have a beer."

Okay, so this is a joke. Phil scowled at the amusement in those twinkling eyes, and then grinned like an idiot as the man lowered his burden to reveal a big old nose set in the coppery skin of a very familiar face.

"Perhaps I should just say 'honey, I'm home' if it—"

Phil smacked into the door as Ankti knocked him aside and wrapped Kay in a fierce hug that staggered the startled man and crushed the aroma of Kung Pao from the remaining bags. She stood on tiptoe to kiss his face like a worried mother finding her lost child, then remembered herself and tried to pull away. But Kay held on with one arm as a brilliant smile lit his face, and she was forced to swing over to stand at his side. Ankti didn't seem to mind and kept her own arm wrapped around Kay's waist.

"You took your sweet time getting back." Phil took the remaining bags and looked down the row of apartments. "I hope you didn't turn our delivery driver into a newt or something."

"Nothing quite so harsh." Kay chuckled. "But I did buy out his remaining deliveries with a hefty tip. I thought I'd surprise you two." He looked past Phil at the bags and suitcase sitting by the couch. "Looks like the party's about over though."

"Yep, the office won't let me lounge around out here forever. So the place has to get closed up. I turn in the keys tomorrow and fly back to New Philly. But on the bright side, the night is young, we have plenty to eat"—he held up the paper sacks, using them to motion the other two inside—"and plenty of beer."

Phil set out dinner and a six-pack on the coffee table. Ankti refused to let go of Kay, and they ended up sitting together on the couch while Phil took the chair opposite. He was glad she'd get some time and closure before the mysterious god disappeared back to his own realm. But the joy shining in her eyes made him worry the crash would be all that much bigger when the time came. That was a problem for later. Simone liked to tease about his inability to enjoy the moment, and if there was ever a time for doing so, this was it.

After everyone got their drinks and plates set up, the small talk commenced, and Phil had to ask the burning question so important to Ankti and the tribes.

"Are the Red Scarfs gone for good?"

"Well, I did lead Erik and Kasandra on a very merry goose chase from which they will not soon return." Kay's hand found its way into Ankti's and their fingers entwined.

"Better than having your goose cooked." Ankti laughed, a joyful chuckle.

God or not, Kay wore an all-too-human expression behind his twinkling eyes as he lifted her hand and slowly kissed each knuckle. Ankti beamed, and a faint blush painted her cheeks.

A can and a half of beer was doing its job, and Phil grinned like an idiot at the unlikely couple. But he wanted a better answer and finally cleared his throat in an attempt to break the spell.

"A merry chase indeed." Kay cocked an eyebrow at him. "And it was your idea."

"Really?"

"Well, you planted the seed by recommending I go back in time." Kay wagged a warning finger. "Highly dangerous to make changes. But I'll tell you what I did do." Kay explained how he lured Kasandra and Erik through time and fooled them into attacking the earlier version of himself because it had already happened. "Your indelicate comments about them besting me the night of the ceremony got me wondering how they'd managed such an effective ambush."

"Sorry about that." Phil hid behind his beer as he took another swig.

"No, you were right. Those two should never have been able to bring that much energy to bear. Digging through my jumbled memories proved no others were involved. But they'd exactly doubled their firepower and rained twice as many spells down as should have been possible—unless there were two of each of them. On top of that, I felt a ghost of my own power as I tumbled to Earth, and I knew what had to be done."

He went on to praise his own ingenuity in executing the trap and how he'd led the older versions of his attackers away from where Phil and Ankti had helped a disoriented Kay. The staff was back in the hands of its rightful owner, who had not pressed charges—or whatever the equivalent was in those supernatural realms. Overall, Kay seemed very pleased with himself, another mannerism not strictly reserved for mere humans.

"And after the attack, what of *our* Erik and Kasandra?" Ankti asked.

"I drew on the Staff of Balance to send them into a time loop. They'll keep emerging a few moments before the attack."

"Stuck in a loop and gone for good." Ankti gave a sharp nod and leaned in close.

"Well…" Kay hedged. "The staff helped me do more than I could on my own, but each interval sending them back takes power from the spell. It will eventually wear down. Then Kasandra and Erik will drop back into this timeline—no time soon, but it will happen eventually."

* * *

Ankti leaned against Kay as they sat on the couch talking with Phil. The beer and good company melted away the cold dread that had grown in the pit of her stomach since the day Kay went missing. She'd felt like a silly schoolgirl pining after a professor. But he'd come back alive and well, and when they'd touched…well, she never wanted to let go.

The hand she held tingled with excited energy. The guy just felt so damn good. She scooted close, letting their hips touch. Whether the little electric jolts came from simple biology or his magic was unclear; she didn't *want* to know and resisted opening her *sight* to investigate. She refused to ruin the moment by overanalyzing. Judging by the way he leaned into her, fingers still entwined, Kay enjoyed the contact as much as she did.

The conversation turned casual as the three gorged themselves and traded friendly banter. Even though he was the odd man out, Phil wore a contented grin, perhaps fueled by one too many beers or the fact he'd soon fly home to see his fiancé. He stifled a yawn, and her stomach fluttered in excitement at the thought of Phil turning in and leaving her alone with Kay.

"I do have one question." Phil cleared his throat, scratched his chin in thought, then cleared it again; this was something big. "I realize you're kind of tapped out as far as helping the locals stave off the C-12 virus, but this Staff of Balance sounds super powerful. Couldn't you use that to undo some of the damage? Raising a family…well, it's what gives a lot of us hope and purpose, making a better future for our children. People *need* that kind of hope, *need* to know a bit of themselves lives on after they're gone."

Though fuzzy from the alcohol, Phil's eyes shone with passion. This was no academic plea. Her friend desperately wanted this, wanted a family. He'd told her before that he and Simone would apply for adoptions, but most families able to bear children hadn't bought into the idea of continuing to do so to help the population crisis. And those that had often took on the task of raising large families that hadn't been seen since early last century. Maybe as a solid citizen employed at the Bureau Phil and his wife-to-be would stand a better chance of moving up the waiting list. She certainly hoped so. He tried to hide it, but true pain lay beneath Phil's bleary gaze.

"Regrettably, the staff cannot help," Kay said gently. "Even if it could, the Neutral Council would never allow it. In their eyes, the damage is done and reversing it would be a shift in the natural balance. I am truly sorry."

"It was worth a shot." Phil stood abruptly and ferried his empties to the kitchen. "Maybe just knowing someone tampered with the genetic engineering back in the day will give the labs a clue on how to beat C-12. I can't exactly call out the Dark Court in my reports, but back channels exist. And the government will want to put safeguards in place to keep something like that from happening again.

"Early flight, so I think I'll turn in." Phil hid his disappointment behind another yawn, stretched theatrically, and held a hand out to Kay. "You're welcome to crash in your old room, or wherever." He managed a sly little grin for Ankti that made her ears warm. "But if I don't see you in the morning, it has been a true honor."

"The honor has been mine." Kay took Phil's hand and bent in close. "Worry not. All will be as it should with your report." Power flowed, subtle blue energy riding the whispered words.

"It's definitely the clean living and diet." Phil scrunched up his forehead as if trying to remember what he'd been saying, then nodded. "I mean for my report. Yep, away from the smog and traditional nutrition. Heck, they've known for years that a Mediterranean diet mitigates medical problems. Why should C-12 be any different?" His enthusiasm built. "I bet the dry climate helps too. I'll have to run the numbers, but they're going to eat this up back at the Bureau. I'll smooth it all out on the plane tomorrow. Well, good night."

With a wave for Kay and a half-wink for Ankti, Phil headed down the hall to his room.

"What was that?" Ankti's curiosity warred with mounting anticipation now that they were alone.

"A simple charm." Kay took her hand as she stood and looked to be certain Phil's door was shut. "He's learned much that should not be repeated. None of it fits his world view, so his mind will happily reject much of what he's seen."

"You made him forget?" Ankti let herself be led toward Kay's room, her giddiness not quite overriding concern for Phil. "How much?"

"My Hopi flower, always worried about others." Kay brushed the back of his hand along her cheek and studied her face, sending new thrills zipping along her spine.

"Stop that and answer the question." She smacked his hand away half-heartedly, and he took it as the playful gesture it was.

This time Ankti did open her *sight*, letting herself see the ebb and flow of energies around her. If Kay had so easily influenced Phil's memory, it seemed prudent in her current state of…interest, to be certain she wasn't being manipulated—at least not by magic.

She gasped. Kay's aura shone brilliant as the sun, glorious and shifting through colors no human bore. He'd hidden this before, but now laid himself bare for her to see. As she caught her breath, relief followed. No magic flowed between the two, no spells of coercion. Her endocrine system might betray her, but Kay did not. She wanted to throw her arms around him but refrained, needing to hear his answer.

"Our friend will forget what needs to be forgotten. Erik, Kasandra, and their demons will fall into a familiar framework as the thugs they were first purported to be. He will recall nothing of my powers nor realm. All memories of magic will slip away with time."

"Maybe that's for the best," Ankti said.

The world wasn't ready to learn about the things she'd seen in the past few weeks. Phil was such a sweetheart. If it might help cure C-12 he'd do his best to spread the word, even if people thought he was crazy. But Kay believed that knowledge would do more harm than good, and she trusted his judgement.

He reached out a tentative hand and smiled broadly when she stepped in close to slip an arm around his waist.

"Now, perhaps we can make a different kind of magic." Kay looked to the bedroom door with a raised eyebrow and an impish smile matching her own.

"Let's see what you've got, old man." Ankti pushed him into the room; neither would be getting much sleep.

24. Expectations

ANKTI FRETTED at the small powder-blue blanket in her lap as she stared at the front door of their small apartment and willed Kay to come home. Sometimes it worked, as though he could hear her across whatever space and time separated them. He'd been away for three full days this time, so she knew things were getting ugly again with the Dark Court. After eighteen wonderful months the pull from the life he'd left grew stronger with each passing day. She'd soon lose him; she could feel it.

Ankti blinked back tears, then giggled imagining his reaction to her news. *Damned mood swings.* Two narrow white stripes framed either side of the little blue blanket, not a traditional design or color. But Grandmother had made it after Ankti's last visit, and Grandmother was never wrong about such things.

It had been strange sitting in her living room with Deedee draped over the back of the tiny couch coughing out puffs of smoky breath in what passed for an affectionate purr. The demon animal had made herself quite comfortable, and Wikiwi treated her just like a housecat—albeit a hundred pound one with glowing red eyes and the ability to bring down a stallion.

On the bright side, Deedee ferociously defended her new territory. Within the first week, three of the flaming animals left behind by the Red Scarfs had been quietly dispatched by Grandmother's new companion, each disemboweled carcass left as a morning offering on the front mat for the old woman to find. As an added benefit, the few pesky coyotes that insisted on poaching chickens and the occasional dog from the locals had decided to ply their wily ways elsewhere. But most importantly, Grandmother was happy.

Am I happy?

Ankti's life was about to change dramatically. Hell, her body was too. And she didn't know where Kay would stand in all this. Shacking up with a god had never been in her life plans, not even as a wishful footnote like winning the lottery or learning to scuba dive. She shook her head at the glib thought. She'd always known their relationship couldn't last, but loved the old man. Ankti was certain he reciprocated, but that didn't change the fact they came from different worlds—literally.

Footsteps sounded outside, and Kay came through the door wearing the ridiculous fur coat and hat he'd grown so fond of. The odd outfit meant he'd been conducting business in human lands. He usually wore traditional buckskin clothes for dealings in other realms.

"Hello, my flower." He swept her into a tight hug and planted a breathtaking kiss on her lips.

Kay tasted of honey and sage, an intoxicating blend that always left her head spinning. But there were important matters to discuss, and she pushed him out to arm's length. In doing so, the blanket dropped to the floor. He bent and retrieved it, running his fingers over the cotton strands and lifting a questioning eyebrow. She took the blanket and walked him to the kitchen where dinner and a serious conversation waited.

"A gift from Grandmother," she explained as she sat and carefully draped the baby blanket over the back of the third chair.

"A boy!" The look of surprise and delight on his face was worth the days of waiting.

As a god of fertility, Kay of course already knew she was pregnant, but apparently had resisted peeking into the future to see if they would have a boy or girl. He might not be able to reverse viral sterility in the general populace, but his very nature had let her conceive a child when such a thing should not have been possible.

After some teary discussion and celebrating, which ended up back in the bedroom—hey, it wasn't as if she could get *more* pregnant—Kay turned serious.

"Things are not going well," he admitted as they lay spent on the bed holding hands.

Dark hair framed worried eyes. Kay looked tired, and she wondered if he'd been in real danger while off doing his otherworldly business. He'd mostly insulated her from those troubles, but occasionally let slip tidbits of information.

Uktena, his once-friend and ally, had defected months ago, and minions of the dark had stepped up their campaign against humanity. Although many shared his concerns, few in the supernatural community were willing to join the trickster god Kokopelli in any sort of organized campaign.

Pina the forest sprite and a handful of lesser beings stood by him, but it just wasn't enough to make much of a difference. The only bit of good news was that Kasandra and Erik remained trapped in their time loop.

"You have to leave for good, don't you?" She held her breath.

"That and worse." He laid a gentle hand on her belly, and dread clenched her chest. "Our son will not be safe."

* * *

Ankti's days became an anguished blur of denial and fruitless arguments, her nights a restless vigil that stole away much needed sleep. Neither was good for the baby. Fighting with Kay was a frustratingly lopsided affair. His calm sorrow in the face of her wrath and pleading only served to drive the wedge between them deeper. He rarely disputed her assertions, remained annoyingly empathetic, and wrapped her in a loving embrace whenever the hormones and stress sent Ankti over the edge. But it was all for naught.

Kay had been too passionate in his defense of mankind, too belligerent toward his opposition. Once they learned he had fathered a human child, nothing would keep their son safe. Civilian authorities were powerless against the magic of the cosmos, and moving could only provide temporary sanctuary.

The only option with any true chance of succeeding would be for Ankti and their son to permanently relocate to Kokopelli's domain, but that was no life for a child. And it *would* be Kokopelli's land, not Kay's. Ankti was no fool. Although she loved him deeply and Kay believed he loved her just as much, he was an immortal and their time together a diversion that could not last.

"I've arranged the adoption," Ankti said quietly at dinner on the Friday of her thirty-fourth week.

Kay had broken away from his commitments to stand vigil over her and their son during the final days. Between her aching back, sore hips, and life on the toilet, Ankti should have been thrilled that she had less than a month left—Kay insisted he knew the exact day and hour their son would be born, though she refused to let him give her too much detail. But a pang of loss overshadowed any joy she took in knowing she would soon bring a healthy child into the world.

Adoption was a long-standing and honored tradition among tribes. The people prided themselves on raising orphaned children as their own and cast no stigma upon parents who decided their children needed a better life than they could offer. Still, the thought of giving up her first child, her only child, left a deep wound she was certain would never truly heal.

"Anonymous and untraceable?" he asked.

"The company has an excellent reputation and prides itself on discretion. Edan will be well cared for on the way to his new parents." She choked on those last two words, thankful for the warm hand he closed over hers.

They'd settled on the name Edan, in homage to the fiery spirit he would need and the pleasure he'd bring. Keeping his birth name was an unenforceable condition of adoption the company had questioned, but she'd insisted it be written into the papers anyway. Edan had excellent parents waiting, good people she knew would honor her request.

"We will make a coming of age gift for him," Kay declared. "A few items to tell him of his parents and to help him on life's journey."

The thought of that future Edan learning about her eased a bit of the anxiety gnawing at Ankti's soul. But quiet power rolled out with Kay's words, and she knew these would be no normal presents.

Epilogue

P HIL'S LITTLE girl scampered across the living room to her toy box, frizzy red hair flowing down over the back of her pajamas. She picked out a fuzzy pink ball the size of her head, hurried back, and plopped her butt down opposite his spot on the floor.

"Now, I'm going to roll the *ball* to you, and *you* roll it back," his four-year-old daughter said in the solemn authoritarian manner of big sisters the world over.

Phil sat with legs splayed, helping Edan sit upright between his knees. At six months old, their new son was able to sit up for short periods with only minimal support. When he clapped and squealed at the ball, Piper gave a curt nod of satisfaction that bounced flame-red curls across her face. She pushed them away with the back of the hand holding her ball, then rolled. The ball stopped at Edan's feet.

"Now, roll it back." She pantomimed the motion.

His son gave a big toothless grin, beat his balled little fists on Phil's thighs, and kicked in excitement.

"See, Daddy, he's drumming again."

"Edan's just happy, Piper." Phil grabbed each chubby little leg and used his son's feet to punt the ball back.

"Dinner's almost ready," Simone called from the kitchen.

"Need any help?"

Before his wife could answer, the phone rang.

"Hello?" Simone's voice drifted through the open doorway. "Yes, this is she…wait a moment. Phil, I do need a hand. It's the adoption agency."

"Coming." He picked Edan up and headed for the crib.

"Oh Daddy, Daddy, can I hold him?" Piper wrapped both arms around his right calf and stared up with pleading eyes. "Pleeaaase! I've been a good girl all week, and you promised."

Simone stood in the doorway, phone in hand, and curling a long strand of black hair around one finger. She wore her blue hospital scrubs, which he always found quite attractive when she cinched them tight to her hips with the apron. Administration put her back on evening training once Edan had settled into his routine. That way they were able to trade off watching the kids. Worry creased her forehead as she waved the phone for him to hurry, but she smiled and nodded in response to Piper's request.

Phil sat his daughter down on a cushion on the floor and put Edan between her legs. She carefully wrapped both arms around his middle and beamed.

"That's it, now just give him support like we practiced with dolly. Edan isn't real good at sitting up yet." He let go, stepped away, and—satisfied—backed to the kitchen door so he could keep an eye on the kids.

"I will, Daddy." Piper cooed and whispered in Edan's ear, making him giggle.

His wife put her phone on speaker and held it flat so the mic would pick up both their voices.

"Phil and Simone Johnson here," he said.

"Hello, this is Rachelle Fox from Blue Bonnet Adoption. I wanted to check to make sure Edan is doing well on his formula and see if you have any questions for us."

"Oh yes, he's a good eater," his wife assured the woman. "I have him on early stage puree too, and his diapers are just fine."

After a few minutes of technical exchange about inputs and outputs that Phil made little effort to follow, the person on the other end seemed satisfied and told them to expect a visit from the social worker Saturday morning.

"Nothing to worry about, just the required follow-up and a quick house safety inspection. Please make certain you are both home and available until noon."

"Not a problem," Phil said. "We've been expecting that."

"Um…there is one last item." Her voice grew hesitant. "You'll be receiving a package next week for Edan from his birth parents. Mrs. Johnson, would you be open to speaking with the mother?"

"Oh?" Simone clutched her apron front, at a loss for words.

"I realize this is unusual, and it would be just this once. 'No' is a perfectly acceptable answer, but I do have her on hold. I can connect you if you have somewhere private to talk and are willing. No offense, Mr. Johnson, but the request is for a private discussion."

Simone sucked in a deep breath and nodded.

"None taken," Phil said. "She'll take the call and boot me out of the room. We're taking you off speaker now."

He gave his wife a reassuring half hug and retreated to the far side of the living room to be out of earshot of whoever came on the line, but still keep a watchful eye on Piper and Edan.

Edan squirmed as if wanting to follow, but big sister clamped down to keep him in place, pulled the ball close with a toe, and got his attention by passing it from one foot to the other.

"Hello, this is Simone." She cradled the phone to her ear, turned away, and gave an occasional nod while listening for several seconds. "No, it's…fine." More silence. "Yes, the agency said that was coming…On his birthday then?" Simone's ear turned bright red, and she twisted the apron into a knot around her free hand. "Oh, honey, it's okay. We just love him so much. I'll be sure—" She nodded vigorously and wiped at her eyes. "I promise we will…goodbye."

Phil rushed to her side as she lowered the phone and sagged against the doorframe. "You okay?"

"Just give me a minute." Simone patted the hand he'd placed on her shoulder, closed her eyes, and drew air through her nose. "Hard call."

He let her lean on him until she was ready to say more. A glance over his shoulder showed Edan still safe with big sister, although Piper stared off at the couch with her little face screwed up in confusion.

"She sounds like a dear." Simone swallowed hard on the heels of the statement. "We obviously didn't get into much, and she didn't give her name. That package we're expecting goes into storage until he's eighteen."

"Birthday present?" Phil asked.

"Guess so." She nodded and gave a weak, fretful smile. "I think she just wanted to…I don't know, connect? Make sure her— Edan was in good hands?"

"You know he is." Phil swept his wife into a fierce hug and kissed her forehead.

"I know it's wrong to worry. We're just so lucky to have been approved for Piper and then be requested by name to adopt Edan."

"Very lucky. Soon it'll be nearly impossible to adopt. There just aren't that many kids to go around." And why on Earth had this woman decided to hand them a lucky lottery ticket named Edan?

"Daddy! Daddy!"

Piper whispered in her brother's ear and tried to wriggle around to face the couch. Phil peered into Simone's eyes to make sure she was okay.

"Duty calls," he said at her weary nod. "I hope not literally."

* * *

Piper did good holding her new baby brother. She told him how they would play and have lots of fun—just as soon as he learned to walk.

Edan slapped her legs with a rat-ta-tat-tat rhythm and gurgled. She wasn't a drum, but she let him do it 'cause he was making music, like Mommy on the piano.

Over by the kitchen, Mommy finished talking on the phone and started to cry.

Oh no!

Piper pulled her squishy ball up and held it tight, wishing she could help. Daddy rushed over and hugged Mommy. She squinted hard but couldn't see Mommy's boo-boo, but Daddy would make it better.

Something tugged at the arm not cradling her ball. She looked to see what and gasped. Edan slipped off her lap and fell toward the floor. She'd forgotten to hold tight!

Just before his curly black hair hit the white tiles, something blurred beneath Edan, and a sparkling cloud lifted her little brother back onto her lap. Piper let go of the bad ball and hugged her baby brother.

Someone peeked around the long comfy chair and giggled, a girl not much taller than Piper—and Piper was a big girl. She had long blonde hair and big green eyes. Really big eyes. And pointy ears! Piper and Daddy had seen movies with pretty fairies and scary monsters.

The fairy girl raised a finger to her lips as if shushing Piper. She wore a funny brown dress with a rope belt and wood shoes. Piper wrapped her arms tighter around her little brother, and the girl smiled.

Then the pretty fairy girl lowered both hands to the floor, and a tiny unicorn made of light trotted over. It touched its horn to Edan's toe, and then the unicorn and girl disappeared in a cloud of sparkles—real magic, just like the stories.

"Mommy says magic is just pretend," Piper explained to Edan as the last few sparkles winked out. "But it's real."

Someday, when she was big, Piper would figure out how magic worked. Then she'd be a fairy princess too.

"Daddy! Daddy!"

~

Loved it, hated it, somewhere in between? Let people know!

I'd be eternally grateful if you'd share your opinion of *Strange Origins* or any other books on my author page at Amazon
https://amazon.com/author/steinjim

Your review need not be long, only takes a minute, and is super helpful to new authors. – Jim

Bonus: Deleted Scene
Chronicles of the Neutral Council

G REASY BLACK fur smeared the polished surface of the low stone table as Uktena, the great horned serpent, slapped three fat black rats down in front of those assembled. Talons raised sparks across the impenetrable surface as his scaled claw withdrew.

Tia sighed, wisps of breath stirring delicate black curls hanging from either side of her plaited hair. Vermin carcasses weren't going to win anyone over, and—judging by the physical and metaphorical hackles rising around the room—this inquiry was about to turn into another circus.

In dragon form, Uktena towered over the handful of players gathered about the sacred stone. Wide-bodied fay warriors, were-creatures, and others less easily classified leaned in from opposite sides of the table, separated by demeanor as much as clothes and form—forms that had little bearing on the power each of these ancient beings might wield. The serpent almost certainly chose the lizard over his snake form in an attempt at intimidation. Such a tactic might have worked on lesser beings, but today it did nothing except raise already brittle tensions to near breaking.

"Blasphemous to bring plague bearers here!" Sakpota spat the words through thick lips in the hard-edged accent of his worshippers.

The god's barrel chest was the color of midnight and as broad as he was tall, with dark weathered bones hanging in a vest over powerful shoulders. Although he was a deity of death like herself, Tia didn't much care for Sakpota. As a god of disease and insanity, he reveled in chaos and pain like so many of the Dark Court. The African people who originally prayed in his name had died or been assimilated into other tribes long ago, so his power waned—a thing that made many of those gathered as dangerous as wounded prey— or more accurately, wounded predators.

"Evidence for those presiding," the dragon rumbled, waves of power and intimidation doing little to quell the smoldering glare of the dark god—although several in the back cringed and many tails tucked tight.

"We welcome all testimony," Damballa, primordial creator of Haitian Vodou culture, proclaimed.

Though mild, the words washed over those assembled with the finality of the grave. Tia didn't know Damballa's gender. The handful of greater spirits that presided over squabbles between the Dark and Light Courts were beyond such simple concepts. Humans were the ones focused on gender roles, and it baffled her as to why such a thing mattered as much as it did to gods and greater spirits. But their existence remained closely linked to that of mortals, so there was a certain ironic sense to it all.

Damballa's words calmed the dozen figures crowding the table and the minions gathered behind them, but they also struck with a muted ring against the shroud surrounding the room.

"Room" was an antiquated concept describing the tableau. This was the hall of petition, where the courts gathered to air grievances or forge the increasingly rare alliance. Curtains of energy contained the area, rising from a stone floor that was always too hot, or cold, or wet, or hard. No one was meant to feel at ease during such proceedings.

Gray mist surrounded them on all sides. The formless Tokpela was the stuff of creation, a substance of nothingness from which all took shape. It separated their individual realms and insulated the human plane of existence from those of the gods.

The power in Damballa's words struck the walls and ceiling of the island brought into existence for the meeting. The swirling Tokpela overhead shifted and lightened, resolving into dappled clouds promising late season rain. The scene around the hall similarly shifted into tightly-packed dwellings and muddy streets filled with people, too many people, an impossible compaction of humanity so dense it was hard to comprehend. And many of them were dead with black boils dripping pus and blood even as hearts stilled, victims of the Black Death.

Death wagons creaked as if in misery under their gruesome loads, splashing mud and worse from deep ruts as they crisscrossed the crowded by-ways in search of passengers. Plague ravaged much of the human world, including the London they now looked upon. This was the reason Tia and the others gathered.

Tiw, son of Odin, pushed past a massive scaly foreleg, sparing a satisfied nod for the group. "Inspect the carcasses for yourselves. Even dead they reek of dark magic. I'll not have you spreading your disease among *my* people."

The accusation shot across the table at the African god, but strafed the entire contingent. Reactions ranged from feigned affront to confusion as the more powerful beings on both sides squared off across the gleaming surface that shifted from variegated gray to crimson as power rippled on the air.

Some reactions were genuine, and she felt for those caught off-guard. The concepts of light and dark were relative and often oversimplified. Neither court presented a unified front; they never did. Those gathered came from diverse cultures and realms that correlated to the varied continents of human lands. As a rule, spirit beings were not skilled at working together. Their lives were too long, treaties and promises too fleeting.

Small groups might band together for a common cause over the millennium, but the majority simply lived their lives and did what they wanted. The former became the nexus for each court, a core of beings who tended to run things and marshal the others in times of need—such as now.

Even Tia could feel the miasma of compulsion that would have driven the rats leaking from the dead rodents, yet Sakpota and his cohorts studied them closely as if the fact was difficult to ferret out.

"This may be a trick," the stocky deity finally said, sitting back on his heels. "There is no denying the power, but others have just as much to gain from this chaos." He pointed out to where dejected humans dumped blistered bodies into a long trench at the edge of the city. The reek flowed across the table like dense wet fog, and Tia found herself running cleansing magics over her shimmering blue dress.

"If this isn't your work, it's clearly one of your minion's!" Tiw slammed his fist on the table, and their pocket of reality rippled as if with dissipated heat from the blow. "Power drives these rats, drawing them to the human populace and bringing plague energies so like the ones dripping from your person."

Tiw had inherited his father's passion, and temper. While not entirely incorrect, speaking so blatantly of another of high stature could easily lead to war. Sakpota's face darkened, and he drew breath to no doubt issue challenge.

A pile of porous black rocks crashed onto the table amidst a splash of lava that drove everyone back. The material simmered and hissed, the cooling edge of molten rock pooling out to touch the brace of rats, which immediately burst into flames and gouts of greasy black smoke.

"What is this, Kokopelli?" Damballa turned ancient, depthless eyes on an old man hobbling up from behind Uktena. The bent newcomer's beady black eyes shone with mischief over an impressive hook of a nose. His clothes were of light buckskin with three feathers rising from a leather band around his head, and he spoke in a dry cackle of amusement.

"More evidence from the great eruption of Mount Tambora in 1810, but the same underlying manipulations can be found in many ancient volcanoes, earthquakes, and tsunamis. This is a systematic extermination attempt." He swung his arms in a wide arch, playing to the captive audience as the scene outside shimmered and changed.

Rocky crags appeared with pyroclastic flows of killing ash and rock that cascaded at incredible speed toward fields and villages below. A massive ejection of deadly material spewed into the atmosphere as the facing slope of a peak in the distance exploded.

Thousands died in those first minutes on the island nation of Sumbawa. Tens of thousands more followed as water and crops failed, and the catastrophe spread. The ejected material circled the northern hemisphere, altering weather and temperatures. Snow fell in summer across the lands of men. Famine and disease followed.

"Stop jumping around in time, old man," yelled a gaunt figure with the narrow face of a ghoul.

The ability to time-travel wasn't unique to the Native American god, but he certainly liked to do it more than most. Tia herself found it a disorienting and draining experience seldom worth the effort. But the old man positively thrived on it.

Clear traces of magic spilled from the mountain, causing the destruction they witnessed. The same magic that currently drove the black rats to seek refuge on outbound ships, forced them to breed, and urged them forth to infiltrate humanity, a compulsion that would not abate until no humans remained.

As explosions and screams rocked the landscape outside their bubble, beings on both sides of the table drew back in disgust at such irrefutable evidence.

"Tia, goddess of peaceful death, what say you?"

She started at the great being's question. Damballa inclined that insect-like head, a praying mantis waiting for her response. She looked to where Kokopelli stood under Uktena's massive wing. Why couldn't the old trickster stay in his deserts, keep to his music and dance? A wooden flute dangled from his belt alongside his medicine pouches. The instrument glowed and pulsed as he drew power to maintain the vison without.

She sighed. Fertility was another aspect of Kokopelli. Perhaps that was what drove him to care so much for the humans, but what the great serpent by his side stood to gain remained a mystery. Not quite a god, yet more than a mere spirit, the massive creature should be hunting meat on the hoof instead of hidden plots. The unlikely pair watched expectantly, silently urging her to lay blame.

"These are not peaceful deaths." She chose her words carefully and stood tall, drawing on every scrap of regal bearing she could muster—a trick that often had others anxiously shifting their stance. "Ta'xet rules over violent death and would better serve these proceedings."

Damballa would have to maneuver someone else into passing judgement. Though a god of duality, she could no more conjure up her other aspect as avoid the coming conflict. Ta'xet would not awake for anything short of glorious battle, and there had not been open war between the courts in three hundred years. Some would say they were overdue.

"Ridiculous!" a beautiful creature with long canines and the tail of a fox called out from the safety of her position behind Sakpota.

The African god turned as if to chastise the fox spirit, but instead nodded with an impertinent grin of superiority. Titters rose from the dark courtiers. Sakpota might think himself powerful. Though his star waned, the sickness he and the others spread made him stronger. But he had no idea of the forces Tia's opposite aspect controlled. There was never a shortage of carnage and destruction to fuel Ta'xet. The rats, the eruptions, the quakes—all of it empowered her other half too. If he came forth to take over their shared body, became the dominant presence, only Damballa would stand a chance of restraining the retribution he'd level for such affront.

Tia would gladly give over and fall into the fitful slumber until needed, but Ta'xet tended to emerge only during great conflict—either in human lands or among the gods. That still might come, but for now she was stuck dealing with this arrogant lot. Or was she?

"I have no special gift of divination. The taint of power radiating from these items is plain for all to see." Uktena and Kokopelli smiled broadly, as did others of the Light Court. "But I recuse myself from casting judgement." The smiles darkened. "Too long have we bantered back and forth nipping at each other's heels in hopes of gaining some small advantage that the millennia easily erase. I declare neutrality and withdraw from the proceedings of this and future courts."

The great Damballa studied her, unmoving, as if carved from granite. In that instant, Tia felt herself being weighed and judged. Perhaps punishment would be meted out. So be it. Her declaration was no rash decision. Court intrigue and battles wearied her; worse yet they served no purpose. If dark or light ever truly prevailed, it would be an end to all they knew. Balance had to be maintained, and history proved no one else was likely to step forward and be an adult. Tia took heart as the silence stretched, driving her to expound.

"I propose the formation of a third entity, a body comprised of those of us wishing to keep the balance and maintain order." She hurried on over the indignant huffs and guffaws from many around the stone. "A neutral party is needed. One that ensures the natural balance is maintained, that no group or individual gains undue sway and power over others. There will ever be the natural ebb and flow of power with the seasons and other factors, but we must guard against tipping so far that order slides from our grasp and all descends into chaos."

The room grew still, and all eyes turned to Damballa. The great deity's narrow face tilted left then right in consideration. Weeks passed between each slow steady breath, years flew by as the impassive stare passed over one court, then the other, and finally settled squarely on Tia. Pain flit through those bulbous eyes, but also a question, "*are you certain?*" The weight of the unspoken words gave her pause, but only for a moment.

She'd been working this through for a long time. Such a move was well overdue. She hated to be the one to venture forth. She had a fair amount of power, but couldn't call on the massive reserves of her other half. When her dual nature took over, she would simply sleep and had no delusions that Ta'xet would uphold a notion like neutrality. If anything, he'd add to the chaos. How in all the heavens could she alone control both courts? Yet what was done was done. There was no backing out now. Tia squared her shoulders and managed an imperial nod by way of response.

"So it shall be!" Damballa boomed.

Tia gasped as a heavy mantle of power and responsibility settled over her. The burnt carcasses on the table flared impossibly bright. The light dimmed, leaving a three-foot staff in their place. The wood gleamed reddish brown, an elegant spiral with an irregular lump of turquoise at one end radiating quiet power. The artifact lay peacefully on the stone slab, patiently waiting for someone to take it up.

"The Staff of Balance," Damballa intoned. "Who will join the goddess of peaceful death in keeping the balance?"

Time stretched again as hesitant looks were exchanged. Sneers from Sakpota's group drew snarls from the Light Court, but then something surprising happened. Individuals began to step forward. True, most of them were from the back row, lesser beings of little power, but at least she wasn't alone in her concerns. Surprisingly, Uktena took a shuffling step, but shook his great head at a scowl from Tiw and stepped back to his place with the Light Court.

Five others joined her at the end of the table, the start of something…different.

"As for you"—Damballa turned to Sakpota and his compatriots—"Your meddling with the humans will cease. They will grow and flourish or weaken and perish according to their own design."

"We haven't—" the African god began.

"You have, and you shall no longer." The elder had spoken.

"It is best." Tia saw it all so clearly. "This is necessary for the balance. Gains you make hurting the humans are only temporary. Succeed in wiping them out and who will be left to harbor the disease and anguish that you and yours need to survive? With no worshipers and no one to suffer you would perish along with those you torment."

"Not such a bad thing," Tiw said, though she saw how he wrestled with the morality of letting humans perish.

"And those of the light would rise." Tia raised both arms high, bringing forth beautiful light, a sublime glow to make souls soar, but the scene without was devoid of anyone to care. Buildings crumbled into ruins, overtaken by forest and raging seas. The brightness flared, angry at being ignored, feeding upon itself and crafting its own glorious pedestal. "Rise and bask in your own glory. Look upon yourself and worship." The light grew unbearable, and those gathered turned away as a super-nova fissure split the air. "And perish in your self-adulation." All went dark.

Whatever had possessed Tia fled into the stunned silence, leaving her drained but satisfied. The darkness resolved again into swirling

Tokpela. She eyed Damballa, searching for a hint of what had brought forth her true vision. The old being simply nodded and turned away as grumbled accusations slipped from players of both courts.

"The path you have chosen will not be as easy as you may have hoped. None will envy the court politics your Neutral Council will be drawn into."

"Wait." She'd meant to leave the intrigue behind.

"Word has gone forth." The declaration drifted back from Damballa's retreating form. "A moratorium upon interference is in place. Tia will see that violations are swiftly dealt with."

And just like that, she and her small cadre of helpers found themselves set upon by the squabbling light and dark courtiers from which she'd meant to distance herself. Tia sighed, reached down, and picked up the staff.

Strange Tidings Excerpt

(Legends Walk book 1)

A COIN FLASHED through the afternoon sun and dropped into my open case. I scowled at the worn bit of silver shining against purple velvet, and an F-sharp slipped from my horn. The old geezer who'd tossed it spat a few vowel-heavy words, tugged down his feathered hat, and turned away. *Honestly, who wears a fedora nowadays?*

Busking the farmers' market made for a tough living. Mr. Fedora was one of the few lingering Saturday shoppers, so I gathered up my trumpet and meager tips. Anger radiated from the hunched old man, but when I turned to glare back, he was shuffling away.

Green flashed near his right hand, two sullen emeralds that winked out immediately. Cufflinks would match his antiquated headdress. But the pair had been set wide, surrounded by the ghost of an outline, an impression of…something. My nerves jangled. The familiar headache stabbed behind my left eye, and the air grew thick and warm despite a fall breeze. I plopped down on the edge of my improvised stage, arms heavy at my sides.

I hadn't had an episode all year. The pain made me want to crawl into a dark, cool corner, though I doubted I had the strength. I closed my eyes and tried to dredge up a happy, silly melody. Instead, a dirge filled my head, somber and relentless. But it distracted me until the pain and fatigue passed.

I wiped at the hair plastered to my face, pulled off my jacket, and counted out my money. The change and two reissued bills didn't amount to much. I sighed and plucked an odd coin from the pile. I figured Fedora tossed in a dime, which was pretty insulting, but the silver disk was larger, its surface worn to the point of illegibility. I could just make out a hint of the original imprint and image, worthless.

The headache threatened to return, and I looked around for a clear path to my car. Pete Easton, an ex-classmate, bustled about nearby, folding up tables that had sagged under his offering of corn and melons.

"Music will be ready in a few days," I called, swallowing my residual nausea. "Chores around the house keep getting in the way, but I'd rather not freeze this winter."

"You just had to live in a mansion." Pete grinned up at me. He pronounced it 'man-shuun', drawling out the long 'yu' sound, mocking the twang his family had kept alive for generations.

At six one, I towered over Pete, but his wide build, straw-colored hair, and chiseled features put my gawky charms to shame. Those sturdy farmer genes were even resistant to the C-12 virus. Working the market rekindled our friendship, but I hadn't been out to Pete's place in years. His family's turn-of-some-century farmhouse probably stayed toasty with just firewood.

"Mom wanted me close." I shrugged. "Can't beat next door."

Abandoned stores ringed the parking lot, silent sentinels. Even the bakery and seamstress were shut tight against the afternoon chill. I slid into my powder blue Toyota RAV4, a car that laughed at snow, but I had hoped for something a little sportier or tougher.

Of course, half the town drove similar cars, and they were all ancient, the cars, that is. Well, and most of the people. As the population declined, manufacturing went belly up. On the bright side, the waterfront housed cargo containers chock-full of brand new, fifty-year-old vehicles, and there's lots of gas. Just my bad luck to start driving when the mini-tanks were doled out.

One stop and ten minutes later found me crunching through leaves by the stone circle in front of my brick colonial. The dried-up fountain was over the top, but the place wasn't all that big. Surprisingly, I found my sister stretched out on the leather couch facing the cold fireplace in my living room.

"Piper? Where'd you park?"

"Hello to you, too, Edan." Piper eyed my white paper bag. "Don't worry. I ate."

I sighed, easing the stranglehold I had on my meal, and plopped down into the armchair to eat most of my day's earnings. "You know it's just Ed now. Car?"

"The shop," she answered absently, twirling two fingers around a strand of dark-red hair.

Sure, "in the shop." Mechanics were a dying breed. More like she abandoned her sleek, black Charger. Sis would have to see what the next riverfront raid yielded.

Piper and I don't look much alike. She's a couple of inches shorter with long, red hair, straight as an arrow. Freckles fleck her round cheeks. Dark, wavy hair frames my olive complexion. She's Irish or Welsh, whereas I have a heavy dose of Latino or maybe Native American, considering my height and regal nose. I'm not as athletic, but hoped my sporadic workouts would soon start adding bulk. Piper claims to be five years older, but it's really only four. My birthday is coming up fast.

Like most everyone, our folks couldn't have their own kids, thanks to the C-12 virus. That was a total screw-up. No one had noticed the gene-spliced contraceptive "medicine" mutating, until birth rates plummeted.

Fifty years later, the world population is back to six digits and everyone's still infected. Only about three percent can bear children, like the Eastons. I know because Dad works at the Census Bureau. His office keeps assessing humanity's viability and trying to build a plan.

We have it good in New Philadelphia: utilities, working traffic lights, you name it. Even a wing of the old Bryn Mawr hospital is still open, an easy commute for Mom. Consolidating southwest of the old city center was genius. Who'd want dilapidated housing over suburban estates?

"Sooooo, there's a job open." Piper smiled wickedly and fell silent.

"Where?"

Her last lead was…less than ideal. Piper contemplated the ceiling with pursed lips. I rolled my eyes and waited. I loved my sister, but it was a fine line sometimes.

"Main Line Studios!" she finally blurted, her feigned indifference shattering.

"Seriously?" The remnant of my headache and dark mood vanished.

Piper rocked in her seat, clapping her hands and grinning. "They need a gofer and sound guy. You might even get to use the studio after hours!"

Okay, it was back to brotherly love.

* * *

In short order, I found myself hustling recordings around the studio, filing, and occasionally working on equipment. The first week had been a confusing whirlwind, but mornings quickly settled into an enjoyable pattern of cataloging old items and feeding news clips to the broadcast room. Afternoons were for planning and maintenance.

Billy, the station engineer, mentored me in spite of my dubious natural ability. I was a wizard with apps and filters, conjuring music from degraded audio, but I was proving fundamentally inept with hardware.

Thanks to Piper, Mr. Conti, the station manager, insisted I use the auxiliary sound room after hours. Professional gear made finalizing my playlist a breeze. I would have *Spiritual Mayhem* ready for the weekend market, despite working with damaged albums scavenged from Old Philadelphia.

Thursday night I put the final track through an acoustic filter to remove background noise and level the volume. Needles in the gauges at my station twitched, fitful and uncertain as the music began.

"Yes," I whispered, coaxing the Trans-Siberian Orchestra's number to life with precise hand gestures and wrist flicks. The opening strains trod atop the preceding piece with staccato complexity, tensions rising. "Wizards in Winter" blossomed to life in my little studio, and the world dropped away.

* * *

A dark form moved beneath the meager streetlamp along Delaware Avenue. The figure pulled its coat tight and approached a pair of glass security doors. A shadow should have fallen across the keypad, but shadows presented certain vulnerabilities, so the dirty white keys remained illuminated by feeble, yellow light.

At the wave of a gnarled hand, the lock let out a reluctant snick, and the doors opened. The feathers atop the black hat rocked in disapproval as the hunched figure entered.

* * *

Throbbing chords filled me, swirling and building. The short, fierce piece was a perfect finale to my mix of progressive rock, metal, and alternative. I left the genreless hip-hop, stained with corporate agendas, moldering in the city ruins. This music was real, powerful.

My hands flew, calling forth a blizzard of notes from the embattled instruments. Legions charged down the thrumming bass line toward their final conflict. Goosebumps rose on my arms as pianos crashed in. Among the cascading chords, the pianos and guitars hesitated, belched forth a final, staccato flourish, and it was done.

"Perfect!" I panted through raised arms.

"Okiw, too dramatic," a voice rasped from behind me.

I whirled, hands thrust defensively forward, my mind halfway between snowy mountains and reality. The man darted right, his fur coat scattering audio disks and my dinner. Sparks, and just a tiny jet of flame, shot from the patch panel by the door. *Crap!* The small figure popped back up in the shadows to my left.

"Mr. Conti?" I looked at the panel and winced. "I can fix that." Hoping it was true, I grabbed a towel. Why had the boss come back?

"You harness the music well." The dry croak was not the station manager's mild tenor.

"Who?" My head snapped up from the spilt iced tea. "How did you get in here?"

"Front door." The man cackled and stepped into the light. He was old and bent.

"This is private property." I scrubbed a scorch mark, paused at the thought of getting zapped, and rounded on the intruder. "New Philly isn't some abandoned town. You can't just go anywhere you want."

"I visit children," he said as if that explained everything.

Family, sure. The vagrant's face was a desert of crags and gullies, his features more leather than skin. An impressive nose hooked out beneath shiny black eyes gleaming with birdlike amusement or beady malice. It was difficult to tell which, with his hat pulled low. My eyes locked on the two feathers tucked in the hat's satin band.

"Fedora!" I blurted. "You threw me that useless coin."

"Ungrateful. You give sour tone. I give nether coin you deserve." I couldn't place his clipped accent. He craned over my work area and started pushing buttons.

"That's it." I used my no-more-crap voice. "Time to go."

He made a grab for my table mic, but I scooped it into my back pocket and shooed the kook toward the entry, trying not to provoke him.

Out front, something scrabbled at the metal trashcans in the alley. Fedora whipped his head toward the sound, hands clenched. The noise subsided in short order, but the angry glint in his eye spoke volumes. If he reacted that way to a few raccoons, I didn't what to see him get riled up.

I was shocked to find my own fists clenched and that I'd taken a step toward the commotion. The old man's antics had me on edge. A pair of unblinking red eyes looked back from the alleyway, then vanished.

The man half shambled, half hopped down the street, and I carefully relocked the front doors, ensuring they were secure this time. After pulling the circuit breaker, I straightened up the studio and scanned the room. The patch panel was dry, but looked—well—fried. I'd have to face the music for that.

Then I noticed a vacant nook by the meters. The microphone! I reached to my back pocket, but could already tell the mic was absent. Instead, I fished out a bit of metal and shook my head. Another faceless coin.

Get *Strange Tidings* and the rest of the Legends Walk series at
https://www.amazon.com/dp/B07P6Z1Z85

About the author

Jim Stein hungers for stories that transport readers to extraordinary realms. Despite sailing five of the seven seas and visiting abroad, he's fundamentally a geeky homebody who enjoys reading, nature, and rescuing old pinball machines. Jim grew up on a steady diet of science fiction and fantasy plucked from bookstore and library shelves. After writing short stories in school, two degrees in computer science, and three decades in the Navy, Jim has returned to his first passion. His speculative fiction often pits protagonists with strong moral fiber against supernatural elements or quirky aliens. Jim lives in northwestern Pennsylvania with his wife Claudia, a grandcat with a perpetually runny nose, and the memory of Marley the Greatest of Danes.

Visit **https://JimSteinBooks.com/subscribe** to get a free ebook, join my reader community, and sign up for my infrequent newsletter.